EZ TALK

聞文新英

2022年度

疫情下的台灣

U0046399

音檔
使用說明

STEP ①

STEP ②

掃描書中 QRCode

快速註冊或登入 EZCourse

STEP ③

STEP ③

STEP ④

STEP ⑤

回答問題按送出

完成訂閱

點選個人檔案

答案就在書中（需注意空格與大小寫）。

該書右側會顯示「已訂閱」，
表示已成功訂閱，
即可點選播放本書音檔。

查看「我的訂閱紀錄」
會顯示已訂閱本書，
點選封面可到本書線上聆聽。

在今年年底台灣終於迎來了戶外口罩解禁，以及出國的禁令亦在今年解除，這個全球大流行疫情終於漸露曙光。多年以前誰也不會想到會有這麼嚴重的疫情，改變了人們的生活型態，其中最辛苦的莫過於位於第一線的醫療人員，每天必須冒著染疫的風險，穿著笨重的防護衣，日以繼夜的照料大量的確診者，在此真的要對他們致上最崇高的敬意與感謝！

今年除了人們已經學習與之共存的疫情之外，在世界各地也同樣有許多事件發生，本書我們就為你精選了三大新聞類型共 40 則國際新聞，其關注度、話題性、重要程度都不在話下。像是今年吵得沸沸揚揚的《Twitter 收購案》、臉書更名《元宇宙》、以及像是《瑞士天王費德勒退休》等等，讓我們在邁向新一個年度的同時，了解過去一年世界是如何轉動，也同時帶入我們讀者最關心的事：英語學習。

不知道你是怎麼想的，但是編輯本人在學習英文的過程，始終是非常愉快的，我也始終相信藉由自己感興趣的議題、書籍、電影、歌曲等，自然而然地吸收學習會比傳統的填鴨死背要有效得多！這也是我們 EZTalk 編輯群一整年在做的事，所有的努力都是為了把最好的素材、最有效的學習方式以及最專業的內容提供給讀者，希望你們在學習英文這條偉大的航道上，一路順遂，與我們同行！

EZ TALK
本期責任編輯

Section 4 • Health News 衛生新聞

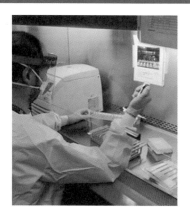

Cover Story 封面故事 — 疫情下的台灣

PART 2   News Reading

Section 5 • International News 國際局勢新聞

Section 6 • Society News 社會氛圍新聞

PART 3 · Life News

Section 11 • Art News 藝文新聞

Section 12 • Educational News 教育新聞

Section 13 • Sports News 體育新聞

Section 14 • Film & Drama News 影劇新聞

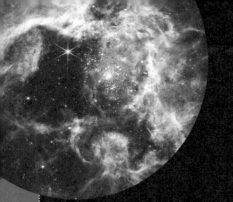

PART 1

News TV

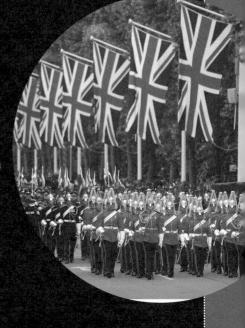
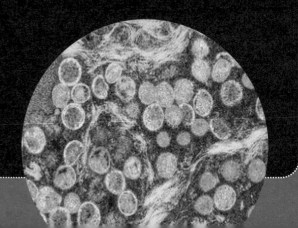

◀ 破金氏紀錄的
巨型草莓

©guinnessworldrecords.com

全文朗讀 🎧 001 | 單字 🎧 002

Giant Israeli Strawberry Sets Guinness Record
以色列巨型草莓破金氏世界紀錄

Vocabulary

1. **declare** [dɪˋklɛr] (v.)
   宣告，宣布

2. **enormous** [əˋnɔrməs]
   (a.) 巨大的，極大的

3. **strain** [stren] (n.)
   品種，品系

4. **researcher** [ˋrisɜtʃɚ]
   (n.) 研究員，調查者

5. **institute** [ˋɪnstəˌtut]
   (n.) 機構，研究院

Tongue-tied No More

put sth./sb. on the map
使……出名

使某地或某人變得有名。

A: What's your favorite
   Katy Perry album?
   你最喜歡凱蒂佩芮哪張
   專輯？

B: *One of the Boys*—it's
   the album that **put** her
   on the map.
   《花樣派對》吧。這張專
   輯令她聲名大噪。

On February 12th, a strawberry grown by Israeli farmer Chahi Ariel was ¹⁾**declared** the world's heaviest by Guinness World Records. When picked early last year on Ariel's farm near the city of Netanya in central Israel, the ²⁾**enormous** strawberry was 18 centimeters long, 4 centimeters thick, and weighed 289 grams.

在 2 月 12 號，一顆由以色列農夫查海亞利爾栽種的草莓被金氏世界紀錄宣布為世界上最重的草莓。亞利爾的農場靠近以色列中部內坦亞市，這顆長達 18 公分，厚 4 公分，重達 289 公克的巨型草莓在去年先被採收。

"We waited for a year for the results," said Ariel. "We kept it in the freezer for a year." The strawberry was of the Ilan ³⁾**strain**, developed by Nir Dai, a ⁴⁾**researcher** at Israel's Volcani ⁵⁾**Institute**. According to Dai, the record-setting fruit was five times the average weight of an Ilan strawberry.

亞利爾表示：「我們等了一年才得到結果。我們將它冰在冰庫一整年。」這顆屬於伊蘭品種的草莓，由以色列沃肯尼研究中心的研究員尼爾戴培育。根據戴的說法，這顆破紀錄的水果比一般的伊蘭草莓重五倍。

"The news has spread all over the world." added Ariel. "I am very proud to put Israel on the map." The previous record was held by a Japanese farmer who grew a 250-gram strawberry in 2015.

亞利爾補充說：「這件新聞傳遍了全世界。我非常驕傲能讓以色列為世界所見。」先前的紀錄保持者是一名日本農夫，他於 2015 年種出了一顆 250 公克重的草莓。

©guinnessworldrecords.com

◀ 栽種出世界第一草莓的以色列農夫

◀ 時尚精品巴黎世家
（Balenciaga）

©Wiki Commons

Balenciaga Sells "Destroyed" Sneakers
巴黎世家販售「破爛版」球鞋

When Balenciaga revealed its new line of "full destroyed" [1)]**sneakers**, they immediately went viral, with many criticizing the shoes for their dirty look and high price tag.

當巴黎世家揭曉其新款的「破爛不堪」運動鞋，這件事隨即被瘋傳，引發許多人批評這雙鞋的骯髒造型及昂貴價格。

The [2)]**luxury** fashion house released the [3)]**shabby** version of its Paris High Top Sneaker on Monday. The limited edition sneaker, which sells for $1,850, features "full destroyed" details like tears, ***scuffs** and what appears to be dirt. That's more than double the price of the standard Paris High Top, which costs $625 for a new, clean look.

這家高檔時尚品牌週一發表其 Paris 高筒球鞋系列的破舊版本。這款限量版球鞋要價 1,850 美元，主打「毀壞程度嚴重的」特色，例如撕痕、磨損，及看似髒汙等。這雙鞋比一般 Paris 高統鞋價格貴上兩倍，一雙新穎乾淨的基本款要價 625 美元。

Balenciaga is selling just 100 pairs of the "full destroyed" sneakers, which were created for an ad [4)]**campaign**. One social media user compared the sneakers to a dirty old pair of Converse high tops his mom begged him to throw away when he was in high school.

巴黎世家只販售 100 雙此款「破爛不堪」球鞋，本商品是為了一個廣告活動所設計。一名網友將此鞋比喻成自己高中時所穿，那雙不斷被媽媽要求丟掉的老舊髒 Converse 布鞋。

◀ 巴黎世家販售的破爛版球鞋

©Shutterstock.com

Vocabulary

1. **sneaker** [ˋsnikɚ] (n.)
   球鞋，運動鞋

2. **luxury** [ˋlʌkʃərɪ] (n.)
   奢華，高貴

3. **shabby** [ˋʃæbɪ] (a.)
   破爛的，破舊的

4. **campaign** [kæmˋpen]
   (n.) 活動，運動

Advanced Words

scuff [skʌf] (n./v.)
磨痕；使磨損

Tongue-tied No More

go viral 瘋傳，
（網路）爆紅

影片或圖片等在網路上經由社群媒體被快速且廣泛傳播

A: Did that video of your cat **go viral** on YouTube?
你貓咪的那隻影片在 Youtube 上有爆紅嗎？

B: Yeah. It has over a million views!
有啊，它的點閱率超過了 100 萬！

▶ 韋伯望遠鏡拍攝
到的宇宙星雲

全文朗讀 🎧 005 | 單字 🎧 006

Webb [1] Telescope Reveals New View of Ancient Universe
韋伯望遠鏡揭開遠古宇宙新面貌

Vocabulary

1. **telescope** [ˈtɛləˌskop]
   (n.) 望遠鏡

2. **galaxy** [ˈɡæləksɪ] (n.)
   星系

3. **capacity** [kəˈpæsətɪ]
   (n.) 能力，能量

4. **remark** [rɪˈmɑrk] (v./n.)
   談到，說；言辭，評論

Advanced Words

infrared [ˈɪnfrəˈrɛd]
(a./n.) 紅外線的；紅外線

briefing [ˈbrifɪŋ]
(n.) 簡報，記者會

Tongue-tied No More

turn heads 引人注目

由於特別有趣、美麗、不尋常
或新穎而引起人們的注意

A: Have you seen
   Barbara's new dress?
   你有看到芭芭拉的新洋
   裝嗎？

B: Yeah. It's gonna **turn
   heads** at the party
   tonight.
   有啊，那在今晚的派對將
   會很吸引人。

The first image from the new James Webb Space Telescope—successor to the Hubble Space Telescope—has been released, and it's <u>turning heads</u>.

新詹姆斯韋伯太空望遠鏡（哈勃太空望遠鏡的接替者）的第一張圖像已經發布，而且引起了巨大轟動。

The image is said to be the deepest, most detailed ***infrared** view of the universe ever captured. Because the image contains light from [2]**galaxies** that has taken many billions of years to reach us, it allows us to look back in time to within a billion years after the Big Bang.

據說這張照片是迄今為止拍攝到的宇宙最深、最詳細的紅外線圖。因為該圖像包含來自數十億年才到達我們的星系之光，它使我們能夠回顧到宇宙大爆炸十億年內的光景。

"These images are going to remind the world that America can do big things, and remind the American people, especially our children, that there's nothing beyond our [3]**capacity**," U.S. President Joe Biden [4]**remarked** when shown the Webb image during a White House ***briefing**.

「這些圖片將提醒世界，美國可以做大事，並提醒美國人民，尤其是我們的孩子，沒有什麼超出我們的能力」，美國拜登總統在一次白宮記者會展示韋伯圖片時說到。

Further pictures from the Webb Telescope are due to be released by NASA on Tuesday.

來自韋伯望遠鏡的更多照片將於週二由美國航太總署發布。

◀ 知名漫畫《獵人》
為冨樫義博代表作之一

全文朗讀 ⌒ 007　單字 ⌒ 008

Good News for Hunter x Hunter Fans
《獵人》粉絲們有好消息囉！

Yoshihiro Togashi, creator of the *Hunter x Hunter* manga series, opened a Twitter account this week, and his fans are <u>jumping for joy</u>. In his first tweet, which included a photo of a manga [1)]**sketch**, the 56-year-old manga artist hinted at the return of *Hunter x Hunter* after a four-year *haitus, revealing that he was working on "four more chapters for now." Within 72 hours, his account had gained over two million followers.

《獵人》連載漫畫的作者冨樫義博，本週開設一個推特帳號，讓他的粉絲開心得手舞足蹈。這位 56 歲的漫畫家，在他的第一則推文附上一張漫畫草圖的照片，暗示《獵人》休刊四年後終於要回歸，並表示他目前正在執筆「四章」內容。發文後的 72 小時，他的帳號已擁有超過 200 萬名追蹤者。

Togashi later [2)]**commented** in Weekly Shōnen Jump magazine—where *Hunter x Hunter* has appeared in *serial form since 1998—that he has finished the rough drafts for 10 chapters, enough for a new volume, of which there are 36 so far. The popular series, which has inspired anime [3)]**adaptations** and video games, follows young Gon Freecss on his journey to become a Hunter—a [4)]**professional** skilled at locating secret treasures and rare beasts.

©Retrieved from Twitter of 冨樫義博

冨樫義博隨後在《週刊少年 Jump》雜誌表示（《獵人》自 1998 年就在此週刊連載），他已經完成 10 章的草圖，足以推出新的單行本，而目前《獵人》漫畫共有 36 集。衍生改編動畫和電玩遊戲的這部熱門連載漫畫，讓大家跟著小傑富力士走上成為獵人的旅程——也就是精通尋找秘密寶藏與罕見怪獸的專家。

Vocabulary

1. **sketch** [ˈskɛtʃ] (n.)
   草稿，草圖

2. **comment** [ˈkɑmɛnt] (v./n.)
   發表意見；意見，評論

3. **adaptation** [ˌædæpˈteʃən] (n.)
   改編，改寫

4. **professional** [prəˈfɛʃənəl] (n.)
   專家，專業人士

Advanced Words

haitus [haɪˈetəs] (n.)
休刊，短暫的中斷

serial [ˈsɪriəl] (n.)
連載系列

Tongue-tied No More

jump for joy 開心得手舞足蹈，歡呼雀躍

極度開心；開心得跳來跳去。

A: Was Tom excited to get accepted to Havard?
   湯姆對於被哈佛錄取感到興奮嗎？

B: Definitely. He **jumped for joy** at the news.
   當然興奮，他聽到消息後，開心得手舞足蹈。

▶ 紅髮艾德於 2017 年發行的《Shape of You》陷入抄襲官司風波

全文朗讀 ∩ 009 ｜ 單字 ∩ 010

Ed Sheeran's Copyright Troubles
紅髮艾德陷入版權風波疑雲

Anchor 1: Next up, in [1]**entertainment** news, pop star Ed Sheeran is back in court again. The award-winning singer is in a [2]**copyright** battle over his 2017 hit song, "Shape of You."

Anchor 2: And what a hit that was! It took the charts by storm, reaching number one in 34 countries, and becoming the most [3]**streamed** song on Spotify. So what is this case about?

Anchor 1: The 31-year-old singer is being [4]**accused** of *plagiarism by grime artist Sami Chokri, who performs under the stage name Sami Switch, and producer Ross O'Donoghue. Chokri claims "Shape of You" *infringes "particular lines and phrases" of his *track, "Oh Why," which was released in 2015. He and O'Donoghue argue that the "Oh I" hook in Sheeran's song is "strikingly similar" to the "Oh why" refrain in their own [5]**composition**.

Anchor 2: This isn't the first time Sheeran's been [6]**involved** in copyright drama, is it? Wasn't he accused of ripping off Marvin Gaye's "Let's Get It On" back in 2018?

Anchor 1: Yes. The company that owns the copyright accused Sheeran of stealing the song's melody in his number one hit, "Thinking Out Loud." The case hasn't gone to trial yet, though.

Anchor 2: Speaking of trials, how's the current one going?

Anchor 1: Well, when Chokri's lawyer accused Sheeran of being a "*magpie" who "borrows" ideas from other artists, the singer denied the charge, saying he didn't remember hearing "Oh Why" before the legal fight. The court also heard about another copyright claim over Sheeran's 2015 hit, "Photograph," which the singer settled out of court for millions of dollars. The case continues.

主播 1： 接下來是娛樂新聞。流行樂歌手紅髮艾德再次出庭。這位獲獎無數的歌手，因為 2017 年的熱門金曲《Shape of You》陷入版權之戰。

主播 2： 這首歌當年超夯的！簡直是席捲全球排行榜，在 34 國都登上冠軍寶座，還是 Spotify 上串流播放最多次的歌曲。所以這個官司是怎麼回事呢？

主播 1： 三十一歲的紅髮艾德，被指控抄襲倫敦污垢樂歌手喬克里（藝名為 Sami Switch）與製作人歐唐納福的作品。喬克里宣稱《Shape of You》侵害他 2015 年發行《Oh Why》歌曲裡「特定歌詞和用語」的版權。他和歐唐納福辯稱，紅髮艾德金曲副歌裡重複的「Oh I」與他們作品的「Oh Why」副歌「極為相似」。

主播 2： 這不是紅髮艾德第一次涉及版權風波，對嗎？2018 年的時候，他不是被指控抄襲馬文蓋伊的《Let's Get It On》？

主播 1： 對。擁有該版權的公司，控告紅髮艾德的冠軍金曲《Thinking Out Loud》剽竊該歌曲的旋律。不過這件官司尚未進入出庭審理的程序。

主播 2： 說到出庭審理，那麼目前的官司進行得怎麼樣？

主播 1： 當喬克里的律師指控紅髮艾德，向其他歌手「借取」點子來東拼西湊自己的作品時，艾德否認此控訴，並表示他在此法律糾紛之前，不記得聽過《Oh Why》這首歌。法院也聽取紅髮艾德另一首 2015 年的神曲《Photograph》的侵權案，當時艾德以支付數百萬美金的方式庭外和解。而這次的官司仍持續進行中。

EZpedia

grime 污垢（音樂類型）

是一種電子音樂流派，於 2000 年代初在倫敦發跡。它從早期的英國電子音樂發展而來，並受到 UK Garage、叢林舞曲、牙買加 Dancehall、Ragga 和嘻哈的影響。這種風格的特色是快節奏、切分音碎拍，一般約為每分鐘 140 次，並且時常伴隨強烈或鋸齒狀的電子音效。主持人是該風格的重要元素，歌詞通常圍繞著對城市生活的粗獷描繪。

hook 吸引人哼唱不已的疊句

指一首歌裡面向鉤子一樣能夠勾人心弦的幾個音。之所以說幾個音，是因為 hook 通常是短小卻具洗腦性的一段歌詞或音樂。

refrain 副歌

是歌曲中一句或一段重複的歌詞及音樂。通常出現在幾段正歌（也稱為主歌）之間，即由第一節正歌唱到副歌後，連接第二節正歌再返回副歌，如此類推。

▲ 紅髮艾德之熱門金曲《Shape of You》

▲ Sami Switch 指控紅髮艾德抄襲其《Oh Why》一曲

MY FANTASTIC SOCIAL MEDIA LIFE   REAL LIFE

NO WAR ♥ ONLY ♥ LOVES

◀ 震驚世界的 2022 奧斯卡
頒獎典禮掌摑事件

©Wiki Commons

全文朗讀 ⌒ 011　單字 ⌒ 012

The Oscars
第 94 屆奧斯卡頒獎典禮

Vocabulary

1. **address** [əˋdrɛs] (v.)
   處理，應付

2. **slap** [slæp] (n./v.)
   甩巴掌，拍擊

3. **comedian** [kəˋmidiən]
   (n.) 喜劇演員

4. **celebrity** [səˋlɛbrəti]
   (n.) 名人，名氣

5. **stride** [straɪd] (v.)
   大步行走

6. **smack** [smæk] (v.)
   掌摑，拍打

7. **incident** [ˋɪnsɪdənt]
   (n.) 事件，事變

8. **script** [skrɪpt] (v./n.)
   寫劇本，安排；（戲劇、
   電影等）劇本

Advanced Words

wrap up (phr.)
結束，落幕

quip [kwɪp] (v./n.)
調侃，打趣地說；妙語

alopecia [ˌæləˋpiʃə] (n.)
脫髮症，掉髮

biopic [ˋbaɪoˌpɪk] (n.)
傳記片

Anchor 1: The 94th Academy Awards ***wrapped up** on Sunday, so let's talk about the big winners.

Anchor 2: But first we should [1]**address** the [2]**slap** heard around the world.

Anchor 1: Of course. Will Smith really stole the show last night, and surprisingly, it wasn't with his Oscar win.

Anchor 2: Yes, and it all started with a joke. After making fun of Penélope Cruz and Javier Bardem, [3]**comedian** Chris Rock turned his attention to another [4]**celebrity** couple, Will and his wife Jada Pinkett Smith, ***quipping**, "Jada, I love you. *G.I. Jane 2*—can't wait to see it."

Anchor 1: For those not familiar with *G.I. Jane*, it's the 1997 movie where Demi Moore's character shaves her head for military training.

Anchor 2: And since Jada revealed last year that she has ***alopecia**, a disease that causes hair loss, the joke really hit a nerve. Will laughed at first, but after he saw his wife's expression, he [5]**strode** onto the stage and slapped Rock across the face.

Anchor 1: And as Will was returning to his seat, Rock said, "Wow, Will Smith just [6]**smacked** the shit out of me!"

Anchor 2: The audience wasn't sure if this was part of the show, but after Will yelled, "Keep my wife's name out your f***ing mouth," it became clear that the [7]**incident** wasn't [8]**scripted**.

Anchor 1: While later accepting his Best Actor award for *King Richard*, the ***biopic** about Venus and Serena Williams' father, Will apologized to the Academy, but not to Rock, explaining, "love will make you do crazy things."

主播 1：第 94 屆奧斯卡金像獎在週日結束了，讓我們談談有哪些大贏家吧。

主播 2：但首先我們應該討論一下驚動全球的「巴掌事件」。

主播 1：當然。令人吃驚的是，威爾史密斯昨晚搶盡鋒頭並不是因為他得了奧斯卡最佳男主角獎。

主播 2：沒錯，這一切都起因於一個玩笑話。拿潘妮洛普克魯茲和哈維爾巴登開玩笑後，喜劇演員克里斯洛克將目標轉往另一對名人夫婦，也就是威爾和妻子潔達蘋姬史密斯。他調侃地說：「潔達，我愛妳。我等不及看《魔鬼女大兵 2》了」。

主播 1：對那些不熟悉《魔鬼女大兵》的人，在這部 1997 年的電影中黛咪摩爾飾演的角色為了軍事訓練而剃光頭。

主播 2：而因為潔達去年表示她患有脫髮症，也就是一種會掉髮的疾病，這個玩笑著實戳中別人痛處。威爾一開始笑笑的，但當他看到妻子的表情後，他邁步走上舞台並給了洛克一記耳光。

主播 1：而在威爾走回座位時，洛克說：「哇，威爾史密斯剛甩了我一巴掌耶！」

主播 2：觀眾們都不確定這是否是典禮的一個橋段，但當威爾大喊：「不准你該死的談到我妻子」時，很明顯這起事件並沒有經過安排。

主播 1：威爾在《王者理查》這部傳記片中飾演 Venus 和 Serena Williams 的父親，當他之後在接受這部片的最佳男主角獎項時，他向學院（而不向洛克）道歉，並解釋說：「愛會驅使你做出瘋狂行為。」

94th Academy Awards 第 94 屆奧斯卡金像獎

2022 年第 94 屆奧斯卡獎是美國電影藝術與科學學會為表彰 2021 年 3 月至 12 月上映的傑出電影所頒發的獎項，並定於 2022 年 3 月 27 日在加州好萊塢的杜比劇院舉行頒獎典禮。本屆入圍名單創下多項影史紀錄，如《犬山記》與《沙丘》等；儘管掌摑事件帶動了收視率飆升，本屆奧斯卡仍是史上收視率第二低的一屆。

©Wiki Commons

▲ 奧斯卡小金人獎座

◀ 韓國男團 BTS 於葛萊美獎
上演出曲目《Butter》

©Getty Images

全文朗讀 🎧 013　單字 🎧 014

The Grammy Awards
第 64 屆葛萊美獎

Vocabulary

1. **kick off** (phr.)
   展開，開球

2. **highlight** [ˋhaɪ,laɪt]
   (n.) 亮點，最精采、有
   趣的一部分

3. **elegant** [ˋɛləgənt] (a.)
   優雅的，高雅的

4. **inspire** [ɪnˋspaɪr] (v.)
   賦予…靈感，激勵

5. **tribute** [ˋtrɪbjut] (n.)
   致敬，表達敬意的言辭、
   事物

6. **nomination**
   [,nɑməˋneʃən] (n.)
   提名，入圍

   nominate [ˋnɑmə,net]
   (v.) 提名

7. **coveted** [ˋkʌvətɪd](a.)
   夢寐以求的，垂涎的

   covet [ˋkʌvət] (v.)
   覬覦，渴望

Advanced Words

bling [blɪŋ] (n.)
金光閃閃

snub [snʌb] (n.)
遺珠

duo [ˋduo] (n.)
雙人組合

Anchor 1: The Grammy Awards [1)]**kicked off** in Las Vegas for the first time ever this year, and Sin City really brought the ***bling**, didn't it?

Anchor 2: It sure did. But before we talk about the [2)]**highlights** of music's biggest night, did any of the red carpet looks catch your attention?

Anchor 1: Well, Justin Bieber did, but not in a good way. A pink beanie and a suit that's five sizes too big? Seriously?

Anchor 2: Ha-ha. My favorite was Olivia Rodrigo's [3)]**elegant** black Vivienne Westwood gown. Now let's move on to the reason everybody watches the Grammys—the performances! Favorites?

Anchor 1: BTS for sure. They may have been ***snubbed** again this year, but their James Bond-[4)]**inspired** performance of "Butter" really brought down the house. How about you?

Anchor 2: Billie Eilish's performance of "Happier Than Ever" was amazing—especially the part where she danced on the rooftop in the rain. And she wore a Taylor Hawkins T-shirt—a [5)]**tribute** to the Foo Fighters drummer, who died recently while the band was on tour in Colombia.

Anchor 1: Right. They were originally scheduled to perform at the Grammys, but still ended up winning three awards—Best Rock Performance, Best Rock Song and Best Rock Album.

Anchor 2: Speaking of awards, Jon Batiste was the big winner, with 11

[6)]**nominations** and five awards, including Best Album. Next was R&B ***duo** Silk Sonic with four Grammys, including Record of the Year and Song of the Year for their hit single, "Leave the Door Open."

Anchor 1: And let's not forget Olivia Rodrigo, who took home the [7)]**coveted** Best New Artist prize.

主播 1：今年的葛萊美獎史上頭一遭在拉斯維加斯舉行頒獎典禮。此罪惡之城金光閃閃的風格，確實錦上添花，不是嗎？

主播 2：完全沒錯。但是在我們論及此音樂盛會的亮點之前，有什麼紅毯上的穿搭吸引你的目光嗎？

主播 1：我有注意到小賈斯汀，但不是正面的吸引到我。一頂粉紅色的毛帽搭配大五號尺寸的西裝？有沒有搞錯？

主播 2：哈哈。我最喜歡奧莉維亞優雅的 Vivienne Westwood 黑色禮服。現在我們來談談大家都看葛萊美獎的原因——那就是現場表演！你喜歡哪一段呢？

主播 1：當然是防彈少年團。他們今年雖然又是遺珠之憾，但是以 007 為靈感的《Butter》現場表演，真的贏得滿堂采。那你呢？

主播 2：怪奇比利的《Happier Than Ever》表演很精彩——尤其是她在屋頂上雨中跳舞的那段。還有她穿的是「幽浮一族」樂團鼓手泰勒霍金斯肖像的 T 恤，藉此向他致敬，因為他最近在樂團到哥倫比亞巡演時過世。

主播 1：對啊。他們本來有安排要在葛萊美獎表演，不過最後還是獲得「最佳搖滾演出」、「最佳搖滾歌曲」與「最佳搖滾專輯」等三個獎項。

主播 2：說到獎項，強巴提斯可是最大贏家，入圍 11 個獎項，抱走 5 個獎項，其中包括「最佳專輯獎」。其次是節奏藍調樂雙人團體「絲綢之聲」，贏得 4 座葛萊美獎，包括「年度唱片」以及由《Leave the Door Open》此暢銷單曲獲得「年度歌曲」。

主播 1：還有別忘了奧莉維亞，她拿下了眾人夢寐以求的「最佳新人獎」。

EZpedia

The Grammy Awards 葛萊美獎

是由國家錄音藝術科學學院（Recording Academy of the United States）頒發的獎項，目的為獎勵過去一年中成就出眾的音樂藝術家。葛萊美獎是美國及全球四個主要表演藝術獎項之一，獎項始於好萊塢星光大道計劃，並於 1959 年 5 月 4 日正式頒發第一屆葛萊美獎以表揚前一年於音樂界有傑出表現的人士。

©Getty Images
▲ 小賈斯汀與其妻海莉鮑德溫

◀ 《捍衛戰士：獨行俠》在
全球票房飆破 13.53 億美金

©Shutterstock.com

全文朗讀 🎧 015　單字 🎧 016

Top Gun: Maverick
《捍衛戰士：獨行俠》

Released back in 1986, the original *Top Gun* became one of the most ***iconic** movies of a decade famous for action movies. Starring Tom Cruise as ***cocky** pilot Pete "Maverick" Mitchell and Kelly McGillis as his gorgeous flight ¹⁾**instructor** Charlie, the movie follows Maverick and other young pilots as they ²⁾**undergo** training at the U.S. Naval Fighter Weapons School, better known as TOPGUN. Although Maverick loses his confidence when his radio intercept officer Nick "Goose" Bradshaw dies in a tragic accident, he still <u>saves the day</u> and gets the girl in the end.

第一部《捍衛戰士》於 1986 年上映後，成為了以動作片聞名的 80 年代最具代表性的電影之一。由湯姆克魯斯飾演代號「獨行俠」的自大飛行員—彼得米歇爾，凱莉麥吉莉絲則飾演美女飛行女教官查莉。劇情描寫獨行俠與其他年輕飛行員，在美國海軍戰鬥機武器學校受訓的經歷（該校別稱為「捍衛戰士」）。雖然「獨行俠」在他的雷達攔截官尼克布雷蕭（代號「呆頭鵝」），於一場悲慘意外罹難後而喪志，他最後還是扭轉頹勢並贏得美人心。

With Tom Cruise's star power, exciting ***dogfights** and classic '80s songs like "Take My Breath Away" and "Danger Zone," it's <u>no wonder</u> *Top Gun* was one of Paramount Pictures' biggest hits of the decade. Fans have been waiting for a sequel ever since, and now, 36 years later, Paramount is finally rewarding them for their patience.

在湯姆克魯斯的明星光環、熱血的近戰纏鬥與《Take My Breath Away》及《Danger Zone》等經典 80 年代歌曲的加持下，《捍衛戰士》無疑是派拉蒙影業在那十年間最賣座的電影之一。粉絲從那時起就引頸期盼續集，如今，36 年過去了，派拉蒙終於滿足了影迷的耐心等候。

Directed by Joseph Kosinski of *Oblivion* fame, *Top Gun: Maverick* ³⁾**hit** theaters on May 27, after a two-year delay due to the pandemic. Returning from the original film are Tom Cruise as Maverick, now a test pilot doing his best to dodge the advancement in rank that would [4]**ground** him, and Val Kilmer as his friend and former TOPGUN [5]**rival** Tom "Iceman" Kazansky, now [6]**commander** of the U.S. Pacific Fleet. When Maverick, cocky as ever, crashes an [7]**experimental** jet, he's sent back to TOPGUN as punishment, this time to train a fresh crop of young pilots for a dangerous mission to destroy a uranium enrichment plant. Will Maverick be able to save the day yet again?

由知名的《遺落戰境》導演約瑟夫科金斯基所執導的《捍衛戰士：獨行俠》，因為新冠疫情而延後兩年，終於在 5 月 27 日上映。故事繼續從湯姆克魯斯於第一集飾演的「獨行俠」來延伸，他現在是一名想盡辦法拒絕晉升、以避免遠離駕駛座艙的試飛員。而方基墨也再次飾演他的朋友，也就是他捍衛戰士時期的對手湯姆卡贊斯基（代號「冰人」）冰人現已任職美國太平洋艦隊司令。「獨行俠」一如往常的自大，當他撞毀一架實驗性噴射機，受到的懲處就是被遣返回捍衛戰士。這一次，他必須訓練一群年輕新血飛行員，執行一項摧毀濃縮鈾煉製場的危險任務。「獨行俠」是否能再次化險為夷呢？

EZpedia

U.S. Naval Fighter Weapons School 美國海軍戰鬥機武器學校

是美國海軍於 1969 年 3 月 3 日在加州米勒馬海軍航空站（現為米勒馬海軍陸戰隊航空站）建立用來培養海軍飛行員空戰技能的學校，現已併入位於內華達州法隆海軍航空站的美國海軍空中打擊與作戰中心，成為該中心的「美國海軍攻擊戰鬥機戰術教學計劃」。

Paramount Pictures 派拉蒙影業

是一家位於美國加州好萊塢的電影製片廠。是全球第五古老以及美國第二古老的電影製片廠，同時它也是「美國五大電影公司」之一。派拉蒙影業公司的總部位於好萊塢的美露斯大街 5555 號。

1916 年，電影製片人阿道夫祖克爾（Adolph Zukor）將與自己簽訂合同的 22 名演員化身為「星星」印製在公司的商標上。2014 年，派拉蒙影業公司成為好萊塢第一家僅以數位形式發行所有影片的電影公司。

派拉蒙影業公司的著名版權作品包括：偷天換日電影系列、教父系列、星艦迷航記系列、印第安納瓊斯系列前四部、不可能的任務系列、捍衛戰士系列、科洛弗檔案系列、變形金剛電影系列、古墓奇兵電影系列前兩部、南方公園系列、七夜怪談系列、癟四與大頭蛋系列、鬼影實錄系列和漫威電影宇宙第一階段前四部電影等等。

派拉蒙影業公司是美國電影協會（Motion Picture Association）的成員之一。

save the day
扭轉劣勢，拯救某人

想要形容某人宛若英雄般扭轉危險局勢、救出某人或是幫了大忙，就可以用 save the day 來表示。

A: Did our team win the game last night?
我們球隊昨晚比賽有贏嗎？

B: Yep. We were behind for most of the game, but a touchdown at the last minute **saved the day**.
有啊，我們幾乎整場都落後，但最後一分鐘的達陣扭轉了局勢。

(be) no wonder
難怪

不意外；「no wonder」可放在句首來表達。

You didn't have breakfast, so it's **no wonder** you're hungry.
你沒吃早餐，難怪會肚子餓。

A: Casey was screaming for the whole concert.
凱西整場演唱會都超級大聲尖叫。

B: **No wonder** she lost her voice!
難怪她失聲了！

▶ 安柏赫德與強尼戴普

©Shutterstock.com

The Trials of Johnny Depp and Amber Heard
強尼戴普和安柏赫德離婚官司不斷

Vocabulary

1. **sensation** [sɛnˋseʃən]
   (n.) 轟動（的人事物）

2. **sue** [su] (v.)
   控告，提出訴訟

3. **abuse** [əˋbjus] (n.)
   虐待，傷害

4. **career** [kəˋrɪr] (n.)
   職業，生涯

5. **countersue**
   [ˋkaʊntəˌsu] (v.)
   反告

6. **physical** [ˋfɪzɪkəl] (a.)
   身體的，肉體的

7. **witness** [ˋwɪtnəs] (n.)
   證人，目擊者

8. **alcohol** [ˋælkəˌhɔl]
   (n.) 酒，酒精

Advanced Words

defamation
[ˌdɛfəˋmeʃən] (n.)
誹謗，誣蔑

Ms. [mɪz]
女士（代替 Miss 或 Mrs.
的字，不指明稱呼人的婚
姻狀況）

testify [ˋtɛstəˌfaɪ] (v.)
作證，證實

In case you've been <u>living under a rock</u>, Hollywood star Johnny Depp and his ex-wife, actress Amber Heard, are in court over a $50 million *defamation case. And because the trial involves a celebrity couple <u>airing their dirty laundry</u>, it's become a media [1)]**sensation**.

以防萬一你已經與世隔絕很久，我們來談談好萊塢明星強尼戴普，和女星前妻安柏赫德因為誹謗案告上法庭，而爭取五千萬美元賠償的事。由於此庭審案件牽涉到名人夫妻所外揚的家醜，因此成為了媒體灑狗血的焦點。

Depp, 58, is [2)]**suing** Heard, 36, for $50 million over a 2018 opinion piece she wrote for the *Washington Post*, in which she described herself as a victim of domestic [3)]**abuse**. The Pirates of the Caribbean actor argues that the piece ruined his acting [4)]**career**. Heard is also [5)]**countersuing** for $100 million, claiming that Depp is attempting to destroy her name.

58 歲的戴普控訴 36 歲的赫德，針對她 2018 年向《華盛頓郵報》發表的社論求償五千萬美金，因為赫德在文章裡表述自己是一名家暴受害者。主演《神鬼奇航系列》的戴普，辯稱該文章毀了他的演藝生涯。赫德亦反告求償一億美金，她宣稱戴普企圖摧毀她的名聲。

Addressing Heard's claims of [6)]**physical** abuse in a Virginia court on Tuesday, Depp said, "Never did I myself reach the point of striking *Ms. Heard in any way. Nor have I ever struck any woman in my life." So far, several [7)]**witnesses** have *testified about the couple's drug and [8)]**alcohol** abuse, as well as their constant fighting.

星期二於維吉尼亞州法院上，戴普針對赫德宣稱的肢體虐待一事表示：「我的怒氣從未到達用任何方式毆打赫德小姐的程度，我這輩子也從未打過任何女人。」目前有多位證人出庭，針對這對夫妻的毒品與酒精濫用以及不斷爭吵的情況作證。

22 2022 年度新聞英文

Quotes

強尼戴普：

My goal is the truth, because it killed me that all these people I had met over the years...that these people would think that I was a fraud.

我的目標就是追求真理，因為這麼多年來，我碰到那麼多人都以為我是個騙子，這件事讓我飽受折磨。

It's been six years of trying times. It's very strange when one day you're Cinderella, so to speak, and then in 0.6 seconds you're Quasimodo.

我已經折騰了六年。好像一下子從灰姑娘變成鐘樓怪人一樣，感覺非常奇怪。

I'm not some maniac who needs to be high or loaded all the time.

我不是什麼必須一直嗑藥或酗酒的瘋子。

If anyone had a problem with my drinking, at any time in my life, it was me. The only person I've abused in my life is myself.

如果有誰對我人生中任何一個階段的酗酒感到困擾，那就是我。我人生中唯一虐待過的人就是我自己。

安柏赫德：

I became a public figure representing domestic abuse, and I felt the full force of our culture's wrath for women who speak out.

我成為了代表家暴的公眾人物，卻發現我們的文化對於挺身而出的女性感到極度憤怒。

Tell the world, Johnny. Tell them I, Johnny Depp—a man—I'm a victim too of domestic violence.

強尼，你跟全世界講啊，你跟大家說，「我，強尼戴普，身為一個男人，我也是家暴的受害者。」

怪奇比莉本屆時尚奧斯卡
的服裝

全文朗讀 🎧 019　　單字 🎧 020

Billie Eilish at the Met Gala
怪奇比莉出席時尚奧斯卡

Vocabulary

1. **amazing** [əˋmeɪzɪŋ]
   (a.) 令人驚豔的，極棒
   的

2. **totally** [ˋtotəli] (a.)
   （口語）當然，沒錯

3. **gorgeous** [ˋgɔrdʒəs]
   (a.) 漂亮的，動人的

4. **thrifting** [θrɪftɪŋ] (n.)
   去二手店（thrift
   store）買衣服等

   thrifter (n.)
   去二手買衣服的人

5. **literally** [ˋlɪtərəli]
   (adv.) 確實地，簡直

6. **fabric** [ˋfæbrɪk] (n.)
   布料，織物

7. **weird** [wɪrd] (a.)
   奇怪的，怪異的

8. **hook up** (phr.)
   連接，搭配

9. **velvet** [ˋvɛlvɪt] (n.)
   絲絨，天鵝絨

Advanced Words

vegan [ˋvigən] (a.)
純素的，植物的

vintage [ˋvɪntɪdʒ] (a.)
經典的，古董的

Emma: Miss Billie.

Billie: You look so good. We were watching in the hotel and I was like, "She <u>killed it</u>."

Emma: Stop. This is so [1)]**amazing**. Tell me about this.

Billie: This is all existing Gucci materials. We got some custom ***vegan** leather Gucci shoes. This is a necessary, like, very needed thing for me.

Emma: [2)]**Totally**.

Billie: And then this is all ***vintage** jewelry. So nothing was wasted.

Emma: [3)]**Gorgeous**. Wait, it's like [4)]**thrifting**, but for the Met. Do you ever go thrifting? Are you a [4)]**thrifter**?

Billie: I only thrifted. I [5)]**literally** don't know the last time I was in a store to buy clothes. When I was eleven, it was, like, Target. Thrifting was the only thing I did. It was my favorite thing. I was so good at it. And it was my world.

Emma: But it takes, like, hours. And you have to <u>have an eye</u> though, too.

Billie: Yeah, you got that eye, too.

Emma: We're twins.

Billie: Oh my God, I used to go to the [6)]**fabric** district and get all these [7)]**weird** fabrics and [8)]**hook them up**. And I made this big shirt with these [9)]**velvet** cuffs. Fashion, man. It's my life. I love it so much.

主持人： 比莉小姐。

怪奇比莉： 妳看起來真美。我們在飯店看到的時候我心想：「她超讚的。」

主持人： 請別再誇獎我了。這身衣服真令人驚豔。談談這身打扮吧。

怪奇比莉： 這都是用 Gucci 現成材料製作的。這雙是訂製的 Gucci 純素皮高跟鞋。我很重視這一點，這很重要。

主持人： 當然。

怪奇比莉： 而這些都是有年代的經典首飾。所以不會浪費任何資源。

主持人： 它們好漂亮。所以這是為了典禮的二手衣物再利用。妳會去二手店尋寶嗎？妳是個尋寶迷嗎？

怪奇比莉： 我只穿二手衣服。我實在不記得上次去店裡買新衣服是什麼時候了。我 11 歲時會去 Target 大賣場，但後來只會買二手衣服。這是我最熱愛的事，而我也很擅長這點。這就是我生活的方式。

主持人： 但去二手店尋寶要花不少時間吧。而且妳也必須要品味獨到。

怪奇比莉： 對啊，妳也很有眼光。

主持人： 我們志氣相投。

怪奇比莉： 我的天哪，我以前常去布料街區買一些奇形怪狀的布，然後再把它們搭配在一起。然後我做了這件帶有絲絨袖口的大襯衫。不得不說，時尚就是我的生活方式，而且我愛死它了。

Quotes

Clothing and fashion are kind of my security blanket, almost.
服裝和時尚幾乎就像我的避風港。

I really like hip-hop and rap; that's my main influence. I really wanna be more of a hip-hop artist.
我很喜歡嘻哈和饒舌，那是最主要的影響。我其實想當個嘻哈藝人。

Getting recognized is insane. It just blows my mind. Like, someone who you don't know at all can just be like, "Oh my God—are you Billie?"
能被認出來簡直令人瘋狂，這讓我非常震撼。像是你完全不認識的某人可能會說「天哪，妳是怪奇比莉嗎？」

EZpedia

Met Gala
時尚奧斯卡

Metropolitan Museum of Art，是紐約大都會藝術博物館的籌款活動。

© Wiki Commons

◀ 10 月 27 日，馬斯克完成以 440 億美元收購推特的交易。

© Sergei Elagin//Shutterstock.com

全文朗讀 ∩ 021　單字 ∩ 022

Musk to Buy Twitter for 44 Billion
馬斯克將以 440 億美元買下推特

After weeks of <u>giving Elon Musk the cold shoulder</u>, Twitter has accepted his offer to buy the social media service for $52.20 per ¹⁾**share**—a deal worth ²⁾**approximately** $44 billion. Musk, who runs **Tesla** and **SpaceX**, is the world's richest person.

推特冷落伊隆馬斯克數週後，終於接受了他提出以每股 52.20 美元買下其社群媒體服務的出價——整個交易價值大約 440 億美元。而經營特斯拉汽車與 SpaceX 太空探索科技公司的馬斯克，是世上最富有的人。

The American ³⁾**tech** ⁴⁾**billionaire** says his goal is to make Twitter a more welcoming platform for free speech. He has also <u>called for</u> a series of changes, from relaxing its ⁵⁾**content** ⁶⁾**restrictions** to removing fake accounts.

這位美國科技億萬富翁表示，他的目標在於讓推特成為更能自由發表言論的友好平台。他亦呼籲一連串的改變，包括放寬內容限制到刪除假帳號。

Some industry experts, however, fear Musk's desire to ⁷⁾**establish** Twitter as a free speech platform without limits could lead to more ***misinformation** and hate speech. Current Twitter policies against such content can cause users to be banned from the service.

然而，有些產業專家深怕馬斯克想要以無極限的方式，將推特建立為自由言論平台的做法，反而可能導致更多的不實訊息與仇恨言論。而目前推特針對此類內容的規定可能讓用戶的帳號被封鎖。

"I hope that even my worst ⁸⁾**critics** remain on Twitter, because that is what free speech means," Musk ***tweeted** just before the deal was announced.

「我希望即使是把我批評得體無完膚的人，也都能留在推特上，因為這才是自由言論的意義。」馬斯克在交易宣布之前的推文如是說。

give sb. the cold shoulder 冷落某人

「cold shoulder」意指對某人或某事物的態度不友善,尤其是刻意忽視或不感興趣;亦可使用「get the cold shoulder」。

- All the girls at the nightclub **gave** David **the cold shoulder**. 夜店的所有女生都冷落大衛。
- Karen **got the cold shoulder** from her classmate when she saw him at a restaurant. 凱倫在餐廳看到同學時,同學卻冷落她。

call for sth. 呼籲某事

公然表示應促成某事物發生或某事物是必要的;「call for」亦可指「要求進行某事」或「在合適或恰當的時機、場合或基於某因素來做某事」。

- Protesters are **calling for** the president to be removed from office. 抗議人士要求總統下台。
- The cake recipe **calls for** two cups of flour. 此蛋糕食譜需要兩杯麵粉。
- You and your boyfriend are getting engaged? This **calls for** champagne! 你和你男友要訂婚了嗎?這要好好用香檳慶祝啊!

EZpedia

Tesla 特斯拉

改名前稱為特斯拉汽車,是美國最大的電動汽車及太陽能板公司,並與松下合作電池業務,產銷電動汽車、車載電腦(FSD 系統),太陽能板及儲能設備與系統解決方案。特斯拉是世界上最早的自動駕駛汽車製造商,至 2018 年,特斯拉汽車已經成為世界最暢銷充電式汽車公司。2021 年 10 月,成為第六家市值破 1 兆美元的巨頭企業。

SpaceX 太空探索科技公司

是美國一家民營航太製造商和太空運輸公司,總部位於美國德州奧斯丁。SpaceX 由企業家伊隆馬斯克於 2002 年創辦,目標是降低太空運輸的成本,並進行火星殖民。SpaceX 現開發出獵鷹系列運載火箭及飛龍系列太空船,用於把太空人和貨物載至地球軌道。

© Tada Images / Shutterstock.com

編按:馬斯克一度開始指責 Twitter 沒有向他提供有關垃圾訊息機器人的足夠的資訊,然後聲稱他完全退出交易。Twitter 官方相當不滿,因此提起訴訟反擊,要求馬斯克完成交易。Twitter 和馬斯克原定於 10 月 17 日在法庭上對決,但在馬斯克讓步同意收購後,以每股 54.20 美元的價格完成收購,共計 440 億美元。

英國女王於今年辭世，享壽 96 歲，她一共在位 70 年

©Shutterstock.com

全文朗讀 🎧 023 | 單字 🎧 024

Queen Elizabeth's Platinum Jubilee
英國伊莉莎白女王在位 70 周年白金禧

Celebrating Queen Elizabeth's 70 years on the [1)]**throne**, the Platinum Jubilee of Elizabeth II was a four-day holiday weekend full of events to honor the [2)]**monarch**'s service to her nation and the *****Commonwealth**.

為了慶祝伊麗莎白女王在位 70 週年，其白金禧是一個為期四天的週末假期，充滿了紀念女王為她的國家和大英國協服務的活動。

On Thursday, the [3)]**celebration** began on the Mall outside Buckingham Palace with Trooping the Colour, which featured 1,400 soldiers, 200 horses, and 400 musicians marching past the Queen in honor of her birthday. The Jubilee brought the Royal Family back together, with Prince William, Kate Middleton, Prince Harry, and Meghan Markle all in [4)]**attendance** at Friday's Service of Thanksgiving at St. Paul's [5)]**Cathedral** in London.

週四，慶祝活動在白金漢宮外的林蔭大道開始，皇家軍隊閱兵儀式中有 1,400 名士兵、200 匹馬和 400 名樂手走過女王身邊以慶祝她的生日。禧年使王室成員重聚，威廉王子、凱特米德爾頓、哈里王子和梅根馬克爾都參加了週五在倫敦聖保羅大教堂舉行的感恩節禮拜。

On Saturday, the [6)]**spotlight** returned to Buckingham Palace for the Platinum Party at the Palace concert, which was headlined by huge acts like Queen, Rod Stewart, and Alicia Keys. Things wrapped up on Sunday with the Platinum Jubilee *****Pageant**, which paid homage to Queen Elizabeth's seven-decade [7)]**reign**. Featuring four acts, the Pageant included a military parade, a [8)]**procession** of double-decker buses representing each decade of the Queen's reign, and a colorful [9)]**carnival** with street theater, music and dance.

週六，焦點回到白金漢宮舉行的皇宮白金派對，這場音樂會由皇后樂隊、洛史都華和艾莉西亞凱斯等大牌明星表演。表演在週日以白金盛會結束，向在位七十年的伊麗莎白女王致敬。盛會共有四幕，包括閱兵式、代表女王統治每十年的雙層巴士遊行，以及充滿街頭戲劇、音樂和舞蹈的豐富多彩嘉年華。

<u>Bringing the Jubilee to a close</u>, Ed Sheeran performed his hit song "Perfect," and the gathered crowd sang "God Save the Queen." Then the Queen, who wasn't able to attend all of the events due to poor health, appeared on the palace balcony and, surrounded by three generations of the Royal Family, waved to her supporters one last time before the weekend ended.

在禧年結束時，紅髮艾德演唱了他的熱門歌曲「完美」，聚集的人群高唱「上帝拯救女王」。隨後，因身體不佳未能出席所有活動的女王出現在宮廷陽台上，在三代皇室成員的簇擁下，在週末結束前最後一次向她的支持者揮手致意。

編按：今年 9 月 8 日，由於醫生擔憂女王健康狀況，讓她在蘇格蘭的巴摩拉堡接受醫療監護，隨後女王於當地時間下午 3 時 10 分逝世，王室於下午 6 時 30 分左右發佈女王死訊。女王在位七十年，是英國歷史上在位時間最久的君主。

EZpedia

Platinum Jubilee 白金禧

是週年紀念之一。在君主制國家，它通常是指 70 週年紀念．

Buckingham Palace 白金漢宮

是英國君主位於倫敦的主要寢宮及辦公處。宮殿坐落在大倫敦西敏市（Westminster），是國家慶典和王室歡迎禮舉行場地之一，也是重要的旅遊景點。在英國歷史上的歡慶或危機時刻，白金漢宮也是重要的集會場所。1703 年至 1705 年，白金漢公爵約翰雪菲爾（John Sheffield）在此興建了一處大型鎮廳建築「白金漢屋」，構成了今天的主體建築，1761 年，喬治三世（King George III）獲得該府邸，並作為一處私人寢宮。1837 年，維多利亞女王（Queen Victoria）登基後，白金漢宮成為英王正式宮寢。19 世紀末 20 世紀初，宮殿公共立面修建，形成延續至今天白金漢宮形象。現在的白金漢宮對外開放參觀，每天清晨都會進行著名的禁衛軍交接典禮（Changing of the Guard），成為英國王室文化的一大景觀。

▲ 前英國女王伊莉莎白二世

全文朗讀 🎧 025　單字 🎧 026

Shanghai's COVID Lockdown Continues
上海因新冠疫情持續封城

©Shutterstock.com

Vocabulary

1. **authority** [əˋθɔrətɪ] (n.)（多為複數）當局，管理機關

2. **resident** [ˋrɛzədənt] (n.) 居民，住戶

3. **transmission** [trænsˋmɪʃən] (n.) 傳播，傳染

4. **community** [kəˋmjunətɪ] (n.) 社區，社群，社會

5. **virus** [ˋvaɪrəs] (n.) 病毒

6. **outbreak** [ˋaʊtˏbrek] (n.) 疫情爆發

7. **shortage** [ˋʃɔrtɪdʒ] (n.) 短缺，匱乏

Advanced Words

lockdown [ˋlɑkˏdaʊn] (n.) 封城，禁閉

quarantine [ˋkwɔrənˏtin] (n.) 隔離，檢疫

disinfect [ˏdɪsɪnˋfɛkt] (v.) 消毒，殺菌

censor [ˋsɛnsə] (n./v.) 審查員；審查

As Shanghai's strict *lockdown approaches the one-month mark, local [1]**authorities** have begun setting up fences around apartment building entrances. Many of the city's 26 million people have been forced to stay at home under China's zero-COVID policy, but the fences, up to two meters tall, only began appearing in the past few days.

隨著上海嚴格的封城措施來到滿一個月的時間，當地政府機關已開始在公寓大樓門口前設置圍籬。在中國清零政策的規定下，2600 萬名上海市民有許多人早已被迫待在家，但高達兩公尺的圍籬，是過去幾天才開始出現。

When photos of the fences were posted on Weibo, some users vented their frustration, comparing the action to locking up animals in cages. Videos were posted as well, with some showing [2]**residents** protesting from their balconies while the fences were set up, and others showing people trying to pull down the fences.

微博上有人貼出圍籬照片時，有些用戶開始發洩受挫情緒，將這樣的措施比喻為把動物關在籠子裡一般。也有人貼出影片，有的顯示政府機關一邊架設圍籬、居民一邊在陽台抗議，有的顯示居民試著拉下圍籬。

In an attempt to limit [3]**transmission**, Shanghai is carrying out COVID-19 testing on a mass scale, with all positive cases forced into *quarantine centers. It has also been reported that whole [4]**communities** are being moved, including people who don't have COVID, so that homes can be *disinfected.

為了試圖限制疫情傳播，上海進行大規模新冠肺炎篩檢，而所有確診者需強制前往隔離中心。甚至有人通報有整個社區居民都被移走，包括沒有確診的人在內，以便當地機關消毒住家。

According to official figures, 39 people died of COVID-19 in Shanghai on April 23, compared to 12 the previous day. But the city did not report any deaths from the [5)]**virus** during the first few weeks of the [6)]**outbreak**, causing some to doubt the government's figures.

根據官方數據，4 月 23 日有 39 名上海確診者死亡，前一天則是 12 名。但是上海市在疫情爆發的頭幾個禮拜，並未通報任何因為新冠病毒而死亡的案例，導致有些人懷疑政府的數據。

As Shanghai's lockdown stretches on, residents are losing wages, families are being separated, and many are experiencing [7)]**shortages** of food and supplies. But in a country where government *****censors** are always <u>on the lookout for</u> any criticism of political leaders, most are afraid to express their anger.

隨著上海封城措施持續進行，居民失去工資、家人分隔兩地，還有許多人經歷了食物和日常用品短缺的情況。但是，在這樣一個政府審查員總是在留意是否有人批評政治領袖的國家，多數人會懼於表達自己的憤怒。

◀ 防疫醫護人員

EZpedia

zero-COVID policy 清零政策

中國大陸常稱作動態清零，是指發現一例新冠確診病例，即在收治的同時進行流行病學調查、隔離一切有接觸可能性人員、控制病毒的影響範圍，以減少傳播和確診人數的一種防疫政策，早先在中國大陸、香港、澳門、台灣、澳洲、紐西蘭及新加坡等地為應對 2019 冠狀病毒疫情實施，但在普及接種疫苗、對病毒的認知加深及病毒的殺傷力下降後，為保住自身經濟，大部分地區於 2021 年陸續退出清零政策。目前中國大陸及澳門仍明確實行清零政策。

Tongue-tied No More

vent one's frustration/ anger/rage 宣洩受挫情緒、怒氣、憤怒

vent 有發洩的意思，此片語指把某人的挫折、怒氣、憤怒發洩出來。

A: Working in customer service must be challenging.
在客服部工作一定很有挑戰性。

B: Yeah. We have to listen to customers **vent their frustration** all day.
對啊。我們必須整天聽顧客宣洩受挫的情緒。

be on the lookout (for) 留心、注意（某人事物）

look out 當動詞片語是叫人小心、注意某種情況，若合成一個字 lookout，則有「瞭望塔」或「監視者」的含意，用於片語中是指「仔細注意以找到／避免……」。

A: I just heard this new CD that I think you'll really like.
我剛聽了這張新 CD，我覺得你會很喜歡。

B: Cool—**I'm** always **on the lookout for** interesting new albums.
太棒了，我一直在找有趣的新專輯。

◀ 猴痘會引起皮膚紅疹

©Shutterstock.com

全文朗讀 🎧 027 ｜ 單字 🎧 028

CDC Raises Monkeypox Alert
美國疾管中心提高猴痘警示風險

Vocabulary

1. **prevention**
   [prɪˋvɛnʃən] (n.)
   預防，防止

2. **precaution**
   [prɪˋkɔʃən] (n.)
   預防（措施），警惕

3. **recommend**
   [ˌrɛkəˋmɛnd] (v.)
   建議

4. **essential** [ɪˋsɛnʃəl]
   (a.) 必要的，基本的

5. **symptom** [ˋsɪmptəm]
   (n.) 症狀

6. **rash** [ræʃ] (n.)
   疹子

7. **infection** [ɪnˋfɛkʃən]
   (n.) 傳染，感染

8. **fatigue** [fəˋtig] (n.)
   疲勞

Advanced Words

nonendemic
[ˌnɑnɛnˋdɛmɪk](a.)
（疾病）非地方性的

lesion [ˋliʒən] (n.)
病灶，損傷

endemic [ɛnˋdɛmɪk] (a.)
（疾病）地方性的

The U.S. Centers for Disease Control and ¹⁾**Prevention** has raised its monkeypox travel alert level, encouraging people to take extra ²⁾**precautions** as global cases of the virus pass 1,000.

美國疾病管制中心（簡稱 CDC）已提高猴痘的旅遊警示等級。由於全球猴痘病毒傳染病例超過一千例，因此勸導民眾特別留意預防。

The CDC changed its alert from level 1 to level 2 on Monday, advising people to practice increased precautions to contain the outbreak, which has spread to 29 *nonendemic countries in the past month. Level 3, the highest alert level alert, would ³⁾**recommend** only ⁴⁾**essential** travel.

CDC 於週一將第一級的警示改到第二級，呼籲民眾加強預防措施以抑制疫情爆發，因為過去一個月以來，猴痘已傳播至 29 個非疫情國家。而最高警示等級的第 3 級，則建議民眾僅能在必要情況下旅遊。

While the CDC said the risk to the general public remains low, the level 2 alert encourages people to avoid close contact with sick people, including those with skin *lesions, as well as sick or dead animals. It also urges those showing ⁵⁾**symptoms** of the virus, such as a skin ⁶⁾**rash** or lesions, to stay away from others and to reach out to their local health authority for guidance.

雖然 CDC 表示一般大眾感染猴痘的風險仍不高，但第二級警示則勸導民眾避免與病人近距離接觸，包括有皮膚病灶的人，以及罹病或死亡的動物。CDC 亦呼籲有染上皮膚疹或病灶等猴痘病毒症狀的人，請遠離他人並求助當地衛生機關，以了解進一步的指示。

Monkeypox is a rare disease caused by ⁷⁾**infection** with the monkeypox virus, with symptoms including rashes, fever, muscle aches, swelling and ⁸⁾**fatigue**. The disease is *endemic to Central and West African countries,

猴痘病毒症狀
MONKEYPOX VIRUS SYMPTOMS
ILLNESS LASTS FOR 2-4 WEEKS

1-3% DEATH RATE WEST AFRICAN STRAIN
10% DEATH RATE AFRICAN STRAIN

西非病毒株 1~3% 致死率
非洲病毒株 10% 致死率

SWOLLEN LYMPH NODES
淋巴結腫脹：天花與猴痘症狀的主要差異在於，猴痘會使淋巴結腫脹，天花則不會。

HIGH FEVER
高燒

BACK AND MUSCLE ACHES
背部與肌肉痠痛

RASH ON FACE
臉部起疹子：高燒 1~3 天後，猴痘的特性就是會起膿皰。並且從臉部開始生長，再擴散至其他身體部位。

INTENSE HEADACHE
劇烈頭痛

RASH ON HANDS
手部起疹子

RASH ON LEGS
腳部起疹子

PUSTULE
膿皰：充滿膿液的疹子

▲ 猴痘常見症狀

but the recent outbreak across North America, Europe and Australia has raised fears of community spread.

猴痘是一種被猴痘病毒感染的罕見疾病，症狀包括紅疹、發燒、肌肉痠痛、腫脹與疲勞。此疾病原本僅流行於中非與西非國家，但近期北美、歐洲與澳洲紛紛爆發疫情，讓大家憂心社區傳播風險。

As of Monday, 1,019 confirmed and suspected cases of monkeypox have been reported in 29 countries, according to CDC data. The U.K. has recorded the most cases by far, with 302 suspected and confirmed infections. Next are Spain with 198, Portugal with 153 and Canada with 80.

截至週一為止，根據 CDC 的資料顯示，已有 29 個國家獲報 1019 例猴痘確診與疑似感染的情況。目前通報最多確診人數的是英國，已有 302 名疑似感染與確診病人。其次是 198 名患者的西班牙、153 名患者的葡萄牙，以及 80 名患者的加拿大。

EZpedia

alert level 警戒層級

因應天災、疾病、恐怖攻擊等因素，國家列出旅遊警戒層級降低災害與保護國人安全。通常將風險層級由低至高層分為 4 大類，一級表示「低」風險，二級表示「中」風險，三級表示「高」風險，四級則是「特殊情況」禁止前往的國家。

Tongue-tied No More

reach out to
努力溝通、求助、協助

努力和某人溝通，或請某人協助；給予某人協助或支援。

The party needs to **reach out to** young voters if it wants to win the election.
政黨如果想贏得選舉，就必須將觸角延伸至年輕選民。

The community was praised for **reaching out to** refugees.
此社區因為救助難民而獲得讚賞。

as of...
自⋯⋯時間開始

從特定時間開始；截至特定時間。

The new application form must be used **as of** January 1.
從 1 月 1 日開始，必須使用新的申請表。

As of 9 p.m., only 60% of votes have been counted.
截至晚上 9 點為止，只有 60% 的選票開出。

1. 在今年的疫情之下，你的工作日常是什麼呢？

What's your work been like during the pandemic this year?

我是於急診工作的第一線護理人員，會面對到因各種不同病痛，來掛急診的病人，當然也包括新冠病毒確診的個案。從重中症呼吸喘、血氧濃度差插管，到輕症感冒症狀的病人，我的工作是提供這些病患們醫療照護。

As a frontline ER nurse, I work with patients who seek emergency treatment for all kinds of medical conditions, which of course includes COVID-19 cases. My job is to provide medical care for patients with moderate to severe symptoms like shortness of breath or low blood oxygen requiring intubation, as well as mild cold-like symptoms.

2. 在這之中，你覺得最辛苦的事情／經驗是什麼呢？

What's been your most difficult experience?

在急診室擠滿新冠病毒感染的輕症病人時，輕症與重症患者會搶時間看診。雖然已告知民眾急診有檢傷分類，中重症病人要優先看診，但還是有輕症病患會表示自己已經等很久了，為什麼還沒輪到自己等等。向病人說明原因後，他們還是會覺得等很久不開心，並在做完新冠 PCR 採檢後，會吵著要馬上拿到健保卡趕著離開急診，不想再繼續等候下去。

When the emergency department is filled with mild COVID cases, they start vying with severe patients for access to treatment. Everybody is informed that under the triage system, severe cases have priority for emergency treatment. But patients with mild symptoms will still say things like, "I've been waiting so long, why isn't it my turn yet?" Even after explaining the reason, they're still frustrated by the long wait, and after their PCR test they want to get their NHI card back and leave the ER immediately instead of sticking around and waiting for treatment.

此外，確診新冠患者的家屬在面對自己的親人不舒服時，會因為種種事情而對醫護人員咆哮，甚至是辱罵，這些都是於急診第一線的醫護人員會遇到的事情。

Also, when the relatives of COVID patients see their loved ones suffering, they'll start screaming at the medical staff for various reasons, and even use foul language. These are all things that frontline medical personnel experience in their work.

看著自己以及身旁一同作戰的同事一一確診，我只能先暫退新冠抗疫的戰場養病，卻被醫院主管要求以篩代隔，在確診的前七天隔離期間回急診上班，繼續照顧同樣為確診新冠的病人。雖然我們是醫護人員，但是我們也是人，也會被感染新冠病毒，感染之後也是需要時間好好休息，才能重新返回戰場為大家努力，不應該被剝奪生病休息的權利。

Watching as me and my colleagues tested positive one by one, all I could do was take a short break from the war on COVID to recover. But then my supervisor at the hospital ordered me to test instead of quarantine, so I spent my seven-day quarantine period back in the emergency department treating patients who, like me, had tested positive for COVID. We may be medical workers, but we're also human beings. We're also vulnerable to COVID, and we need plenty of rest after we catch it before we can return to the fight and serve the public. We shouldn't be denied the right to rest and recuperate.

3. 在這波疫情之中，你碰過最感動的事情是什麼呢？

What's been your most moving experience during the pandemic?

在這場新冠疫情中，雖然見識過各式各樣的台灣刁民，但還是有配合合作、有禮貌的病人及家屬，很感謝這些病人及家屬給我們苦撐下去的力量。

Although I've seen all kinds of entitled behavior during the pandemic, there have also been patients and family members who are cooperative and polite, and I'm grateful to them for giving us the strength to keep going.

4. 關於疫情，請給自己或臺灣人一句話。

Regarding the pandemic, what would you say to yourself or the people of Taiwan?

面對新冠病毒抗疫時期，台灣人民應一同共體時艱，而不是只靠防疫醫療人員苦撐下去。這個時候不該群聚、遊行、聚餐、出國，全國人民應當一起共同努力遵守防疫規定！

In the fight against the COVID pandemic, the people of Taiwan need to work together to overcome adversity, and not just expect healthcare workers to bear the entire burden. At this time, people shouldn't gather in groups, hold demonstrations, have dinner parties or travel abroad. All our citizens need to come together and do their best to follow COVID guidelines.

台北基督教醫院第一線急診護理人員

ER Nurse

Taipei Adventist Hospital

> **1. 在今年的疫情之下，你的工作日常是什麼呢？**

What's your work been like during the pandemic this year?

在交接班結束後，要用漂白水消毒護理站、護理工作車、走廊及各種會觸碰到的地方。消毒完畢後，開始穿著隔離裝備，例如：兔寶寶裝、防水隔離衣、鞋套、護目鏡、髮帽及手套，通常著裝時間大約需要 5 分鐘左右。著裝完畢後，就開始一系列的護理治療工作。

At the beginning of my shift, I use bleach to disinfect the nursing station, carts, hallways and everything else that gets touched. After disinfection, I put on my PPE, including my coveralls, isolation gown, shoe covers, goggles, hair cover and gloves. This usually takes about five minutes. Then I start making my rounds.

首先，先測量每床病人的生命徵象，並給予藥物。巡視過程中遇到吃飯時間也會順便發餐點及倒水，並協助清潔病人使用後的垃圾，完成病人的日常生活所需。若遇到日常生活無法自理，或者臥床的病人，則需協助翻身、由鼻胃管灌食、抽痰及換尿布等。完成後才可脫下裝備、喝水、吃飯及上廁所，並完成每日的護理紀錄。通常一個班別需進行兩次治療，而以上是沒有突發狀況時的工作日常。

若遇突發狀況，則需要儘速穿好裝備進入病室處理。

First, I take all the patients' vital signs and give them their medicine. At meal times, I bring the patients their meals and pour water for them, and then clear away the trash afterwards, making sure their daily needs are met. Patients who can't care for themselves or are bedridden need to be turned over, fed by tube, have mucus suctioned and diapers changed, etc.

> **2. 在這之中，你覺得最辛苦的事情／經驗是什麼呢？**

What's been your most difficult experience?

在此次疫情中，我覺得最辛苦的事情應該是上班 8 小時內完全沒有脫下裝備，無法進食喝水及上廁所；因為此次疫情中有許多病人都是在護理之家感染的年長者，很多都是日常生活無法自理的臥床病人，所以護理人員必須在穿著裝備的情況下，協助病人翻身，並且還要注意避免他們皮膚壓傷，協助灌食牛奶、抽痰及換尿布等。

During the pandemic, the most difficult thing has been the times when I had to keep my PPE on for my whole eight-hour shift, which means I can't drink water or go to the bathroom. Because there have been many elderly patients who caught COVID in nursing homes, a lot of them have been bedridden and unable to take care of themselves. So the nursing staff has had to turn them over to prevent bed sores, feed them milk through a tube, suction mucus, change diapers, etc., all in full PPE.

因為此類病人眾多，所以有幾次我都是整個上班 8 小時都穿著裝備，沒有進食也沒有上廁所。這是我覺得最辛苦的經驗。

Because there have been many patients like this, there have been a few times where I had to keep my PPE on throughout my eight-hour shift, meaning I couldn't drink water or go to the bathroom. These have been my most difficult experiences.

3. 在這波疫情之中，你碰過最感動的事情是什麼呢？

What's been your most moving experience during the pandemic?

我認為這次疫情中最感動的事就是外界的支持與照顧。這次疫情中時常有一些藝人、公司及善心人士捐贈的食物餐點，讓我們在忙碌之餘，還有熱騰騰的飯菜能夠飽餐一頓，真的很感動。

For me, the most moving thing has been all the support and assistance we've received from society. Thanks to meals donated by celebrities, corporations, and good Samaritans, we've been able to enjoy hot food during our hectic schedules, which is really moving.

4. 關於疫情，請給自己或臺灣人一句話。

Regarding the pandemic, what would you say to yourself or the people of Taiwan?

願我們都能戰勝病毒的襲擊！台灣加油！

Let's all do our part to defeat COVID! Go Taiwan!

Coco Chan

Registered Nurse

護理師

1. 在今年的疫情之下，你的工作日常是什麼呢？

What's your work been like during the pandemic this year?

因為台灣各大醫院的急診大部分皆全年無休，在新冠肺炎疫情蔓延後，全年無休的急診更是被各種確診病人湧入。在今年疫情之下，原先我的急診工作從原本的抽血、打針、照 X 光、做醫療處置，變成開始戴 N95 口罩、戴髮帽再穿全套防護衣（PPE)，但做的依舊是抽血、打針、照 X 光如同前述一樣的工作，工作負荷量直直攀升。

The emergency departments at all major hospitals in Taiwan operate 24/7, and as the COVID pandemic spread, COVID patients began flooding into these emergency departments at all hours. During the pandemic this year, my ER duties have still included drawing blood, giving shots, taking X-rays and providing medical treatment, but now while wearing an N95 mask, hair cover and full PPE.

除了例行性工作之外，還要加上由警衛協助拉封鎖動線，以及再加上放射師著裝等過程，中間所花費的人力與時間成本，遠遠高於政府所估計。

In addition to our regular duties, we've also had to assist hospital security staff in setting up cordons to control foot traffic, and help radiation technologists put on their protective garments. The manpower and cost involved has been much higher than government estimates.

2. 在這之中，你覺得最辛苦的事情／經驗是什麼呢？

What's been your most difficult experience?

我相信在疫情中，最令醫護人員覺得辛苦的地方，是多出非常多的專有名詞，包含：居家隔離、居家檢疫、居家照護、自主防疫、自主健康管理等等的匡列類別。這些專業名詞皆有不同規範，因此我們必須要想辦法，如何用最簡單的方式衛教病人及家屬。

I believe that during the pandemic, the most difficult thing for medical personnel has been getting used to so much new terminology, like the following identification categories: home isolation, home quarantine, home care, self-initiated epidemic prevention, self-health management. Each of these categories has different guidelines, so we've had to come up with simple methods to educate patients and family members about them.

隨著防疫規範滾動式調整，院內病人以及家屬皆有不同的採檢規定，而醫院各項規範也會隨著政府政策一再調整。

As COVID guidelines changed, so did the testing rules at our hospital, which were different for patients and family members, and various hospital guidelines had to be adjusted again and again in accordance with government policy.

3. 在這波疫情之中，你碰過最感動的事情是什麼呢？

What's been your most moving experience during the pandemic?

我遇到了一位確診且造成血氧快速下降，引發身體器官多重衰竭嚴重併發症的爺爺。爺爺用僅存的力量開啟視訊鏡頭，請家人別為他擔心，不要害怕疫情，因為他的情況不代表所有的人的情況。雖說最後的結局不像童話故事一樣，但他勇敢面對了疫情，縱然留下遺憾，但是至少還能好好和家人說再見。

I encountered an elderly male patient who contracted COVID, resulting in a rapid drop in blood oxygen, which in turn led to multiple organ failure. The elderly patient used his last remaining strength to make a video call and tell his family not to worry or be afraid of the pandemic, because most people weren't in serious condition like him. Although his story didn't have a fairytale ending, at least he got to say goodbye to his family.

視訊結束後，爺爺對我說：「我能不能握著妳的手，陪我走完人生最後一段路？」伴隨著爺爺呼吸漸弱，病房內留下眼眶泛紅的我。

After the video call ended, he asked me, "Do you mind if I hold your hand so you can accompany me in my final moments?" His breath gradually faded, leaving me in the ward with tear-filled eyes.

4. 關於疫情，請給自己或臺灣人一句話。

Regarding the pandemic, what would you say to yourself or the people of Taiwan?

經歷了無數個穿脫隔離衣，汗水濕了又乾，乾了又濕的日子，雖然中途曾經想放棄，但還是謝謝自己能堅守崗位，堅持在一線的急診工作。看夥伴們彼此在崗位上一起努力，我堅信團隊能一起挺過疫情。

During endless days of putting on and taking off my PPE, soaking them with sweat and letting them dry, only to soak them with sweat again, there were times when wanted to just give up. But I'm grateful to myself that I was able to do my job and stick it out in the ER. Watching my colleagues working together to fulfill their duties, I'm confident that our team can make it through the epidemic.

我是急診護理師，我以自己為驕傲，也請台灣人對彼此有信心，一切終將會雨過天晴。

I'm proud to be an ER nurse, and if the people of Taiwan can only trust each other, we'll have a bright future ahead of us.

Nana
急診護理師
ER Nurse

1. 請簡述一下你確診的經歷與心路歷程。（如發現確診、確診後過程與心情等等）

Please describe your experience with COVID (testing positive, the subsequent process, your state of mind, etc.)

剛開始覺得喉嚨有點癢癢的，那整天瘋狂喝水。後來聽到前幾天接觸過的朋友確診，心裡有點害怕，覺得自己該不會是中標了。下班回家之後我趕快跟主管回報，開始在家隔離，隔離第一天快篩，沒想到竟然是陽性。當下我立刻帶起口罩，跟我先生保持距離，然後上網查詢 PCR 的地點並預約掛號，隔天一早就到現場等候。等待時的心情有點複雜，因為害怕若真的確診，會讓公婆不開心，也怕影響到他們的身體健康。

At first my throat felt a little scratchy, so I drank water all day. Later I heard that a friend I'd had contact with a few days earlier tested positive, and I began to worry that I may have caught it too. After I got home from work, I reported my contact to the health authority and started my home quarantine. On my first day of quarantine, I took a rapid test and, wouldn't you know it, I tested positive. I put on a mask right away and kept away from my husband. I went online to find a PCR testing site and register for a test, then went to the test location early the following morning to wait my turn. As for my state of mind while I was waiting, I was afraid that if I tested positive my husband's parents would be angry, and I worried about endangering their health.

做完 PCR 回來之後我整天關在房間休息，一直流鼻涕也有點頭暈，還好婆婆很照顧我，每天幫我準備午餐和晚餐，還泡維他命 C 給我喝。確診當天晚上因為非常不舒服而睡不著，甚至有一點呼吸不過來。第二天喉嚨開始沙啞，講不出話來，整天就是吃飯和睡覺，大概這樣過了三、四天左右，終於沒有那麼疲倦，可以在房間玩遊戲和看劇了，但聲音還是很沙啞，頭也很暈，玩一下就累了。大概到了第五天之後情況才開始好轉。

After I got back from taking the test, I spent the whole day resting in my room. I had a runny nose and felt a little dizzy. Fortunately, my mother-in-law took good care of me, cooking lunch and dinner for me every day, and even making vitamin C drinks for me. That night, I felt so bad I couldn't sleep, and I even had a little trouble breathing. I was hoarse the next morning, and couldn't speak. All I did all day was eat and sleep. After three or four days like that, I finally didn't feel quite so tired. I could play games and watch TV in my room, but my voice was still hoarse, I felt dizzy, and I got tired after playing just a little while. It probably wasn't until the fifth day that my condition started to improve.

2. 請分享在確診後，與醫護人員或疫調人員的互動或經驗。

Please share your experience interacting with medical workers or public health staff.

PCR 後大概一天就收到結果，也馬上收到疫調單，但過了八天都沒有收到隔離通知書。為此我有打電話給 1922，等了很久才終於有人回應請我留電話。因為客服太忙，表示之後才會回撥給我，隔天就突然收到隔離通知書了。

I received my result about a day after taking the PCR test, and got my risk assessment form right away, but after eight days I still hadn't received my home isolation notice. I called the 1922 hotline about it, and after waiting a long time somebody finally got back to me and took my phone number. Because the phone lines were so busy, they said they'd call me back later, and then I received my home isolation notice the next day.

3. 在這波疫情之中，你碰過印象最深刻的事情是什麼呢？

What's been your most memorable experience during the pandemic?

因為我其實很少感冒，印象最深刻的應該就是確診後的不舒服感。但公婆對我的關心和先生的照顧真的讓我很感動。

Because I rarely catch colds, the most memorable thing is probably the discomfort I felt after I was diagnosed with COVID. But I was really touched by the care and concern I received from my husband and his parents.

4. 關於疫情，請給自己或臺灣人一句話。

Regarding the pandemic, what would you say to yourself or the people of Taiwan?

雖然我們最後沒有好好守住這波疫情，對於那些在疫情中離去的人真的很讓人不捨，但我相信大家都能克服這次的難關，希望不戴口罩的日子能夠儘快到來。

Although we weren't able to keep out the pandemic in the end, and it's hard to let go of the people lost in the pandemic, I believe that we can overcome the current crisis, and I hope the day when we no longer have to wear masks will come soon.

Chloe Wei

「疫情下的台灣」口述訪談

> **1. 在今年的疫情之下，你的工作日常是什麼呢？**

What's your work been like during the pandemic this year?

我是一名警察。

I'm a police officer.

> **2. 在這之中，你覺得最辛苦的事情／經驗是什麼呢？**

What's been your most difficult experience?

在疫情之中，有許多對於員警來說相對不便與辛苦之處。首先，我們需要在接獲通報或日常巡邏時，在路上取締未戴口罩的民眾，並且在居家隔離者電子圍籬顯示離開居隔範圍時，需要到現場查看是否真的離開住處，亦或只是訊號異常或手機關機等。

There have been a number of inconveniences and difficulties for police officers during the pandemic. First of all, when responding to calls or while on daily patrol, we have to enforce the mask mandate when we see people not wearing them. And when the electronic fence system indicates that people in home quarantine have left their quarantine area, we have to go to their homes to see if they've actually left, or if there's just a problem with their phone signal or their phone is turned off.

另外，上班時要清查因疫情暫停歇業的場所，更須承受與民眾接觸可能造成的感染風險等心理上的壓力。

In addition, while on duty, we have to check up on businesses temporarily shut down due to the pandemic, and deal with the mental pressure of knowing we may become infected though contact with the public.

最後，員警們也需要面對疫情下暴增的業務（例如有些是衛生局的業務，但卻是警察要去處理）。這些是對我來說較為辛苦的地方。

Lastly, police officers have had to deal with a big increase in their workloads due to the pandemic. For example, the police have had to take on work normally handled by public health departments. These are things I've found difficult.

What's been your most moving experience during the pandemic?

2021 年剛開始三級警戒時，最感動的是台灣人民自律的表現。疫情爆發後，可以感覺到民眾明顯降低在外的活動，連逛商圈的人都銳減，這大大降低了前線作戰人員的業務量。

At the beginning of the Level 3 epidemic alert in 2021, the most touching thing was the self-discipline displayed by the Taiwanese people. After the outbreak started, you could tell that people greatly reduced their activities outside the home. Even the numbers of people visiting shopping areas dropped sharply, which really helped our frontline workers from being overwhelmed.

4. 關於疫情，請給自己或臺灣人一句話。

Regarding the pandemic, what would you say to yourself or the people of Taiwan?

到了後疫情時代，我們應學會在影響最小的前提下，與病毒學會共存。官方政策雖有諸多不妥，但也並非完全無可取之處。最重要的是練習獨立思考，判斷如何讓自己的生活在防疫與便利之間取得平衡。防疫路上一路走來如履薄冰，相當不易，但若能堅守最後的時刻，就能準備迎向全新生活，期待解封的那天。

In the post-pandemic age, we need to learn how to coexist with the virus in a way that has a minimal impact on our lives. Government policy may have many flaws, but it's not entirely without merit. The most important thing is to practice independent thinking and determine how to create a balance between epidemic prevention and convenience in our lives. Our journey in fighting the pandemic has been dangerous and difficult, but if we're able to stand firm till the end, we can look forward to our new lives after pandemic measures are lifted.

派出所基層一線三
Substation Police Officer

專欄撰稿 / 張簡晴瑩醫師

疫情之下，家長和孩子們，你們好嗎？

新冠疫情剛開始時，我們雖然擁有 SARS 的經驗，但這病毒來勢洶洶，在全球四處蔓延，一開始的重症和死亡率，讓大家人心惶惶。

政府很快就有相關防疫措施，所以開始要求個人防護，不能群聚、外出要戴口罩、要勤洗手，這些對我們來說似乎很簡單的事情，對於正值好奇年紀的孩童，一下子突然不能出門、不能上課、不能跟朋友玩，還要求出門必須要戴口罩，家長們生活重新洗牌，陪孩子練習防疫操作、和孩子一起學習上網課，假日陪孩子一起在家打發時間。這幾年出生的小孩，從媽媽在懷孕就開始擔心有沒有確診的可能，到生都在擔心如果自己或是剛出生的寶寶感染，該怎麼辦？

在醫師這個職位上，我們除了看到很多無助與擔心的家長外，更多是無奈的孩童…。孩子出生後，幾乎都待在家裡，好不容易上學又必須面臨三不五時停課，口罩成為日常…，這短短三年，孩子們更安靜了，也活在某種未知的恐懼之中，陸陸續續，身邊的人開始確診消息一一傳出，這些孩子及家長，在解脫與擔心間掙扎。面臨打疫苗時也是，各種拉扯不斷在這三年上演。

在我們臨床觀察這三年的孩子，很明顯是懂事許多，小小年紀就知道出門要戴口罩，要記得洗手才不會有壞病毒上身，就連面對打疫苗孩子們也相當勇敢，知道有打疫苗才可以保護自己和身邊的

人。而在第一線的我們，這三年除了面對焦急的家長，更多是臨床的挑戰！

{ 晴晴醫師，為什麼我家小孩會確診？}

在 2022 年 5 月以後，Omicron 正嚴重傳播的時期，每天確診人次高達 5 萬以上，幾乎每一天都有家長來我的門診問：『晴晴醫師，為什麼我家小孩會確診？』往往我還沒回答完，自責的家長又很緊接著補充：『晴晴醫師我跟你說，疫情一開始，我跟老公就去打新冠疫苗，把自己關在家裡。口罩也是，口罩正缺我熬夜排隊，就是要家裡小還可以確定受到完整地保護。台灣開始有社區感染，我就讓孩子們跟學校請假，讓他們在家裡上網課，為什麼還是確診了？』

站在家長的角度，我很理解…，

站在醫師的角度，我不意外…。

怎麼防都很難，終究還是要走上這條路。

坐在門診椅子上，我拍著家長的肩膀：『你已經做得很好了，真的…。』

時間拉回疫情剛開始，大家還對這個病毒不太理解，國外的疫情一直提醒著國人，這病毒對人類的威脅有多強。在前線工作的我們，戴上了全套裝備，

開　快篩防疫的工作。全套裝備密不透風，又濕又悶又熱，一整天的工作，臉上滿滿的壓痕外，也擔心自己會不會消毒不徹底，而去影響到身邊的人。

台灣防疫做得很好，全民也很配合政策，不群聚不隨意外出，但病毒是狡詐的，變異到很容易在宿主存活。其實台灣做得很好也很幸運，在疫苗施打率到達一定時，才開始慢慢有疫情。在臨床的我們工作轉換，開始跟這病毒正面對決，正開始理解這病毒的臨床表徵之時，重症孩童的案例開始現身。

對於這狡詐的病毒，我們醫療端不斷在把最新的訊息，帶給家長和孩童。期待著，因為我們的訊息，能讓家長點少一份擔心和自責，能讓孩子得到更完整的照顧。

{ 晴晴學姊，你不害怕病毒嗎？ }

在鐵皮屋的急診快篩站，一個學弟問我為什麼願意來急診上班，順勢提出這個問題。我笑一笑說還好耶，因為 N 95 增加說話的難度，沒機會分享當醫師的心路歷程。在我們訓練的過程，幾乎天天都住在醫院，所以要說不被孩童感染根本不可能。邊吐邊打點滴邊顧急診，邊發燒邊咳邊值班，這些都是過去的真實經歷。在這未知的病毒要來前，我想所有的醫師也做好準備，瞭解病毒保護好自己，其餘交給上天了…。

學弟工作告一個段落，他看著我透過厚厚的快篩板看診一會兒，好奇著我怎麼能夠『隔空問診』？因為疫情，我們要學習視訊看診，在沒辦法做任何理學檢查，怎麼能看出這個孩童的狀況好不好？

我指了指前面的家長『他們會告訴我』，

學弟不死心又問『他們不是都很焦慮很擔心都會說很嚴重嗎？』

我又指了指小孩『他會告訴我』。

學弟說得很對，一開始在急診工作時，面對焦慮的家長，我們雖然有自己專業的判斷，但是還是要給家長一個滿意的答案。尤其現在，隔著這麼大的距離，我們要怎麼做能讓家長安心且讓孩童得到最理想的照顧。而且，孩子不會說自己有哪裡不舒服，我們只能透過自己的眼睛判斷，說穿還是要靠過去累積的經驗。

『有問題隨時回來！』我笑著跟學弟說，你就跟家長這樣說…。

很多人會說，兒科醫師很難，尤其害怕孩童家長的情緒。人因為擔心焦慮，這些情緒是可以被接受的，但是情緒之下，我們還是要把觀念傳遞清楚。我常常會跟我病童的家長說，你讓自己好好睡一覺，我告訴你的衛教有做，其他事情就交給我。在疫情下，我發現多數人不是故意要為難醫療人員，而是因為不理解而產生憤怒，是因為無助而產生的焦慮，這些事情釐清楚了，醫病關係似乎也不是這麼困難了。

身為兒科醫師今天邁入第十年，前輩常常笑著說『我們在小兒科的事』。在疫情中，更加明白自己『小兒科的事』的獨一無二性和重要性。

也是因為這病毒帶給大眾的恐慌，大家比較能將心比心理解我們工作的壓力，醫病關係似乎比起過往更好。

然而因為這疫情，讓我們本來就很稀薄的醫療人力受到重擊。身處高風險區，有人確診不是太意外，但僅存的人力就必須吃下所有的工作。已經數不清幾天沒有休假，也慶幸自己沒有太多後顧之憂，可以單純把醫療工作做好就好。但是看著許多家長，因為疫情，家裡人力的分配出現問題而疲於奔命。

我們很感恩政府把防疫做好，但也深深覺得有些政策真的很需要滾動。在臨床，我們面對家裡沒有後援的人，全家確診後該怎麼打理生活必需？也遇到自己確診的家長，因為太擔心孩子的狀況，即便有視訊門診，不顧防疫規定直直往醫療院所衝，而本身因為害怕受罰也沒有明確告知自己確診的事實，我們該如何責怪起？

『晴晴醫師，我聽說…』

這段時間，最大的挑戰之一，是面對各方面的訊息。孩子要補充什麼好？要打什麼疫苗能夠避免這樣的疾病感染又可以安全？還有，在得病之後的孩子我們還能做什麼？染疫有這樣的臨床表徵是正常的嗎？染疫康復之後，又擔心會不會有可能是 MIS-C 或是再次確診？當然有很可愛的問題，包括新冠快篩綿棒是不是安全，能否自己買滅菌的綿棒？還有怎麼能讓孩子成為天選之人？

其實，大家相信嗎？我們能做的事情其實很簡單，與其大家抱這個吃那個，我們更強調在預防的工作，能怎麼做才能讓這些小小幼童避免過多的身體負擔。除了健康飲食以及運動外，疫苗也是在這疫情中的一道曙光。

面對這麼多聽說，我們雖然擁有專業的知識，但是這也是個全新的病毒，我們也跟著家長孩童一起在學習成長。在這艱困的疫情年，守護著各位孩童的家長們，真心辛苦了！

疫情下之臺灣中西醫藥觀察

專欄撰稿 / 彭溫雅中醫師

2019 年 12 月，中國大陸武漢市發現原因不明的肺炎感染，2020 年 1 月，世界衛生組織 (WHO) 隨即公布此為公共緊急事件，並將此病毒命名為 SARS-CoV-2 (Severe Acute Respiratory Syndrome Coronavirus 2)，將所引起的疾病稱為 COVID-19 (Coronavirus Disease-2019)，臺灣在 2020 年 1 月 21 日時確診第一例由境外移入的個案，之後便展開全島緊急防疫作戰狀態。

其實早在 2003 年 3 月時，臺灣就曾經爆發過 SARS-CoV，起初因為經驗不足，對於疾病致病原、傳染途徑及防疫措施皆狀況不明，處於措手不及的狀態，許多輿論壓力及防疫物資的缺乏，加上封院的管制，導致當時的臺灣瀰漫一股人心惶惶的氛圍。

也幸好有當時的經驗，再加上多年來對於冠狀病毒努力不懈的研究，這一次，臺灣一遇到類似狀況，立即宣布此為第五類法定傳染病，並明確公布相關防疫措施，包括配戴口罩、勤洗手、維持社交距離等，加上隨即成立的中央流行疫情指揮中心，每日舉行記者會，宣布最新確診例、最新防疫措施並清楚闢謠等政策，對於建立民眾防疫信心很有幫助。加上上千床的負壓隔離病房、日產上千片的口罩產能等具體醫療物資，及合成美國實驗室抗新冠肺炎藥物瑞德西韋 (Remdesivir) 的成功，讓臺灣無論是在快篩、疫苗、治療用藥上，皆是有備而來，並以「清零」為目標，讓國際間譽為「防疫模範生」！

可惜，隨著病毒變種的速度越來越快，從 Beta、Delta、Omicron，到目前的 BA.4、BA.5，臺灣的確診數量也達到單日破萬的狀態，2022 年 5 月，更創下臺灣當日確診人數破四萬人的驚人數量。在當時快篩試劑不足，無症狀帶原者過多的情況下，衛生福利部國家中醫藥研究所根據 2003 年對抗 SARS 的經驗及中醫的傳統理論，提出「新型冠狀病毒病中醫臨床分期治療指引」，並根據明朝嘉靖年間醫書《攝生眾妙方》中之「荊防敗毒散」為處方基礎，考量瘟疫治療臨床需求，依照病邪入肺化熱為主要表現，進行加減複方，研發出中藥抗病毒方劑「清冠一號」(NRICM101)，與全臺四所醫學中心合作治癒 21 位確診患者，隨即同步緊急授權國內多家 GMP 藥廠進行製造，臨床上發現對於防止輕症轉重症的效果顯著，經過臨床實驗也證實可以縮短病患住院天數及縮短三採陰的時間。

隨著臺灣清冠一號、二號的研發，各家醫學中心也紛紛推出不同成分的防疫方劑，例如國立陽明交通大學與臺北市立聯合醫院中醫院區的「淨冠方」、花蓮慈濟醫院的「淨斯本草飲」、恩主公醫院的「正冠飲」、長庚醫療體系的「益氣飲」等，也是因為 2003 年 SARS 肆虐時，臺灣中醫發現金銀花、板藍根等中藥材具有對抗冠狀病毒、提升免疫力的作用，才能讓中醫藥在這次 COVID-19 蔓延時發揮功效、並外銷至美國、德國及新加坡等，造福更多需要的人，這真的是臺灣的一大特色，以中西醫聯手對抗病毒，不但造福了人類，更為防疫付出很大的貢獻！

PART

2

News Reading

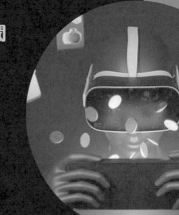

The Ukraine-Russia Conflict
烏俄戰爭

全文朗讀 | 🎧 029   單字 | 🎧 030

Vocabulary

1. **ongoing** [ˋɑnˌgoɪŋ] (a.)
   進行中的，持續的

2. **emerge** [ɪˋmɜdʒ] (v.)
   出現，崛起

3. **revolution**
   [ˌrɛvəˋluʃən] (n.)
   革命，變革

4. **communist**
   [ˋkɑmjənɪst] (n.)
   共產黨員，共產主義者

5. **fraud** [frɑd] (n.)
   舞弊，詐欺

6. **protest** [ˋprotɛst]
   (n./v.) 抗議

   protestor [prəˋtɛstə]
   (n.) 抗議者

7. **economic**
   [ˌɛkəˋnɑmɪk] (a.)
   經濟的

8. **occupy** [ˋɑkjəˌpaɪ] (v.)
   佔領，佔據

9. **parliament**
   [ˋpɑrləmənt] (n.)
   國會，議會

10. **flee** [fli] (v.)
    逃跑，逃脫

©Shutterstock.com

If you've found the news on the ¹⁾**ongoing** conflict between Ukraine and Russia confusing, you're not alone. The two countries have a complex relationship dating back to the Middle Ages, when they ²⁾**emerged** from the ancient state of Rus, ruled from Kyiv—now Ukraine's capital. Ukraine was part of the Russian Empire for centuries before becoming a Soviet republic after the Russian ³⁾**Revolution**, finally winning independence after the Soviet Union broke up in 1991.

若你不解烏克蘭和俄羅斯間持續衝突的新聞，很多人都跟你一樣。這兩個國家的複雜關係可追溯到中世紀，當時兩國都源自於古羅斯，而古羅斯的統治中心——基輔——也成了現今烏克蘭的首都。烏克蘭幾世紀以來一直是俄羅斯帝國的一部分，在俄國革命後成為蘇聯的共和國之一，最終在 1991 年蘇聯解體後贏得獨立。

Since then, Ukraine has gradually moved away from Russia towards closer ties with the West. Ukraine's first two presidents were former ⁴⁾**communists**, but when pro-Russian Viktor Yanukoviych became president in 2004, claims of voter ⁵⁾**fraud** caused a wave of ⁶⁾**protests** known as the Orange Revolution. In a second vote, pro-Western Viktor Yushchenko was elected on promises to lead Ukraine closer to the European Union and NATO—the organization created during the Cold War to protect Western Europe from the Soviet Union.

此後，烏克蘭逐漸脫離俄羅斯，轉向與西方建立更緊密的關係。烏克蘭首兩位總統是前共產黨員，但 2004 年親俄的亞努科維奇就職總統時，選舉舞弊的指控引發「橙色革命」的抗議浪潮。在第二次選舉中，親西方的尤申科當選，因為承諾帶領烏克蘭走向歐盟和北約（此組織建立於冷戰時期以保護西歐免受蘇聯侵害）。

Yanukovich finally did <u>come to power</u> in 2010, but by then Western Ukraine was firmly pro-Europe. When Yanukoviych backed out of a planned trade agreement with the EU in favor of [7]**economic** ties with Moscow in late 2013, thousands filled the streets of Kyiv in protest. As clashes between protestors and police became violent in February 2014, the protests turned into the Maidan Revolution—named after Kyiv's central square. After [6]**protestors** [8]**occupied** government buildings and [9]**parliament** voted to *impeach him, Yanukoviych left Kyiv and [10]**fled** to Russia.

亞努科維奇終於在 2010 年上台，但當時西烏克蘭已堅定親歐。2013 年底，亞努科維奇退出與歐盟計劃簽訂的貿易協定，轉而支持與莫斯科拉近經濟關係，於是數千人在基輔街頭抗議。2014 年 2 月，隨著抗議者和警察衝突暴力相向，抗議演變成以基輔中央廣場為名的「廣場革命」。抗議者佔領政府機關、國會投票通過彈劾案之後，亞努科維奇離開基輔，逃亡俄羅斯。

Just days later, Russian president Vladimir Putin sent troops to occupy Crimea, which was [11]**transferred** from Russia to Ukraine during Soviet times. A *referendum was then held, in which 96.7% of [12]**participants**—mostly Russian speakers—voted to join Russia. And when pro-Russian [13]**rebels** began an [14]**armed** *insurgency in the industrial region of Donbas in eastern Ukraine, Moscow supported them with weapons and possibly troops. Although a 2015 *cease-fire agreement helped end [15]**large-scale** battles, the fighting continued, leaving over 14,000 dead.

就在幾天後，俄羅斯總統普丁派兵，佔領克里米亞半島（蘇聯時期克里米亞管轄權從俄羅斯轉移至烏克蘭）。 隨後舉行公投，96.7% 的選民（主要為俄語人口）支持加入俄羅斯。東烏克蘭的工業地區頓巴斯，親俄叛軍開始武裝暴動，莫斯科提供武器支持，甚至可能提供軍隊。儘管 2015 年停火協議協助終止大規模戰役，但戰鬥仍持續，造成 1 萬 4 千多人死亡。

11. **transfer** [ˋtrænsfɝ] (v./n.) 轉移，轉換

12. **participant** [pɑrˋtɪsəpənt] (n.) 參與者

13. **rebel** [ˋrɛbəl] (n.) 反叛者，反抗者

14. **armed** [ɑrmd] (a.) 武裝的

15. **large-scale** [ˋlɑrdʒˋskel] (a.) 大規模的

16. **invasion** [ɪnˋveʒən] (n.) 入侵

    invade [ɪnˋved] (v.) 入侵，侵略

17. **expansion** [ɪkˋspænʃən] (n.) 擴展，擴大

18. **guarantee** [ˏgɛrənˋti] (v./n.) 保證，擔保

Advanced Words

impeach [ɪmˋpitʃ] (v.) 彈劾

referendum [ˏrɛfəˋrɛndəm] (n.) 公投

insurgency [ɪnˋsɝdʒənsi] (n.) 暴動，暴亂

cease-fire [ˋsisˏfaɪr] (n.) 停火

ballistic [bəˋlɪstɪk] (a.) 彈道的

The Ukraine-Russia conflict heated up again when Moscow began massing troops on Ukraine's eastern border in late 2021. U.S. officials stated that there were over 100,000 Russian troops on the border, and that an [16)]**invasion** of Ukraine could happen as early as mid-February. Moscow claimed there were no plans to [16)]**invade**, and insisted the troops were a response to NATO's growing ties with Ukraine, which hopes to become a NATO member. Putin, who sees NATO's eastward [17)]**expansion**—it now includes most of Central Eastern Europe, and will soon have *ballistic** missiles in Poland—as a threat to Russian security, asked for [18)]**guarantees** that Ukraine won't join NATO, but Western leaders refused. On February 10, 2022, U.S. president Joe Biden warned all Americans remaining in Ukraine to leave immediately. Just two weeks later, on February 24, the Russian invasion of Ukraine became a reality.

▲ 俄羅斯總統普丁

▲ 俄羅斯與烏克蘭的軍事糾紛示意圖

2021 年底，莫斯科開始在烏克蘭東部邊境部署大批軍隊，烏俄衝突再次升溫。美國官員表示，邊境有超過十萬名俄羅斯軍隊，最早二月中可能入侵烏克蘭。莫斯科聲稱沒有入侵的計畫，並堅稱軍隊是對北約與烏克蘭關係日益密切的回應，烏克蘭希望成為北約成員國。普丁認為北約東擴——已包含中東歐大部分地區，且即將在波蘭部署彈道飛彈——對俄羅斯安全造成威脅，他要求西方保證烏克蘭不會加入北約，卻遭西方領袖拒絕。2022 年 2 月 10 日，美國總統拜登呼籲所有留在烏克蘭的美國人應立即離開。而在兩週後的 2 月 24 日，俄羅斯入侵烏克蘭成為現實。

Phrase

come to power 上台

被任命在高階職位，例如國王、總統或總理。

• The Republicans **came to power** in 2020. 共和黨在 2020 年開始執政。

雙破折號，強調附加訊息

雙破折號（em dash）的用法安插在句子中間，用來補充資訊，且更能聚焦讀者的注意力。

(A) A referendum was then held, in which 96.7% of participants, mostly Russian speakers, voted to join Russia.

(B) A referendum was then held, in which 96.7% of participants—mostly Russian speakers—voted to join Russia.

which 關係代名詞，指 referendum，補充說明公投中 96.7% 選民站贊成加入俄羅斯；再補充選民大部分為俄語人口。(A) 使用太多逗號不易閱讀；(B) 則可以凸顯資訊重點。

EZpedia

Russian Revolution 俄國革命

第一次世界大戰，俄羅斯帝國難擋德國攻勢，傷亡慘重、經濟潰敗，加劇人民對百年來帝俄專制的不滿。1917 年 3 月（俄曆 2 月）二月革命爆發，推翻尼古拉二世，建立俄國臨時政府。同年 11 月（俄曆 10 月）以列寧（Vladimir Lenin）為首的布爾什維克黨（Bolsheviks）發動十月革命，推翻臨時政府，建立俄羅斯蘇維埃共和國（Russian Soviet Republics）。1922 年納入烏克蘭、白俄羅斯、波羅的海三國、中亞五國、高加索三國，組成「蘇維埃社會主義共和國聯邦」（Union of Soviet Socialist, USSR）。

Orange Revolution 橙色革命

2004 年烏克蘭總統大選，官方公布亞努科維奇以 3% 領先尤申科，民調卻顯示尤申科領先 11%。烏克蘭各城市爆發大規模抗議、罷工，尤申科支持者穿著橙色衣物（尤申科競選代表色），或舉橙色旗幟，抗議選舉舞弊。烏克蘭最高法院宣布選舉無效，並規定 12 月 26 日重新選舉。第二次選舉受到國際監督，最終尤申科獲 52%、雅努科維奇 44%。2005 年 1 月尤申科入職，橙色革命落幕。

North Atlantic Treaty Organization, NATO 北大西洋公約織（北約）

北美洲及歐洲國家防禦合作的軍事組織，擁有核武器和軍隊。二戰後，美國為首的西方國家為抵擋蘇聯共產主義擴張，1949 年成立北約。1955 年蘇聯為首的華沙公約組織（Warsaw Pact）成立。1991 年蘇聯解體，華約解散，北約持續運作，並加入波蘭、捷克、波羅的海三國等前華約成員，至今共 30 個國家。北約軍事開支佔全球國防預算 70% 以上。

Maidan Revolution 烏克蘭廣場革命

2013 年 11 月時任總統亞努科維奇中止與歐盟簽署政治和自由貿易協議《聯繫協定》（Association Agreement），並強化和俄羅斯的關係。烏克蘭親歐洲人士集聚基輔獨立廣場（Maidan Square），展開反政府示威，至次年 2 月國會投票通過罷免亞努科維奇結束。期間示威鎮暴至少 125 人死亡，1,890 多人受傷。2014 年 6 月烏克蘭新任總統波羅申科（Petro Poroshenko）簽署《聯繫協定》。

North Korea Launches Ballistic Missiles
北韓發射彈道飛彈

Vocabulary

1. **launch** [lɑntʃ] (n./v.)
   發射（飛彈等）

2. **deterrence** [dɪˋtɜəns]
   (n.) 遏止

   deter [dɪˋtɜ] (v.)
   遏止，制止

3. **nuclear** [ˋnukliə] (a.)
   核子的，原子彈的

4. **presume** [prɪˋzum] (v.)
   推定，假定

5. **maximum**
   [ˋmæksəməm] (a.)
   最大的，最多的

6. **altitude** [ˋæltəˌtud] (n.)
   高度，海拔

7. **shift** [ʃɪft] (v./n.)
   改變，轉變

8. **component**
   [kəmˋponənt] (n.)
   （機械設備的）零組件

9. **satellite** [ˋsætəˌlaɪt]
   (n.) 衛星

10. **peninsula** [pəˋnɪnsələ]
    (n.) 半島

©Shutterstock.com

全文朗讀 | 🎧 031   單字 | 🎧 032

North Korea fired three ballistic missiles, including a suspected **intercontinental ballistic missile**, toward the Sea of Japan early on Wednesday, South Korea's military said. The 1)**launches** came on the heels of U.S. President Joe Biden's five-day trip to the region, where he promised to increase 2)**deterrence** against the growing 3)**nuclear** threat from North Korea.

南韓軍方表示，北韓週三一早往日本海方向發射了三枚彈道飛彈，包括疑似的洲際彈道飛彈。美國總統拜登到該區拜訪五天，就緊接著發生此飛彈事件。拜登此行承諾會加強遏止北韓與日俱增的核武威脅。

In Pyongyang's 17th missile test this year, the three missiles were launched from Sunan, just north of the capital, between 6 a.m. and 7 a.m., according to the South Korean military. The first ***projectile**, 4)**presumed** to be an ICBM, reached a 5)**maximum** 6)**altitude** of 550 km, leaving the atmosphere, before falling 300 km east into the Sea of Japan. The second, a short-range ballistic missile, was lost after reaching an altitude of 20 km. The third, also a short-range ballistic missile, reached an altitude of 50 km and traveled 750 km, appearing to 7)**shift *trajectory** before falling.

根據南韓軍方表示，今年平壤的第 17 次飛彈測試中，有三枚飛彈於早上 6 點至 7 點之間，從北韓首都北邊的順安發射。被推定為洲際彈道飛彈（ICBM）的第一枚彈體，距地面最高高度達 550 公里而離開了大氣層，往東飛行了 300 公里後掉落日本海。而第二枚短程彈道飛彈則在抵達 20 公里高度後失蹤。同樣是短程彈道飛彈的第三枚飛彈，則到了 50 公里高度並飛行 750 公里，才疑似變化彈道而墜落。

The first missile was likely the Hwasong-17, North Korea's largest ICBM, which was first ***unveiled** at a military parade in October 2020, a South Korean national security official said on Wednesday. North Korea started testing 8)**components** of the system in February under the guise of a 9)**satellite** launch, and claimed to have tested the full missile on March 24.

南韓國安官員於週三表示，第一枚飛彈很有可能是北韓於 2020 年 10 月軍事演習首次揭露的最大 ICBM「火星 17」。北韓二月開始在偽裝發射衛星的情況下，測試此飛彈系統組件，並宣稱在 3 月 24 日完整測試飛彈。

Shortly after North Korea's Wednesday missile test, the South Korean and U.S. militaries each fired a surface-to-surface missile into the sea off the Korean 10)**Peninsula**—the first joint response to a North Korean missile launch since July 2017, when the North tested an ICBM. The South Korean air force also conducted an "elephant walk" on Wednesday, 11)**taxiing** 30 fully armed F-15K fighter jets on the runway as a show of strength, the South's Joint Chiefs of Staff said.

北韓週三的飛彈測試結束不久後，南韓和美國軍方各發射一枚地對地飛彈至朝鮮半島沿海——這是自 2017 年 7 月以來，雙方第一次針對北韓試射飛彈而聯手回應，當時北韓試射了 ICBM 飛彈。南韓參謀本部表示，南韓空軍亦於週三進行「大象漫步」演習，30 架全副武裝的 F-15K 戰鬥機在跑道滑行以展示軍力。

There are also signs North Korea could soon conduct its first nuclear test in nearly five years. South Korea's presidential office said Wednesday that North Korea recently tested a ***detonation** 12)**device** in possible preparation for a nuclear test. Satellite images have shown increased activity at North Korea's Punggye-ri nuclear test site in recent weeks.

亦有跡象顯示，北韓可能即將舉行近五年以來第一次核武試爆。南韓總統府於週

11.taxi [ˋtæksi] (v.)
（飛機）在地面滑行

12.device [dɪˋvaɪs] (n.)
裝置，設備

13.condemn [kənˋdɛm]
(v.) 譴責，責備

14.violate [ˋvaɪə‚let] (v.)
違反，侵犯

15.resolution
[‚rɛzəˋluʃən] (n.) 決議，
正式決定

Advanced Words

projectile [prəˋdʒɛktəl]
(n.) 彈體，拋射體

trajectory [trəˋdʒɛktəi]
(n.) 彈道

unveil [ʌnˋvel] (v.)
揭露，揭幕

detonation [‚dɛtənˋeʃən]
(n.) 起爆，引爆

三表示，北韓最近測試起爆裝置的舉動，有可能是在為核武試爆做準備。衛星影像顯示北韓位於豐溪里的核試場，最近幾週的活動增加。

▲ 北韓領導人金正恩

In Seoul over the weekend, Biden and newly elected South Korean president Yoon Suk-yeol agreed to hold bigger military exercises if necessary to ²⁾**deter** North Korea's nuclear and missile threats. The United States and South Korea have ¹³⁾**condemned** North Korea's launches, noting they ¹⁴⁾**violate** United Nations Security Council ¹⁵⁾**resolutions**. But China and Russia, North Korea's most powerful supporters, have instead criticized the U.S. for refusing to make concessions to the North.

而週末的時候，拜登和南韓新任總統尹錫悅同意，倘若有必要遏止北韓核武與飛彈威脅，即可舉行更大規模的軍事演習。美國和南韓譴責北韓發射飛彈的行為，指出此舉違反聯合國安全理事會的決議。但是北韓最強大的支持者中國和俄羅斯，反而批評美國拒絕對北韓讓步。

Phrase

(come) on the heels of 緊接在後

亦寫作「follow on the heels of」，意指緊跟在後、在後方靠得很近。

• The new California gun law came **on the heels of** similar laws in Nevada and Utah.
內華達州和猶他州發佈類似法律後，加州亦緊接著公佈新槍枝管制法。

under the guise of 在……偽裝下

假裝某事物；對外表示或裝作某事物不是它真正的樣貌。

• The con artist cheats his victims **under the guise** of friendship. 這個騙徒以友情之名欺騙受害者。

a show of strength 示威

政府、組織等示威、展現自己實力 / 能力的某種舉動。

• Workers marched in front of the factory in **a show of strength**. 工人在工廠前面遊行來示威。

make concessions 讓步

亦可寫作單數形式「make a concession」；允許某事物或放棄某事物，通常是指終結異議。

• The company will have to **make concessions** if it wants to avoid a strike. 此公司如果要避免罷工問題，就得讓步。

同位語

同位語的功能是「補充說明」，提供額外的資訊。而同位語的位置則是「緊接在先行詞之後」。例如：

• My brother Ben is going swimming next week. 我的哥哥班下週要去游泳。

• Donald Trump, the U.S. former president, is trying to make a comeback in the next presidential election.
唐納川普，美國前總統，正嘗試要在下次總統大選東山再起。

這兩句當中的 My brother 與 Donald Trump 就是先行詞，而之後的 Ben 和 the U.S. former president 是用來補充說明先行詞的，就是所謂的同位語。

EZpedia

intercontinental ballistic missile 洲際彈道飛彈

一種超遠程彈道飛彈，設計用途為投射一枚或多枚的核彈頭，威力強大，常被設想成導致世界末日的核戰中使用的武器。其具有比中程彈道飛彈、短程彈道飛彈和新命名的戰區彈道飛彈更長的射程和更快的速度。

世界上試射成功的第一枚洲際彈道飛彈是蘇聯的 R-7，北約代號 SS-6「警棍」。這枚飛彈於 1957 年 5 月 15 日從位於加盟共和國哈薩克的拜科努爾航天發射場試射成功，飛行了 6,000 公里。

Hwasong-17 火星 17

是朝鮮民主主義人民共和國在 2020 年 10 月 10 日朝鮮勞動黨建黨 75 週年閱兵式上公佈的新型導彈，這種導彈被視為火星 15 彈道飛彈的新版本，它於 2022 年 3 月 24 日首次發射。

F-15K fighter jet F-15K 戰鬥機

是一款美國麥道公司（現波音公司）開發生產的全天候制空戰鬥機。針對獲得與維持空優而設計，是美國空軍現役的主力戰鬥機之一。F-15 是自 1962 年展開的 F-X（Fighter-Experimental）計劃發展而來，在戰鬥機世代上被劃分為第四代戰機。

Joint Chiefs of Staff 參謀本部

為現代軍隊中提供人事行政、軍事情報、軍事訓練、後勤補給、政戰與計劃的幕僚部門。

十八世紀晚期以前，上述功能全部由軍隊統帥管理，但法國大革命後出現徵兵制，大量軍隊的管理使統帥的職責十分沉重。在 1795 年，路易 - 亞歷山大·貝爾蒂埃將軍率先創立了參謀系統。一年後，拿破崙接管改制軍隊。從此以後，總參謀部成為法軍的正式組織，並隨拿破崙戰爭走遍歐洲。

Former Japanese PM Shinzo Abe Assassinated
前任日本首相安倍晉三遇刺

▲ 日本前首相安倍晉三

Vocabulary

1. **stun** [stʌn] (v.)
   使震驚、目瞪口呆

2. **issue** [`ɪʃu] (n.)
   議題，問題

3. **nevertheless**
   [ˌnɛvəðəˋlɛs] (adv.)
   仍然，然而

4. **faction** [`fækʃən] (n.)
   （政黨的）派系，派別

5. **influential**
   [ˌɪnfluˋɛnʃəl] (a.)
   有影響力的，有支配力的

6. **ring out** (phr.) 響起

7. **collapse** [kəˋlæps] (v.)
   倒下，昏倒

8. **tackle** [`tækəl] (v.)
   制伏，撲倒

9. **helicopter**
   [`hɛləˌkɑptə] (n.)
   直升機

10. **vital** [`vaɪtəl] (a.)
    生命的，維持生命所必需的

全文朗讀 | 🎧 033　　單字 | 🎧 034

Shinzo Abe, Japan's longest serving prime minister, died after being shot on Friday in the city of Nara in western Japan. The attack, which occurred while Abe was giving a campaign speech on behalf of a Liberal Democratic Party candidate in the *upcoming Upper House elections, [1)]**stunned** a nation with some of the world's strictest gun laws.

日本首相任期最久的安倍晉三，週五於日本西部奈良市遭槍擊不治死亡。安倍當時幫即將參選上議院的自由民主黨候選人站台發表演說。過程中遇刺則震驚全國，尤其日本又是全球槍械管制法律最嚴格的國家之一。

The 67-year-old Abe served two terms as prime minister before stepping down in 2020 due to health [2)]**issues**. [3)]**Nevertheless**, as leader of the LDP's largest [4)]**faction**, he remained an [5)]**influential** presence in Japanese politics.

67 歲的安倍當過兩任首相，並於 2020 年因健康問題而辭職。然而，身為自民黨最大派系的領導人，他仍對日本政治具有一定的影響力。

Several minutes into Abe's speech in front of Nara's Yamato-Sadaiji Station, at around 11:30 a.m., two shots [6)]**rang out**, and he [7)]**collapsed** to the ground holding his chest. According to witnesses and video *footage, a man in a gray shirt approached from behind and fired twice at close range with what looked like a homemade gun. Moments later, the suspect was [8)]**tackled** by security guards.

安倍在奈良市大和西大寺車站前演講幾分鐘後，大約早上 11 點半的時間，響起兩次槍聲，他隨即摀住胸口不支倒地。根據目擊者和錄影片段，身穿灰色襯衫的男子從後方靠近，並使用看似自製的手槍近距離開槍兩次。過不久，警衛就制伏了嫌犯。

Abe appeared to be in cardiac arrest when he was transported to nearby Nara Medical University Hospital by [9)]**helicopter**. He showed no [10)]**vital** signs on arrival, and suffered a wound to his neck and internal bleeding in his chest, said a doctor who treated him. After four hours of emergency treatment, including [11)]**massive** blood *transfusions, Abe was declared dead at 5:03 p.m. "I'm at a loss for words," said Prime Minister Fumio Kishida on hearing the news.

安倍被直升機送往附近的奈良縣立醫科大學附屬醫院時，似乎已心臟驟停，到院已無生命跡象。救治安倍的醫師表示，安倍的頸部有傷口且胸腔內出血。經過四小時的急救，包括大量輸血，醫師仍於下午 5 點 03 分宣布安倍死亡。首相岸田文雄聽聞表示：「我震驚得難以言喻。」

Police at the scene of the shooting arrested 41-year-old Tetsuya Yamagami on suspicion of murder, and [12)]**retrieved** his weapon, a gun made of two metal barrels taped to a wooden board. During a search of his apartment, police recovered several other homemade guns, as well as what appeared to be [13)]**explosive** devices.

警方在槍擊現場以殺人未遂嫌疑逮捕 41 歲山上徹也，並找回他的武器，也就是用膠帶將兩個金屬管貼在木板上的自製槍。警方在搜查嫌犯公寓時，亦發現其他幾把自製槍，以及疑似具有爆炸殺傷力的裝置。

A former member of the Maritime Self-Defense Force, Japan's navy, Yamagami was [14)]**unemployed** at the time of his arrest. The suspect admitted attacking Abe, telling police he held a grudge against him because of his ties to a certain organization. Later media reports identified the organization as the Unification Church—a South Korean

11. **massive** [ˋmæsɪv] (a.)
大量的，龐大的

12. **retrieve** [rɪˋtriv] (v.)
找回，取回

13. **explosive** [ɪkˋsplosɪv] (a.) 爆炸性的

14. **unemployed** [͵ʌnɪmˋplɔɪd] (a.) 失業的

15. **tragedy** [ˋtrædʒədi] (n.) 悲劇，慘劇

16. **outstanding** [͵aʊtˋstændɪŋ] (a.) 出色的，傑出的

17. **mourn** [mɔrn] (v.) 哀悼，哀痛

Advanced Words

upcoming [ˋʌp͵kʌmɪŋ] (a.) 即將來臨的

footage [ˋfʊtɪdʒ] (n.) 影片片段，連續畫面

transfusion [trænsˋfjuʒən] (n.) 輸血

bankruptcy [ˋbæŋkrəptsi] (n.) 破產，倒閉

religious group famous for its mass weddings—which Yamagami blamed for his mother's *bankruptcy.

▲ 安倍晉三遇刺不僅衝擊日本全國，更是震驚國際

曾是日本海上自衛隊成員的山上，被逮捕當下處於失業的狀態。嫌犯坦承襲擊安倍，他告訴警方因為安倍與特定組織的關聯，使他對安倍懷恨在心。媒體爾後報導指出，嫌犯所說的組織為「統一教」。該南韓宗教團體以集體配婚聞名，而山上將母親的破產歸咎於此宗教。

Following Abe's assassination, the first of a Japanese prime minister since the 1930s, tributes from other world leaders began pouring in. "This is a 15)tragedy for Japan and for all who knew him," said U.S. President Joe Biden. Indian Prime Minister Narendra Modi praised Abe "an 16)outstanding leader," and European Commission President Ursula von der Leyen called Abe "a wonderful person," saying, "I 17)mourn with his family, his friends and all the people of Japan."

▲ 安倍遇刺後，許多民眾前往事發地奈良獻花弔唁

自 1930 年代以來，安倍是第一位遇刺的日本首相。事件發生後，世界各地的國家領袖紛紛致意。美國總統拜登表示：「對於日本以及認識他的所有人而言，這是一場悲劇。」印度總理莫迪則讚譽安倍「是一名出色的領袖」，歐盟委員會主席馮德萊恩則表示：「安倍是一個很棒的人，我和他的親友和全日本人民一起哀悼。」

Phrase

on behalf of 為了某人 (做某事)，代替某人

為他人的利益或支持而做某件事情，或是代表該人的利益，"behalf" 是代表、利益的意思。

• Can you go to the meeting **on his behalf** and report back to me? 你能代表他去開會，再向我回報會議結果嗎？

at close range 近距離

距離非常近，通常用以形容射擊目標，"range" 用於軍事用法是射程、距離的意思。

• The murder victim was shot with a pistol **at close range**. 此謀殺案受害者是被手槍近距離射殺身亡。

at a loss for words 不知道該說什麼好

震驚到無言以對的程度，無法思考該說什麼；亦可用「lost for words」來表達。

• I was so surprised to see Jake that I was **at a loss for words**. 我看到傑克的時候，驚訝到說不出話。

Quotations 引用的用法

英文中的引用會把對方說話的內容，前後加上 quotation marks(引號)，然後在前或後方指出說話的人或是出處，另外，引用的句子後方的逗點或是句點，需放在引號的裡面。例如本文中的：

• "I'm at a loss for words," said Prime Minister Fumio Kishida on hearing the news.
  首相岸田文雄聽聞表示：「我震驚的不知該說什麼好。」

Liberal Democratic Party 自由民主黨

是日本大型政黨，成立於 1955 年。2012 年起與公明黨組成執政聯盟「自公連立政權」，並在執政聯盟中占主導地位。

自民黨自 1955 年因保守合同建黨以來，與日本社會黨形成長期「保革對立」的 55 年體制，在 1993 年細川內閣成立以前執政長達 38 年，是日本一黨優勢制度的核心。戰後長期支配日本政治，創黨以來僅在 1993 － 1996 年、2009 － 2012 年短暫失去政權。自民黨總裁（黨魁）由於長期擔任日本內閣總理大臣（首相）的職務，因而被稱為「總理總裁」。

cardiac arrest 心臟停止

是指心臟突然停止跳動的狀況，這是一種醫療緊急情況，如果不立即接受醫療處置，將在幾分鐘內導致心源性猝死（英文：sudden cardiac death）。症狀包含喪失意識、呼吸異常或中止，有些患者在心搏驟止前還會胸痛、呼吸困難，以及噁心等症狀心搏停止後若無獲得治療，一般會在數分鐘內死亡。

Maritime Self-Defense Force 海上自衛隊

是日本自衛隊的海上部隊，成立於 1954 年 7 月 1 日，全體武職人員稱「海上自衛官」。由於現行日本國憲法的限制，因此編制上跟武器都是偏重防衛，原則上不配備具侵略性的艦種（如航空母艦、巡洋艦和核子動力潛艇等）以及兵種（如海軍陸戰隊），編制有限的防衛預算並透明化，其艦隊中的中大型水面作戰艦船也都會被冠以「護衛艦」的名號。其主要任務是防衛日本領海，1992 年開始參與聯合國維和行動。

Unification Church 統一教

世界和平統一家庭聯合會，簡稱統一教，原名世界基督教統一神靈協會，是由文鮮明於 1954 年在韓國創立的新興宗教。

The Canadian Trucker Protests
加拿大卡車司機抗議

Vocabulary

1. **depart** [dɪ`pɑrt] (v.)
   出發，啟程

2. **organizer**
   [`ɔrgə,naɪzə] (n.)
   組織者，發起人

3. **federal** [`fɛdərəl] (a.)
   聯邦政府的

4. **vaccinate** [`væksə,net]
   (v.) 注射、接種疫苗
   vaccine [væk`sin] (n.)
   疫苗

5. **province** [`prɑʒvɪns]
   (n.) 省，州

6. **atmosphere**
   [`ætʒməs,fɪr] (n.)
   氣氛，氛圍

7. **honk** [hɑŋk] (v.)
   鳴按喇叭

8. **hockey** [`hɑki] (n.)
   曲棍球

9. **occupation**
   [,ɑkjə`peʃən] (n.)
   佔領，佔據

10. **demand** [dɪ`mænd]
    (n./v.) 要求

▲ 今年初加國因疫苗規定引發的貨車司機抗議事件

全文朗讀 | 🎧 035   單字 | 🎧 036

On January 22, hundreds of trucks—from pickups to big rigs—formed ***convoys** in British Columbia and ¹⁾**departed** for Ottawa, Canada's capital. Called the "Freedom Convoy" by ²⁾**organizers**, their stated goal was to protest new ³⁾**federal** rules requiring truckers crossing into Canada from the United States to be ⁴⁾**vaccinated** against the coronavirus. Cross-border truckers were originally given an ***exemption** to COVID-19 ⁴⁾**vaccine** requirements, but that exemption ended on January 15.

一月 22 日，從皮卡車到連結車等上百台卡車，在不列顛哥倫比亞省集結成車隊，駛向加拿大首都渥太華。發起人稱此為「自由車隊」，他們的既定目標在反抗新的聯邦法令，該規定要求卡車司機若要從美國越境至加拿大，須施打預防冠狀病毒的疫苗。跨境卡車司機原先擁有新冠疫苗施打的豁免權，但此項特例只維持到 1 月 15 日。

By the time the convoy reached Parliament Hill in downtown Ottawa on January 29, they'd been joined by truckers from other Canadian

⁵⁾**provinces**, as well as thousands of protestors on foot. The protest that day had a party-like ⁶⁾**atmosphere**, with trucks blocking traffic and ⁷⁾**honking** their horns, and protestors barbecuing, drinking beer and playing ⁸⁾**hockey**. But as the protest turned into an ⁹⁾**occupation**, the protestors' ¹⁰⁾**demands** began to change. Some stated they wouldn't leave until vaccine ***mandates** for all Canadians were lifted, and others called for an end to restrictions ¹¹⁾**banning** the ⁴⁾**unvaccinated** from restaurants, bars and gyms. Some protestors even demanded that Parliament be ¹²⁾**dissolved** and Prime Minister Justin Trudeau be removed from office.

當車隊於1月29日抵達渥太華市的國會山莊時，來自加拿大其他省分的卡車司機，以及數千名步行抗議者也加入隊伍行列。當日，遊行隊伍充滿歡樂氣息，卡車阻斷交通，喇叭聲此起彼落，示威民眾在一旁烤肉、喝啤酒與玩曲棍球。但當抗議轉變成佔領，抗議者便逐漸改變對政府的要求。一些人表示，除非解除強制全加拿大人施打疫苗的命令，他們才會離開；有些人則呼籲廢除沒打疫苗就不能進餐廳、酒吧及健身房的規定；而有些抗議者甚至要求解散國會，並認為總理賈斯汀杜魯道該下台。

In the days that followed, Freedom Convoy truckers took their traffic-blocking ¹³⁾**tactics** to other Canadian cities, including Toronto, Quebec City and Calgary, as well as major border ¹⁴⁾**crossings** like the Ambassador Bridge, which connects Windsor, Ontario, with Detroit, Michigan, and carries up to $300 million worth of goods a day between Canada and the U.S. The tuckers' ***blockade**, which began on February 7, forced some auto plants, especially on the Canadian side, to reduce ¹⁵⁾**production** and cancel ¹⁶⁾**shifts** because parts couldn't be delivered. After receiving a court order, Canadian officials sent police on February 12 to remove protestors and vehicles from the Ambassador Bridge, which fully reopened the following day.

之後的幾日，自由車隊的司機們將阻斷交通這一抗議方法延用至加拿大其他城市，包括多倫多、魁北克市、卡加利，以及大使橋等主要邊境口岸。大使橋連接加拿大安大略省溫莎以及美國密西根州底特律，每天運輸往返兩國間的貨物價值多達三億美元。卡車司機們從2月7號開始這場封鎖，由於零件無法運送，迫使了一些汽車廠（多為加拿大的）降低產量並減少班次。收到法院命令後，加國官員在2月12日出動員警來驅離大使橋上的示威民眾與車輛，隔天大使橋便恢復通行。

11. **ban** [bæn] (v./n.)
禁止，取締

12. **dissolve** [dɪˋzɑlv] (v.)
解散，使終結

13. **tactic** [ˋtæktɪk] (n.)
策略，戰術，手法

14. **crossing** [ˋkrɑsɪŋ] (n.)
渡口，岸口

15. **production**
[prəˋdʌkʃən] (n.)
產量，生產

16. **shift** [ʃɪft] (n.)
輪班，班次

17. **chaos** [ˋkeɑs] (n.)
混亂，雜亂

18. **criticize** [ˋkrɪtəˏsaɪz]
(v.) 批評，指責

19. **lawful** [ˋlɑfəl] (a.)
合法的，法定的

20. **operation** [ˏɑpəˋreʃən]
(n.) 行動，活動

Advanced Words

convoy [ˋkɑnˏvɔɪ] (n.)
車隊，航隊

exemption [ɪgˋzɛmpʃən]
(n.) 免除，豁免

mandate [ˋmænˏdet] (n.)
命令，指令

blockade [blɑˋked]
(n./v.) 封鎖

gridlock [ˋgrɪdˏlɑk] (n.)
（無車能動的）交通壅塞

invoke [ɪnˋvok] (v.)
訴諸、行使（法律等）

Under pressure to end the weeks of [17]**chaos** and ***gridlock** caused by the protests in downtown Ottawa, on February 14 Trudeau became the first leader to ***invoke** Canada's Emergencies Act. This decision, which was [18]**criticized** by the Canadian Civil Liberties Association, gave the police broad powers to arrest protestors and even allowed banks to freeze accounts used to support the protests. "This has gone on for far too long," the PM said. "It is no longer a [19]**lawful** protest against federal government policy. It is now an illegal occupation. It's time for people to go home."

杜魯道迫於壓力，要結束示威者在渥太華市中心引起為期數週的混亂與僵局，於是他在 2 月 14 日成為首任啟用緊急狀態法的加拿大領袖。此次決議受到加國公民自由聯盟的批評，因為該法給予警察過多權力來逮捕抗議者，甚至允許銀行凍結支持抗議者所用的帳戶。總理表示：「這起事件已經拖太久，已經不是聯邦政府法令之下合法的抗議行動，而是非法佔領。民眾是時候該打道回府了。」

On February 18, hundreds of police officers began to remove protestors and vehicles from downtown Ottawa. By February 20, the main streets around Parliament Hill were largely deserted. During the [20]**operation**, police arrested nearly 200 individuals, filed about 400 criminal charges, and towed over 100 vehicles. Although the protests are over, the truckers didn't go home empty-handed. Five Canadian provinces have lifted their vaccine mandates, and the federal government has relaxed its COVID border restrictions—the original source of the truckers' anger.

在 2 月 18 日，數百名員警開始驅離渥太華市中心的抗議者與車輛。到了 2 月 20 日，國會山莊周邊的主要道路大部分皆已淨空。在行動中，警察逮捕了近 200 人，發起約 400 起刑事案件，並拖走 100 多台車輛。儘管抗議事件結束，卡車司機們並沒有白費心血。有五個加拿大省廢除了強制施打疫苗的規定，而聯邦政府也放寬了新冠肺炎邊境限制——這也是引發司機們不滿的導火線。

▲ 各類卡車加入遊行隊伍

Compound Words 合成詞

英文中，合成詞是由兩個或以上的字相連組成的一個詞，用來修飾或限制後一個詞。例如：

horse-riding 騎馬（構成名詞）　　　　　　daughter-in-law 兒媳（構成名詞）

quick-charge 快速充電（構成動詞）　　　　peace-loving 熱愛和平的（構成形容詞）

well-known 著名的（構成形容詞）

以及本文中的：

cross-border 跨境的（構成形容詞）　　　　party-like 歡樂的（構成形容詞）

traffic-blocking 阻斷交通的（構成形容詞）

EZpedia

Parliament Hill 加拿大國會山莊

位於加拿大安大略省渥太華市中心，坐落渥太華河南岸，為加拿大國會建築群所在。國會建築呈哥德復興（Gothic Revival）風格，加上其政治核心地位，每年吸引 300 萬人次的訪客到此遊覽。

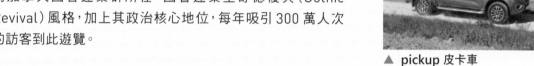

▲ pickup 皮卡車

Emergencies Act 緊急情況法令

是加拿大國會於 1988 年通過的一項法律，根據該法律，加拿大聯邦政府在遇到緊急情況和戰爭情況時可以採取特別臨時措施加以應對，例如政府可以下令金融機構暫停以及凍結個人賬戶資金。不過政府的任何行為繼續受《加拿大權利與自由憲章》和《加拿大權利法案》的約束。該法令通過後，1914 年通過的《戰爭措施法令》（War Measures Act）同步廢除。

▲ big rig 連結車

Canadian Civil Liberties Association 加拿大公民自由協會

是加拿大的一個非營利組織，致力於捍衛公民自由和憲法權利。

▲ trucker 貨車司機

Texas School Shooting Claims 21 Lives
德州校園槍擊案釀 21 死

©Getty Images

▲ 執法人員在事發後於洛伯小學大門外談話

全文朗讀 | ∩ 037　　單字 | ∩ 038

At least 19 children and two adults were killed on Tuesday after a shooting at a Texas 1)**elementary** school, according to authorities. Texas Governor Greg Abbott said the suspect was also dead, adding that law enforcement officers shot and killed the 18-year-old shooter.

根據當局表示，週二發生的德州小學槍擊事件，至少有 19 名兒童與 2 名成人死亡。德州州長艾伯特表示，執法人員亦開槍將 18 歲槍手擊斃。

President Joe Biden ordered <u>flags to be flown at half-staff</u> at the White House, military bases, and U.S. 2)**embassies** as a sign of respect for the victims of the mass shooting. Biden, just back from a trip to Asia, delivered an emotional address later that day. "As a nation, we have to ask when <u>in God's name</u> are we going to <u>stand up to</u> the gun 3)**lobby**?" he said, referring to the failure of Congress to pass gun control 4)**legislation**. The blocking of gun control bills is often blamed on pressure from the powerful National 5)**Rifle** 6)**Association**.

拜登總統下令白宮、軍事基地和美國大使館均降半旗，為此大規模槍擊事件犧牲者表達敬意。剛出巡亞洲而返美的拜登，當天稍晚即發表感言。他表示：「以一個國家的角度而言，我們不禁想問，到底什麼時候才能挺身對抗槍枝遊說團體？」此發言暗指國會無法通過槍枝管制立法。而常有人把槍枝管制法案受阻撓的情況，歸咎於勢力強大的美國步槍協會所施加的壓力。

The shooting took place at Robb Elementary School in Uvalde, a mostly Latino city of 15,000 between San Antonio and the U.S.-Mexican border. The 18-year-old suspect, [7)]**identified** as Salvador Ramos, was a Uvalde resident. Authorities said the gunman first shot and wounded his grandmother before fleeing the scene in her Ford truck. He later crashed the truck in a ditch outside the school and entered the building wearing ***tactical** [8)]**gear** and carrying an AR-15 style rifle.

槍擊血案發生在尤瓦爾迪鎮的羅伯小學，此鎮位於聖安東尼奧與美墨邊界之間，一萬五千名居民多為拉丁裔。18 歲嫌犯名叫薩爾瓦多拉莫斯，是尤瓦爾迪鎮居民。當局表示此槍手先開槍射傷祖母，再駕駛福特卡車逃離現場。卡車不久後撞進該小學外的水溝，槍手穿著戰術裝備、帶著 AR-15 式步槍而進入大樓。

The victims who died in the shooting—19 students and two teachers—were all killed in a fourth-grade classroom, where the suspect ***barricaded** himself, authorities told the media on Wednesday. The gunman "just began shooting [9)]**numerous** children and teachers that were in that classroom, having no regard for human life," said [10)]**Lieutenant** Christopher Olivarez, a [11)]**spokesperson** with the Texas Department of Public Safety. Law enforcement officers were later able to force their way into the classroom, where they killed the gunman.

當局於週三告知媒體，此槍擊案遇害的 19 名學生與兩位老師，均於四年級教室身亡，且嫌犯將自己一同關在裡面。德州公共安全局發言人克里斯多夫奧利瓦雷茲副警監表示：「槍手無視人命，開始射殺該教室裡的無數孩童與老師。」執法人員爾後才有辦法強行進入該教室，並擊斃槍手。

The Uvalde [12)]**massacre** was the 27th school shooting in the U.S. this year, and the [13)]**deadliest** attack at a grade school since 28 people were killed at Sandy Hook Elementary School in Newtown, Connecticut nearly a decade ago. "We have another Sandy Hook on our hands," said Connecticut [14)]**senator** Chris Murphy. "Our kids are living in fear, every single time they set foot in a classroom, because they think they're going to be next."

---

11. **spokesperson**
[`spoks.pɜsən] (n.)
發言人

spokesman
[`spoksmən] (n.)
男發言人

spokeswoman
[`spoks.wumən] (n.)
女發言人

12. **massacre** [`mæsəkɚ]
(n.) 大屠殺，殘殺

13. **deadliest** [`dɛdliəst]
(a.) 最致命的

deadly [`dɛdli] (adv.)
致命地

14. **senator** [`sɛnətɚ] (n.)
參議員

15. **annual** [`ænjuəl] (a.)
每年的，一年一次的

16. **convention**
[kən`vɛnʃən] (n.)
會議，大會

17. **republican**
[rɪ`pʌblɪkən] (a./n.)
（大寫）共和黨的；共和黨員

Advanced Words

tactical [`tæktɪkəl] (a.)
戰術的

barricade [`bærə.ked]
(v./n.) 擋住，堵住；障礙物

forum [`fɔrəm] (n.) 論壇

此尤瓦爾迪鎮大屠殺是美國今年第 27 起校園槍擊案，也是桑迪胡克槍擊案之後最致命的小學校園槍擊案，桑迪胡克槍擊案則是將近十年前於康乃狄克州紐敦鎮桑迪胡克小學發生的 28 人血案。康乃狄克州參議員克里斯墨菲表示：「現在又有另一起桑迪胡克血案算在我們頭上。我們的孩子每次踏入教室就等於活在恐懼之中，因為他們覺得自己可能就是下一名受害者。」

▲ 民眾於事發後前往洛伯小學獻花哀悼

The Uvalde shooting comes days before the National Rifle Association's 15)**annual** 16)**convention** is due to begin in Houston. Governor Abbott, along with both senators from Texas, are among 17)**Republican** officials scheduled to speak Friday during a leadership *forum.

尤瓦爾迪鎮槍擊案發生後的幾天，就是美國步槍協會即將在休士頓舉辦的年會。而身為共和黨黨員的艾伯特州長與兩名德州參議員，預計在此年會的週五領導人論壇發表演說。

▲ 多年來，槍制安全管制一直是美國民眾抗議的議題之一

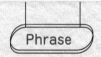

Phrase

(flag) fly at half-staff 降半旗

降半旗意指將旗幟降低至旗桿中間，通常用以表達對往生者的敬意；「fly at half-staff」就是將旗幟降到旗桿一半位置的舉動。

• Government **flags flew at half-staff** following the terror attack. 政府在恐怖襲擊事件發生後降半旗。

in God's name 到底

in God's name 會和 wh 開頭的詞搭配使用，來讓問句更有張力，或表達驚訝、生氣等情緒。

• What **in God's name** are you wearing? 你到底穿的是什麼？

stand up to 挺身對抗

以積極的態度對抗某人或某事；以對立角度來與某人或某事對質；不允許某人被錯待。

• Wow, I can't believe you **stood up to** the boss like that. 哇，我不敢相信你敢挺身對抗老闆。

set foot in 踏入

進入某處，開始進入。

• I'm never **setting foot in** that restaurant again. 我再也不會踏入那家餐廳了。

regard 的用法

regard 可以有三種詞性：名詞、及物動詞、和不及物動詞，意思上也有一些區別。當名詞時有關心、尊重、問候…等意思，例如：

- No one showed any **regard** for her feelings. 沒有人關心她的感受。
- Please give my best **regards** to your mom. 請代我向您的母親問好。

當及物動詞時有把…視作、尊重、注重、凝視、與…有關等意思，例如：

- I will always **regard** her as one of my best friends. 我會永遠視她為我最好的朋友之一。
- William is highly **regarded** as a lawyer. 威廉是一個備受尊敬的律師。

而當不及物動詞時，則有注重、注視的意思。

- Carol **regarded** at the photo thoughtfully. 卡羅沈思地注視著這張照片。

AR-15 style rifle AR-15 式步槍

是一款輕量化氣動式中央底火的半自動步槍，以彈匣供彈發射 0.223 雷明頓小口徑步槍彈，其軍用型可以選擇射擊模式，功能可切換半自動和全自動模式，該槍由美國武器設計師尤金斯通納設計並由阿瑪萊特和柯特公司生產。

由於美軍青睞其設計的先進性和良好的彈道性能，其衍生型被國防部發展成軍用型 M16 突擊步槍並在越戰中首次服役，其後更出現從 M16 槍族發展而成的 M4 卡賓槍，柯特公司更因其良好的口碑而於美國國內民用市場大幅產銷其半自動型號；在柯特的專利於 1977 年過期後，美國國內各大廠商更爭相仿製，導致其最終變成了一個涵蓋了精確射手步槍、短管步槍、手槍口徑卡賓槍、「AR 手槍」等各種不同模式的龐大槍族，亦令其成為美國民間最常見的槍械之一及美國槍械文化的代表，甚至被美國全國步槍協會冠以「國槍」（America's rifle）美譽。亦因其可塑性極高可任意組合、市場基數極大令廠商願意生產種類繁多的配件，而成為世上最容易及最常被改裝的槍種，引領槍械模組化的先驅，更被稱為「成人樂高」（LEGOs for adults）。

grade school 小學

為孩子提供第一部分教育的學校，孩子通常 5 到 11 歲，是 elementary school 較口語化的說法。

Supreme Court Overturns Roe v. Wade
最高法院推翻羅訴韋德案

全文朗讀 🎧 039　單字 🎧 040

In a 5-4 vote on Friday, the U.S. **Supreme Court** ¹⁾**overturned** *Roe v. Wade*, the ²⁾**landmark** decision that established a ³⁾**constitutional** right to ⁴⁾**abortion** nearly 50 years ago. The move puts the court <u>at odds with</u> a majority of Americans who favored preserving Roe, according to opinion polls. Since 1973, Roe had permitted abortions during the first two ***trimesters** of ⁵⁾**pregnancy**.

美國最高法院週五以 5 比 4 的投票結果，推翻了將近 50 年以來讓墮胎權受到憲法保護的劃時代「羅訴韋德案」裁決。根據民意調查，此裁決使法院和多數贊成保留「羅訴韋德案」的美國人意見分歧。而自 1973 年以來，「羅訴韋德案」使婦女可以在第一和第二孕期墮胎。

The new ruling came in the case of *Dobbs v. Jackson Women's Health Organization*, which challenged a 2018 Mississippi law that ⁶⁾**prohibits** abortions after 15 weeks of pregnancy—much earlier than the 24-week limit established under Roe. The Mississippi law allows ⁷⁾**exceptions** for medical emergencies, but not for ⁸⁾**rape** or ***incest**.

此新裁決起因自「多布斯訴傑克森婦女健康組織案」，該案是針對 2018 年密西西比州一項禁止婦女懷孕 15 週後墮胎之法律的訴訟案——此規定比羅訴韋德案所規定的 24 週限制還早。密西西比州法只允許醫療緊急狀況等特例情況下可墮胎，但如果是強暴或亂倫導致懷孕，仍無法墮胎。

The *Dobbs* decision has been expected since May, when an early [9]**draft** of the ruling was leaked to the media. In Friday's majority opinion, Justice Samuel Alito wrote that *Roe* was "wrong from the start," and that because the Constitution <u>makes no mention of</u> abortion, "the authority to[10]**regulate** abortion must be returned to the people and their elected representatives."

自五月以來，外界已知多布斯案的裁定結果即將出爐，因為有人將裁決草案洩漏給媒體。週五公佈的多數意見書裡，大法官阿利托表示「羅訴韋德案從一開始就是個錯誤」，且基於憲法從未提及墮胎，「因此管制墮胎的權力，務必交還給民選代表處理。」

Alito was joined in his decision by four other conservative justices—Clarence Thomas, Neil Gorsuch, Brett Kavanaugh, and Amy Coney Barrett. The last three justices were [11]**appointed** by former president Donald Trump. Chief Justice John Roberts didn't join his conservative [12]**colleagues** in overturning *Roe*, but did vote with the majority (6-3) to [13]**uphold** the Mississippi abortion ban.

其他四位保守派大法官——湯瑪斯、戈蘇奇、卡瓦諾和巴瑞特——均支持阿利托的裁定。而最後提及的三位大法官，是由前總統川普所任命。首席大法官羅伯茲並未加入他保守派同仁的行列來推翻羅訴韋德案，不過他卻在密西西比反墮胎案投下多數的支持票（票數 6 比 3）。

In their ***dissenting** opinion, the court's three liberal justices, Stephen Breyer, Sonia Sotomayor and Elena Kagan, rejected the majority's position. "With sorrow—for this court, but more, for the many millions of American women who have today lost a [14]**fundamental** constitutional protection—we dissent," they wrote, warning that pro-life politicians could now pursue a national abortion ban "from the moment of [15]**conception** and without exceptions for rape or incest."

在不同意見書裡，法院的三名自由派大法官布雷爾、索托瑪約和凱根，則反對多數意見書的立場。意見書裡表示：「懷著對最高法院以及美國數百萬婦女的悲痛情緒，她們從今天起失去受憲法保障的基礎權利——我們不同意此裁決。」他們警示，現在支持胎兒生命權的政治人物，將能名正言順成立全國通用的反墮胎法，而且是「從受精的那一刻開始就禁止墮胎，並且即使因為被強暴或亂倫而懷孕都不能有例外。」

11. **appoint** [əˋpɔɪnt] (v.)
任命，指定

12. **colleague** [ˋkɑlig] (n.)
同事，同仁

13. **uphold** [ʌpˋhold] (v.)
支持，擁護

14. **fundamental**
[ˌfʌndəˋmɛntəl] (a.)
基礎的，根本的

15. **conception**
[kənˋsɛpʃən] (n.)
受精，懷孕

16. **condemn** [kənˋdɛm]
(v.) 譴責，責備

17. **tragic** [ˋtrædʒɪk] (a.)
悲劇（性）的，悲慘的，
不幸的

As a result of the Supreme Court's decision, almost half the states are expected to outlaw or further restrict abortion. Thirteen, mainly in the South and Midwest, have "trigger laws" designed to ban abortion <u>in the event that</u> *Roe* is overturned. Others still have old abortion bans <u>on the books</u> that could now be enforced again. These changes will affect tens of millions of women, who may have to cross state lines to seek an abortion.

因為最高法院的裁決，全美將近半數的州預計將取締或進一步限制墮胎。多在南部和中西部的 13 州，均立有「觸發法」，目的在於假使「羅訴韋德案」被推翻的情況發生時，就會禁止墮胎。而本來就有法律明訂禁止墮胎的州，則可再次加強禁令。上述改變將影響成千上萬的婦女，她們可能會需要跨州來尋求墮胎之道。

While supporters of abortion bans praised a decision they had long hoped for, pro-choice politicians immediately [16]**condemned** the ruling. Speaking from the White House on Friday, President Joe Biden called the decision "a [17]**tragic** error by the Supreme Court" that put women's health and lives "at risk."

雖然墮胎禁令的支持者十分讚賞終於看見夢寐以求的裁決，但支持選擇權的政治人物卻立即譴責此裁定。總統拜登週日於白宮發言，表示此裁決是「高等法院所犯下的悲劇性錯誤」，將婦女的健康和生命置於「風險之中。」

Phrase

at odds (with/over) 意見相左

不認同對方、處於不認同的狀態。這裡的 "odds" 是不合的意思。

• The two political parties have always been **at odds with** each other. 此兩個政黨一直不認同對方。

make mention of 提及

論及、寫到相關的資訊或是簡短參考某事物 / 某人意見、提及 。

• Most history books **make no mention of** the event. 多數歷史書籍並未提及此事件。

in the event that/of 假使發生某事

若某事發生；用以討論可能的未來情況 。

• **In the event that** the performance is canceled, your money will be returned. 假使此演出被取消，你會拿到退款。

on the books 明訂，記錄在案

有官方記錄，尤其是法律；有納入法律制度。

• The death penalty is still **on the books** in most states. 多數州法律仍明訂死刑的相關法律。

result 的用法

result 有結果、成果的意思，常見的片語有 as a result of...、result in、result from 等等，例如：

- **As a result of** Elon Musk's decision, almost one-third of Twitter's employees are being laid off.
  由於馬斯克的決定，將近三分之一的推特員工將被裁員。
- Greenhouse gas emissions **result in** global warming. 溫室氣體排放造成了全球暖化。
- Global warming **results from** greenhouse gas emissions. 全球暖化起因於溫室氣體排放。

由例句可知，三種片語的用法大致如下：

As a result of 原因…，結果…。　　　　原因 result in 結果。　　　　結果 result from 原因。

EZpedia

Supreme Court 最高法院

是現代最高層級的司法機構，通常有對訴訟的最終審判權（即不可推翻的）和對法律（包括憲法）的最終解釋權，但實際權力及名稱在各個地方不盡相同。

Roe v. Wade 羅訴韋德案

是一起已被推翻的美國聯邦最高法院案例，裁定孕婦選擇墮胎的自由受到憲法隱私權的保護。但裁定也引發了一場長期持續的社會爭議：焦點在於墮胎是否應合合法或在多大程度上合法，由誰決定是否合法，以及道德和宗教應在政治方面扮演怎樣的角色；並引發了社會上對最高法院在憲法相關的判決中應如何判斷的爭議。該案由珍羅（真名諾爾瑪麥科維，因保障個人隱私關係於法律程序上使用化名）提起。羅在 1969 年懷了第三胎，但她不想要這個孩子。羅住在德州，該州的法律規定只有在孕婦的生命受到威脅時才允許墮胎。她的律師薩拉韋丁頓和琳達科菲代表她向美國聯邦法院起訴當地的地方檢察官亨利韋德，並指控德州的墮胎法違憲。美國德州北區聯邦地區法院由三名法官組成的判決小組作出了有利於羅的判決，並宣布德州的相關墮胎法違憲。德州相關團體隨即將該案上訴至美國聯邦最高法院。1973 年 1 月 22 日，最高法院以 7 比 2 表決通過判決，認為美國憲法第十四條修正案的正當法律程序條款為女性提供了基本的「隱私權」，故女性的墮胎權受憲法保護。2022 年 6 月 24 日，最高法院在多布斯訴傑克森婦女健康組織案中，以 5 比 4 的表決正式推翻了羅訴韋德案的判決。

Dobbs v. Jackson Women's Health Organization 多布斯訴傑克森婦女健康組織案

是一起美國最高法院案件，針對 2018 年密西西比州禁止在懷孕 15 週後墮胎的法律是否符合憲法進行裁決。下級法院在臨時禁令中裁定阻止該法律的執行，理由是該法律違反了在計劃生育聯合會訴凱西案中所確立的允許女性在懷孕前 24 週自由選擇墮胎的權利。2022 年 6 月 24 日，美國最高法院以 6-3 的裁決推翻下級法院的裁決。多數意見指出，墮胎不是一項憲法權利，此案推翻了羅訴韋德案和計劃生育聯合會訴凱西案，並且各州在規範墮胎方面應該有自由裁量權。由大法官塞繆爾阿利托撰寫的多數意見與洩露的草案基本相似。

Could Partygate Be the End for Boris Johnson?
英國首相強森會因派對門下台嗎？

©Shutterstock.com

全文朗讀 ∩ 041　　單字 ∩ 042

British **Prime Minister** Boris Johnson has ¹⁾**weathered** many
²⁾**scandals** during his long political career, but could the latest—which
³⁾**involves** *allegations of rule-breaking ⁴⁾**gatherings** at **10 Downing
Street** and other government buildings during COVID-19 lockdowns
in 2020 and 2021—finally cause his *downfall? A little partying may
not seem like a big deal, but the leader of the country's **Labour Party**
says the PM should ⁵⁾**resign**, and some members of Johnson's own
Conservative Party agree.

英國首相強森漫長的政治生涯中，經歷了許多醜聞，但近期涉及 2020 年至 2021
年新冠疫情封城期間，政府被指控在唐寧街 10 號和其他政府機關違反防疫規定
聚會，是否最終會導致他的執政生涯急轉直下？稍微辦個派對看似沒什麼大不了，
但英國工黨黨魁表示，首相應該辭職下台，強森所屬的保守黨其中一些黨員也表
示同意。

Although the parties in question took place from mid-2020 to mid-2021,
the scandal itself—*dubbed Partygate—didn't begin until November

2021. On November 30, the Daily Mirror published a story ***alleging** that three parties had taken place at Downing Street in late 2020 as the country entered its second lockdown, including a small gathering in Johnson's flat "where they were all getting ***plastered**" on November 13, and a Christmas party, which the PM didn't attend, on December 18. A week later, following an official [6)]**denial**, ITV broadcast a video showing Johnson [7)]**staffers** joking about their "cheese and wine" Christmas party.

儘管這些派對發生在 2020 年中至 2021 年中，但這個稱為「派對門」的醜聞直到 2021 年 11 月才被報出來。 11 月 30 日《每日鏡報》發表了一篇報導，指控 2020 年底當英國進入第二次封城時，共有三場派對在首相官邸舉辦，包括 11 月 13 日在強森的公寓舉行的小型聚會上「眾人都在那裡喝得酩酊大醉」，以及 12 月 18 日首相沒有參加的耶誕派對。在官方否認此事的一周後，ITV 電視台公布一段影片，顯示了強森的執政團隊拿他們的「乳酪和紅酒」耶誕派對開玩笑。

Addressing Parliament on December 8, Johnson [8)]**apologized** for the [9)]**offense** caused by the video. "I was also [10)]**furious** to see that clip," said the PM, adding "I have been repeatedly [11)]**assured**, since these allegations [12)]**emerged**, that there was no party and that no COVID rules were broken." That same day, Johnson asked Cabinet Secretary Simon Case to [13)]**conduct** an [14)]**inquiry**. But when it was revealed that Case had thrown his own office party the day before the December 18 bash, he was removed from the inquiry and replaced by civil servant Sue Gray.

12 月 8 日強森向國會表示，因影片引發社會觀感不佳而道歉。首相說：「看到那段影片我也很生氣」，並補充說：「自從這些指控出現以來，我一再得到保證，沒有任何派對舉辦，也沒有違反防疫規定。」同一天，強森要求內閣秘書西蒙凱斯進行調查。然而，當凱斯被揭露在 12 月 18 日派對前一天，在自己的辦公室辦派對後，他從調查中被除名，由公務員蘇格雷接任。

And reports of additional parties at government offices kept coming in— eight in the fall of 2020, including a photo of Johnson next to staffers in ***tinsel** and Santa hats at a Christmas quiz, breaking a rule [15)]**forbidding** people from different [16)]**households** from mixing. Next came news of a Downing Street BYOB garden party on May 20, 2020, at which Johnson was photographed drinking wine with his girlfriend, now wife, Carrie. Even worse, however, were reports of [17)]**farewell** parties for two Downing

11. **assure** [əˋʃʊr] (v.)
保證，使放心

12. **emerge** [ɪˋmɝdʒ] (v.)
出現，浮現

13. **conduct** [kənˋdʌkt] (v.) 進行，管理

14. **inquiry** [ˋɪnkwəri] (n.) 調查，探問

15. **forbid** [fɚˋbɪd] (v.) 禁止，不許

16. **household** [ˋhaʊs.hold] (n.) 家庭，戶

17. **farewell** [.fɛrˋwɛl] (a.) 告別 (的)

18. **funeral** [ˋfjunərəl] (n.) 喪葬，葬禮

19. **potential** [pəˋtɛnʃəl] (a.) 潛在的，可能的

20. **ally** [ˋælaɪ] (n.) 盟友，同盟者

Advanced Words

allegation [.ælɪˋgeʃən] (n.) （未證明的）指控

allege [əˋlɛdʒ] (v.) 宣稱，指控

downfall [ˋdaʊn.fɑl] (n.) 垮台，衰敗

dub [dʌb] (v.) 給予…封號，幫…取綽號

plastered [ˋplæstəd] (a.) 爛醉的

tinsel [ˋtɪnsəl] (n.) 金蔥彩帶

breach [britʃ] (n./v.) 違反，破壞

Street staffers with drinking and dancing on April 16, 2021, the day before Prince Philip's [18]**funeral**, during the third national lockdown.

隨後政府辦公室的其他派對報導層出不窮。在 2020 年秋季共有八場，其中一張耶誕節猜謎的照片顯示，強森站在圍著金蔥圈、戴著耶誕帽的職員旁，違反禁止不同家庭成員聚會的規定。接著是 2020 年 5 月 20 日首相官邸的自帶酒水花園派對新聞，當時強森被拍到與女友（現任妻子）凱莉一起飲酒。然而，更糟的是，有報導指稱，在第三次全國封城期間的 2021 年 4 月 16 日，即菲利普親王葬禮前一天，有場為了兩名官邸職員舉行的飲酒與跳舞餞行派對。

Johnson, who didn't attend the two parties personally, apologized to Queen Elizabeth on January 14, 2021. At this point, Labour leader Keir Starmer called for his [5]**resignation**—as did some members of his own party. On January 25, building on Sue Gray's inquiry, the Metropolitan Police opened its own investigation into [19]**potential *breaches** of COVID rules at government buildings. So far in February, five senior staffers have resigned over the scandal. Johnson is expected to face growing calls to resign if he is fined for his role, but his [20]**allies** have insisted he is going nowhere.

強森本人並未出席這兩場派對，並於 2021 年 1 月 14 日向伊莉莎白女王致歉。此時，工黨領袖基爾斯塔默要求他辭職，強森自己政黨的某些成員也跟進。於 1 月 25 日，在蘇格雷的調查基礎上，倫敦警察廳針對違反政府機構防疫規定的潛在行為展開調查。到今年 2 月為止，已有五名高級職員因醜聞辭職。如果強森因目前處境而被懲處，要求他下台的聲浪應會升高，但他的盟友堅稱他不會離開崗位。

©Wiki Commons

編按：面對黨內外施加的各種壓力，前英國首相強森已宣布於 7 月辭去黨魁一職，但將暫任該職位至 9 月選出新首相為止。由於英國首相是由議會多數席位政黨的領袖擔任，而目前保守黨仍為國會最大黨，因此本次新任英相選舉僅由黨內互選，並非全國大選。黨魁選舉獲勝者將直接接任英國首相。新任英相為前外交大臣麗茲特拉斯（Liz Truss）。但她在上任不足兩個月後，同年 10 月 20 日宣布辭任首相一職，成為英國歷史上任職時間最短的首相，但仍留任看守首相至保守黨選出里希蘇納克（Rishi Sunak）為新黨魁為止。

倒裝句

通常英文直述句的組成為 "S. + V."，但也有例外的時候，會以動詞先出現，這種情況我們稱作倒裝句。但使用倒裝句也要有先決條件與特殊功能的需求，像是 1. 否定意味的副詞放句首、2. Neither/Nor/So 之後、3. 條件句 (should/had)、4. 方向副詞在句首…等等，而文章中的例子，則符合了英文中的「尾重原則」：

• Next came news of a Downing Street BYOB garden party on May 20, 2020, at which Johnson was photographed drinking wine with his girlfriend, now wife, Carrie.
接著是 2020 年 5 月 20 日首相官邸的自帶酒水花園派對新聞，當時強森被拍到與女友（現任妻子）凱莉一起飲酒。

「尾重原則」是英文的一種修辭學，也就是把最複雜的成份或意念放在後面，避免頭重腳輕，如例句中形容這則新聞的成份過多，所以使用倒裝句放在後面。

EZpedia

prime minister 首相

指一個國家或地區的政府首腦，負責統領政府的行政工作，可通用於君主制或共和制國家。現代多數實行議會制、雙首長制、君主制以及其他虛位元首制度的國家都有首相或類似的政府首腦職位，有些國家總理的正式職稱為部長會議主席，但在一些總統制國家（例如美國、巴西和印尼等），國家元首兼任政府首腦，亦負此職責，因此無須另設政府首腦官職。

©Wiki Commons
▲ 10 Downing Street 唐寧街 10 號，即英國首相官邸

Labour Party 英國工黨

是英國一個包含社會自由主義與社會民主主義以及民主社會主義理念的中偏左政黨，與保守黨並列為英國兩大主要政黨。

Conservative Party 英國保守黨

是英國中偏右政黨，也是英國歷史最悠久的政黨，與工黨並列為英國兩大主要政黨。目前為英國下議院第一大黨。

Metropolitan Police 倫敦警察廳

是英國首都大倫敦地區的警察機關，1829 年在內政大臣羅伯特皮爾主導下成立，負責重大國家任務，包括配合指揮反恐、保衛英國皇室及政府高層官員和倫敦居民及遊客等。倫敦警察廳的非正式英文縮寫有許多版本，包括「the Met」、「Met Pol」或「the MPS」等。在成文法中常以小寫形式寫做「metropolitan police force」或「metropolitan police」，沒有加上「service」的字樣。此外，倫敦警察廳亦時常因其原先的總部位於白廳大蘇格蘭廣場（Great Scotland Yard），而代稱蘇格蘭場。倫敦警察廳目前的總部大樓位於西敏市內的新蘇格蘭場。

Macron Beats Le Pen to Win Second Term
馬克宏戰勝勒龐贏得法國總統連任

▲ 法國總統當選人馬克宏

全文朗讀 | ∩ 043   單字 | ∩ 044

Vocabulary

1. **defeat** [dɪˋfit] (v./n.)
   擊敗，戰勝

2. **candidate** [ˋkændɪˌdet]
   (n.) 候選人

3. **moderate** [ˋmɑdərɪt]
   (a./n.) 溫和派的；溫和派

4. **despite** [dɪˋspaɪt]
   (prep.) 雖然，儘管

5. **concession** [kənˋsɛʃən]
   (n.) 認輸，讓步

6. **urge** [ɜdʒ] (v.)
   催促，力勸

7. **parliamentary**
   [ˌpɑrləˋmɛntəri] (n.)
   議會的，國會的

8. **immigration**
   [ˌɪməˋgreʃən] (n.)
   移民，移居

9. **welfare** [ˋwɛlˌfɛr] (n.)
   社會福利

10. **vow** [vaʊ] (v./n.)
   發誓；誓言

French President Emmanuel Macron comfortably won a second term in office on Sunday, April 24, ¹⁾**defeating** far-right ²⁾**candidate** Marine Le Pen in a closely watched ***runoff** election. Final results released on Monday show that ³⁾**moderate** Macron gained 59% of the vote, while Le Pen earned 41%. Macron, 44, is the first French president in 20 years to be elected to a second term. He and Le Pen, 53, emerged as the top candidates in the 2022 French presidential election after a first round of voting on April 10. ⁴⁾**Despite** Macron's victory on Sunday, the gap between the two candidates was much smaller in comparison to the 2017 election, in which he beat Le Pen by a landslide.

法國總統馬克宏 4 月 24 日周日在備受注目的第二輪選舉中打敗極右派候選人勒龐，輕鬆贏得第二任期。週一公佈的最終結果顯示，溫和派的馬克宏得票率為 59%，而勒龐則得到 41% 票數。44 歲的馬克宏是法國 20 年來首位成功連任的總統。他和 53 歲的勒龐在 4 月 10 號的第一輪投票後，成為 2022 年法國總統選舉中兩大候選人。儘管馬克宏在週日獲勝，兩名候選人的票數差距卻比 2017 年選舉中來得更小，當時馬克宏獲得壓倒性勝利。

Right after the exit polls came out, Le Pen accepted defeat in a [5)]**concession** speech delivered at the Bois de Bologne in Paris. Calling her result—the strongest ever for a far-right candidate—a victory for her National Rally party, the former lawyer [6)]**urged** her supporters to turn their attention to the [7)]**parliamentary** elections that take place in June. While Le Pen ran on promises to end [8)]**immigration** and leave the euro in 2017, she placed bread-and-butter issues like the cost of living and [9)]**welfare** benefits at the center of her platform this time around.

就在公布選後民調後，勒龐在巴黎布洛涅森林公園舉辦的敗選演講中承認本次選舉的失敗。她把選舉結果——極右派候選人中得票數最高的一次——稱為國民聯盟黨的勝利。這位前律師呼籲支持者們將重心放在六月的議會選舉上。儘管勒龐在 2017 年大選中承諾要禁止移民並退出歐元區，但她將民生物資及社會福利等日常議題作為本次選舉的核心政見。

In his victory speech later that evening in front of the Eiffel Tower, where a crowd of supporters waved French and EU flags, Macron [10)]**vowed** to unite his divided country. "I am no longer the candidate of one side, but the president of all," he said, promising that "nobody will be left by the wayside." [11)]**Acknowledging** that many had only voted for him to keep Le Pen out of office, Macron also promised to address the sense of many French that their living standards are [12)]**declining**. His challenge over the next five years will be to heal the *rifts in the country, improve the economy, and *overhaul social policies.

當晚於艾菲爾鐵塔前，馬克宏在勝選演說中誓言將分裂的國家團結為一，支持群眾在場揮動法國及歐盟國旗。他說：「我不再是某一黨派的候選人，而是全國人民的總統。」他也保證「不會背棄任何人」。馬克宏承認許多選民投給他只是為了阻止勒龐上任，也承諾將解決法國人民感受生活水準降低此一問題。他在未來五年間將面臨弭平國內紛爭、促進經濟、提升社會福利政策等挑戰。

Macron's victory was welcomed by [13)]**relieved** European leaders, who had feared a far-right president in the Élysée Palace. German *Chancellor Olaf Scholz was first to [14)]**congratulate** him, expressing his hope that the close relationship between Germany and France would continue. U.S. President Joe Biden also said he looked forward to [15)]**cooperation** in providing support to Ukraine. While Macron has played a key [16)]**diplomatic** role in the war, Le Pen has been accused of having

11.acknowledge
[əkˋnɑlɪdʒ] (v.) 承認

12.decline [dɪˋklaɪn]
(v./n.) 下降，衰退

13.relieved [rɪˋlivd] (a.)
寬慰的，放心的

relieve [rɪˋliv] (v.)
舒緩，減輕

14.congratulate
[kənˋgrætʃə͵let] (v.)
恭喜，道賀

15.cooperation
[koͺɑpəˋreʃən] (n.)
合作，協力

cooperate [koˋɑpə͵ret]
(v.) 合作

16.diplomatic
[͵dɪpləˋmætɪk] (a.)
外交的，外交人員的

Advanced Words

runoff [ˋrʌn͵ɔf] (n.)
決選投票

rift [rɪft] (n.) 分裂，裂痕

overhaul [͵ovəˋhɔl] (v.)
修正，改進

chancellor [ˋtʃænsələ]
(n.) 總理，大臣

close ties to the Kremlin.

©Wiki Commons

馬克宏獲勝一事受到歐洲領袖們支持,他們恐懼極右派總統搬進愛麗舍宮,因此對選舉一事放下了心。德國總理蕭茲是首位恭喜馬克宏當選的人,他表明希望持續德法之間的緊密關係。美國總統拜登也說他很期待在援助烏克蘭上兩國彼此合作。馬克宏在烏俄戰爭中扮演關鍵外交要角,勒龐卻被指控和俄羅斯政府關係太密切。

▲ 溫和派的馬克宏和極右派的勒龐在第二輪投票中競爭

Phrase

beat/win by a landslide 大勝

大敗其他候選人;在得票數上大勝並贏得選舉。除了名詞外,landslide 也可做形容詞,a landslide victory 表示「壓倒性勝利」。

- The candidate **beat** his opponent **by a landslide**. 那名候選人大勝他的對手。
- The Democrats **won by a landslide** in the last election. 民主黨在上次的選舉中獲得大勝利。

bread-and-butter issue/concern 民生議題,為生之道

有關人們生計基本且重要的議題,在此做形容詞用。名詞片語可寫做 bread and butter。

- The candidate mostly talked about **bread-and-butter issues** in his campaign speech.
  那名候選人在競選演講中大多在談論民生相關議題。
- Wedding photos are the photographer's **bread and butter**. 拍攝婚照是那名攝影師的維生之道。

leave by the wayside 背棄,棄……不顧

棄置或拋棄某人事物(wayside 的意思是路邊)。更常用的片語為 fall by the wayside,表示失敗、落後或丟棄。

- Many independent voters feel **left by the wayside**. 許多獨立選民覺得自己被棄之不顧。
- When the economy worsened, the governor's plan to build roads **fell by the wayside**.
  經濟惡化後,州長要增建道路的計畫就擱置了。

look forward to 期待,盼望

這個句型後面加上名詞使用,表示對某個人事物非常喜悅而殷切的期待。一般可以在信件結尾加上這個句型,例如 I'm looking forward to your e-mail / reply,表示「我很期待收到你的電子郵件/回覆/消息」。

- A: I'll be arriving in San Francisco on the 25th. 我會在二十五號抵達舊金山。
- B: Great! I'm really **looking forward to** your visit. 太好了!我很期待你的到訪。

while 的用法

英文中的 while 出現頻率很高,在句子中的位置不同意思也不一樣,主要有三大用法:**1.** 放在句首意同「雖然…」**2.** 放在句首或句中表達「但…」**3.** 放在句首或句中,引導時間副詞子句,常與進行式連用,表示「在這段時間」。例如:

- **While** Lily hasn't lived abroad before, she still speaks great English.
  雖然 Lily 以前沒有在國外住過,但她還是說一口流利的英文。

- This week it rained three days in Taipei **while** it was sunny every day in Pingtung.
  本週台北下雨了三天,但屏東卻是天天晴朗。

- **While** most of us were struggling through the pandemic, Evergreen Marine Corporation gave out a 60-month year-end bonus.
  在我們大多數人努力對抗疫情期間,長榮海運卻給出了 60 個月的年終獎金。

National Rally 法國國民聯盟

2018 年 6 月前稱為民族陣線(National Front),是法國的一個極右民粹主義政黨,1972 年由老勒龐(Jean-Marie Le Pen,Marine Le Pen 之父)成立。國民聯盟為民族主義、民粹主義、極右翼組織,該黨曾因作風保守、政策充滿偏見與歧視而飽受批評。瑪麗娜勒龐接任後,略為調整走向,以反移民、反歐盟及反伊斯蘭為其政治基調。

EU 歐洲聯盟

簡稱歐盟(European Union),是歐洲多國共同建立的政治及經濟聯盟,現有 27 個成員國,正式官方語言有 24 種,是世界第三大經濟體,會員國多為北大西洋公約組織成員。歐盟的歷史可追溯至 1952 年建立的歐洲煤鋼共同體,當時只有六個成員國。1999 年 1 月推出共同貨幣「歐元」,並於 2002 年 1 月正式啟用。

Élysée Palace 艾麗舍宮

是法國總統的官邸與辦公室所在地,位於巴黎市,鄰近香榭麗舍大街。其名稱「Élysée」來自希臘神話中的至福樂土。1873 年起至今作為法國總統官邸,並供接待重要外賓,除特定日(如歐洲文化遺產日)外,平常並不對外開放參觀。

©Wiki Commons

▲ 法國總統官邸

Kremlin 克里姆林宮

為俄羅斯國家最高權力的象徵,是俄羅斯聯邦政府行政總部,同時也是俄羅斯總統的辦公場所,位於俄羅斯首都莫斯科市。它是世界上現存最大的建築群之一,四周由四座宮殿、四座大教堂、十九座塔樓而成,是俄羅斯克里姆林式建築的代表之作。

Anthony Albanese Defeats Scott Morrison in Australian Election
艾班尼斯於澳洲聯邦大選中擊敗莫里森

▲ 2022 法國總統當選人馬克宏

全文朗讀 | 🎧 045   單字 | 🎧 046

Australia's **Labor Party** ¹⁾**secured** its first election win in over a decade on Saturday, May 21, after ²⁾**conservative** PM Scott Morrison ³⁾**conceded** defeat to ⁴⁾**opposition** leader Anthony Albanese. Though millions of votes have yet to be counted, Morrison acted quickly so the new prime minister can attend a **Quad** summit in Tokyo on Tuesday, along with U.S., Japanese, and Indian leaders.

保守派總理莫里森承認選輸在野黨領袖艾班尼斯，使澳洲工黨於 5 月 21 日週六贏得其十年來首次勝選。儘管有數百萬張票尚待計票，莫里森仍快速承認敗選，以便新任總理可以參加周二在東京舉辦的澳洲、美國、日本及印度領袖四邊安全會談。

It's not clear, however, whether Albanese's center-left party will win a full majority or be forced to ⁵⁾**negotiate** with independent and **Greens** candidates to form a government. With 60% of the votes counted, Labor had 72 seats in the 151-seat parliament, four short of a majority.

然而仍不確定艾班尼斯的左派政營是否會贏得最多數選票，亦或需要與獨立黨派及綠黨候選人協商以組成政府。目前百分之 60 的票數已開出，工黨在議會 151 個席次中贏得 72 席，要成為最大黨還差 4 個席位。

Speaking at Liberal Party headquarters, Morrison claimed his 6)**administration** has left the country in a "stronger position" than when he took office in 2018. "I think on a night like tonight, we can 7)**reflect** on the greatness of our democracy," he said. "It's a difficult night for Liberals and Nationals around the country, as nights like this always are," the ***outgoing** PM admitted, adding that he was stepping down as party leader.

莫里森在自由黨總部宣稱比起 2018 年就任時，他的內閣已使澳洲「地位變得更穩固」。他表示：「我想在今晚這樣的夜晚，我們可以反思我國民主的偉大。這對全國的自由黨及國家黨員來說是個艱難的一晚，而敗選的夜晚總是如此。」這名即將卸任的總理承認，並表示他將辭去黨魁一職。

The mood at Labor headquarters, where an 8)**emotional** Albanese addressed the crowd, was much different. "Tonight the Australian people have voted for change," said the ***incoming** PM. "It says a lot about our great country that a son of a single mom who was a 9)**disability *pensioner**, who grew up in public housing <u>down the road</u> in Camperdown, can stand before you tonight as Australia's prime minister. Every parent wants more for the next 10)**generation** than they had," he added. "My mother dreamed of a better life for me. And I hope that my journey in life inspires Australians to <u>reach for the stars</u>."

工黨總部的氣氛則大為不同，情緒激動的艾班尼斯對著群眾說到：「今晚，澳洲人民以投票來換取改變。」這名新任總理表示：「這個被領取殘疾撫卹金的單親母親扶養，成長於坎伯當的社會住宅之子，今晚能夠站在眾人面前成為澳洲總理，這大大證實了我們國家的偉大。每一名父母親都希望下一代能得到比自己更好的」，他補充說，「我的母親盼望我能有更好的生活，我也希望我的生命歷程能夠啟發澳洲人民勇於追求夢想。」

As Australia struggles with 11)**soaring** 12)**inflation** and 13)**real estate** prices, Albanese's Labor Party has promised higher wages for workers, more 14)**financial** 15)**assistance** for those who need it, and a stronger social safety net. Australians have also expressed increasing concern about climate change, a result of extreme bush fires and flooding

11. soar [sor] (n.)
高漲，激增

12. inflation [ɪnˈfleʃən] (n.) 通貨膨脹

13. real estate (phr.)
房地產，不動產

14. financial [fɪˈnænʃəl]
(a.) 財務的，金融的

15. assistance [əˈsɪstəns]
(n.) 援助，協助

16. ambitious [æmˈbɪʃəs]
(a.) 野心勃勃的，雄心壯志的

17. reduction [rɪˈdʌkʃən]
(n.) 減少，降低

18. defense [dɪˈfɛns] (n.)
國防，防禦

Advanced Words

outgoing [ˈaʊtˌɡoɪŋ] (a.)
即將卸任的，離開的

incoming [ˈɪnˌkʌmɪʒ]
(a.) 新任的，新當選的

pensioner [ˈpɛnʃənʒə]
(n.) 領養老金者，退休人員

during Morrison's two terms in office. Labor plans to fight climate change with an [16)]**ambitious** 43% [17)]**reduction** in greenhouse gas emissions by 2030 and **net zero** emissions by 2050.

©Wiki Commons

▲ 工黨領袖艾班尼斯就任澳洲新任總理

澳洲正處於嚴重通膨及房地產價格飆漲，艾班尼斯領導的工黨允諾將提高勞工薪資，提供有需要者更多經濟援助，並更加強化社會安全網。澳洲人民也表達出對於氣候變遷的更多不安，這導因於莫里森政府兩屆任期內發生的極端森林大火及水災。工黨承諾將在 2030 年前大幅降低 43% 溫室氣體排放量，以及在 2050 年達到排放量淨零以對抗氣候變遷。

On the foreign policy front, the Labor Party proposed the establishment of a Pacific [18)]**defense** school to train armies from neighboring countries in response to China's potential military presence in the Solomon Islands on Australia's doorstep.

在外交方面，工黨提出建設太平洋國防學校訓練鄰近國家軍隊，以應對澳洲鄰近的所羅門群島上中國潛在的軍事部署。

Phrase

down the road 鄰近的，將來

字面上來說 down the road 意思指非常接近，可能就在同一條街上；另一個層面來說，它指的是將來，通常用在談論可能性上。

• If you're hungry, there's a diner **down the road**. 如果你肚子餓了，這附近有家餐廳。

reach for the stars 胸懷壯志

設立遠大的目標或志向；嘗試獲得或達成非常困難的某件事。

• They always taught me to **reach for the stars**. 他們總是教導我要胸懷大志。

on the...front 至於………，在……方面

front 指的是在某項活動或興趣上，因此這個片語代表「有關於……」。

• How's everything going **on the** work **front**? 工作上一切如何？

on one's doorstep 近在咫尺

距離某人居住或所在地非常近。

• A: You must love living in San Diego. 你一定很喜歡住在聖地牙哥。
• B: Yes. The weather's great, and the beach is right **on our doorstep**! 對啊。天氣很舒服，且海灘就在家門附近！

As 的用法

英文中的 as 也很常見，但是意思卻有很多種，如下表所示：

介系詞	以…的身份，當作
連接詞	由於，因為
	當…時
	隨著…
	如同，像是，和…一樣
	雖然，即使

如本文中的例句，"It's a difficult night for Liberals and Nationals around the country, as nights like this always are," 這裡的 as 是當作連接詞，翻譯為如同、像是，而另一個例句，As Australia struggles with soaring inflation and real estate prices, Albanese's Labor Party has promised higher wages for workers, 這裡開頭的 As 也是當作連接詞，意指當…的時候。

EZpedia

Labor Party 澳洲工黨

是澳洲歷史最悠久的社會民主主義政黨，政治立場中間偏左。工黨是澳洲兩大政黨之一，其長期競爭對手是中間偏右的保守派自由黨 - 國家黨聯盟。工黨建黨於 1891 年，為進步聯盟成員。自 2019 年 5 月起至今，該黨領袖是眾議院議員安東尼阿爾巴內塞，副領袖為眾議院議員理察馬爾斯。該黨是澳洲當下的執政黨（自 2022 年 5 月始），黨領袖安東尼阿爾巴內塞和副領袖理察馬爾斯目前是聯邦政府的正、副總理。

Quad 四邊安全對話（Quadrilateral Security Dialogue）

是美國、日本、印度和澳洲之間的非正式戰略對話，依靠成員國之間的對話維持。四邊安全對話是 2007 年由時任日本首相安倍晉三發起的，得到時任美國副總統迪克錢尼、印度總理曼莫漢辛格、澳洲總理約翰霍華德的支持。四邊安全對話還進行了名為馬拉巴爾（始於 1992 年美印合作開始）的軍事演習。
2021 年的聯合聲明「四方精神」強調了對自由開放的印度 - 太平洋的共同願景，這是東海和南海基於規則的海事秩序，並承諾應對 COVID-19 的經濟和健康影響。

Greens 澳洲綠黨

是澳洲的左翼環保主義政黨，澳洲參議院第三大黨。

net zero 淨零排放

其指的是溫室氣體淨排放為零，在近幾年更常被使用。與碳中和不同的是，淨零排放包含所有溫室氣體，且抵銷排放的做法只考慮能實際將溫室氣體從大氣移除的方式（如：植樹造林、碳捕集與封存）。

Here Comes the Metaverse
元宇宙的時代來了

全文朗讀 🎧 047　單字 🎧 048

Imagine putting on a virtual reality (VR) ***headset** and going to a meeting, playing a board game with friends, or attending a live concert—all while sitting in a 1)**cozy** chair in your living room. Sound like something you'd like to try? Big Tech thinks so, and that's why they're betting big on the future of the metaverse.

想像一下，戴上虛擬實境眼鏡開會、和朋友玩桌遊或參加現場演唱會──一切都只需要坐在你客廳裡舒服的椅子上進行即可。你聽完有想試試看嗎？科技巨擘都認為你會想，這就是他們在元宇宙的未來下大賭注的原因。

But what exactly is the metaverse? The term has been a ***buzzword** in the tech and business worlds for several years now, but people didn't really sit up and take notice until late 2021, when Mark Zuckerberg announced he was changing his company's name from Facebook to Meta and shifting its focus from social media to the metaverse. "We believe the metaverse will be the 2)**successor** of the mobile 3)**Internet**," Zuckerberg said. "We'll be able to feel present—like we're right there with people no matter how far apart we actually are."

但是元宇宙到底是什麼？此名詞已經是在科技業和商業圈流行幾年的潮流用語，但是大家一直沒有真的當一回事，直到 2021 年底，馬克祖克伯宣布要將公司名稱從「臉書」改名為「Meta」，並將營業重心從社群媒體轉移到元宇宙，大家才開始對此名詞刮目相看。祖克柏表示：「我們相信，元宇宙會成為手機網路的接替者。我們將會覺得身歷其境—無論實際上與他人的距離有多遙遠，都會好像跟彼此待在一起。」

If this sounds like science fiction, that's because it is. The word "metaverse" was 4)**coined** by sci-fi author Neal Stephenson in his 1992 novel Snow Crash, which describes a *dystopian future where people escape from reality into a virtual world 5)**accessed** through computer 6)**terminals** and special headsets. Inside the metaverse, they use 7)**digital *avatars** to 8)**interact** with other users and explore the Street—which wraps all the way around a virtual planet and is lined with shops, clubs and 9)**neon** signs.

如果你覺得聽起來像科幻小說，原因在於確實如此。「元宇宙」一詞是尼爾史蒂芬森於 1992 年的小說《潰雪》所命名。故事描述一個反烏托邦的未來世界，大家為了逃避現實，而透過電腦終端機與特殊眼鏡進入虛擬世界。在元宇宙裡，大家使用數位化身來與其他使用者互動並探索「街道」，也就是一個環繞虛擬星球、充滿商店、俱樂部與霓虹燈招牌的世界。

But Stephenson was way <u>ahead of his time</u>. It's taken 30 years to develop the technology—like VR headsets and AR (augmented reality) glasses—necessary to turn the metaverse into reality. And we're not there yet. In Zuckerberg's own words: "The best way to understand the metaverse is to experience it yourself, but it's a little 10)**tough** because it doesn't fully exist yet."

不過史蒂芬森簡直是思想超前。現實世界花了 30 年才發展出他故事裡的科技——例如虛擬實境眼鏡和擴增實境眼鏡——這些都是將元宇宙化為現實的必要設備。而且我們還沒真正達到那樣的境界。以祖克伯親口說的話來看：「最能好好了解元宇宙的方式，就是親身經歷，但是目前有點難，因為元宇宙尚未完全存在。」

That may be true, but 11)**glimpses** of what the metaverse may look like can be seen in video games. In Second Life, which was launched in 2003, users can create avatars for themselves and live virtual lives inside a virtual world. 12)**Residents** can do just about anything they can in real

11.**glimpse** [glɪmps]
(n./v.) 一窺，瞥見

12.**resident** [ˋrɛzədənt]
(n.) 居民，住戶

13.**evolve** [ɪˋvɑlv] (v.)
演變，進化

14.**realistic** [ˌriəˋlɪstɪk]
(a.) 逼真的，寫實的

15.**socialize** [ˋsoʃəˌlaɪz]
(v.) 交際，參與社交

16.**predict** [prɪˋdɪkt] (v.)
預測，預言

Advanced Words

17.**headset** [ˋhɛdˌsɛt]
(n.) 頭戴式裝置

18.**buzzword** [ˋbʌzˌwɝd]
(n.) 流行詞，行話

19.**dystopian** [dɪsˋtopiən]
(n.) 反烏托邦的

20.**avatar** [ˋævəˌtɑr] (n.)
化身

life—hang out with friends, go shopping, and even buy and sell real estate. A more recent example is Fortnite, which started out as a **first-person shooter** and has ¹³⁾**evolved** into a social network where users can participate in virtual events—like an Ariana Grande concert that was attended by 12 million fans.

▲ 馬克祖克柏將臉書與其母公司更名為 Met 顯示了他對於元宇宙市場投入的野心。

或許沒錯，不過我們已經可從電玩遊戲窺探元宇宙的可能樣貌。在 2003 年推出的《第二人生》裡，使用者可自行創造化身，並於虛擬世界過著虛擬生活。居民可以進行現實生活裡可做的幾乎任何事——和朋友共度時光、購物、甚至是買賣房地產。更近期的例子是《要塞英雄》，這款遊戲一開始是第一人稱射擊遊戲，但後來演變成社群網絡，讓用戶可參加虛擬活動，例如有 1200 萬名粉絲參加的亞莉安娜演唱會。

So how long will it be until we can truly experience the metaverse, putting on VR headsets or AR glasses and using ¹⁴⁾**realistic** 3D avatars to work, shop and ¹⁵⁾**socialize**? Zuckerberg ¹⁶⁾**predicts** that one to two billion users will be spending time—and money—in the metaverse by 2030.

那麼要等到多久以後，我們才能戴上虛擬實境眼鏡或擴增實境眼鏡、使用擬真 3D 化身來工作、購物與社交而真正體驗元宇宙呢？祖克伯預測到 2030 年，將會有十億到二十億用戶，會在元宇宙裡花時間和金錢。

(Phrase)

bet big (on sth./sb.) 在某事物 / 某人身上下大賭注、希望全放在某事物 / 某人

投資大筆金錢或冒險將大筆金錢投注在相信某事物會發生的信念；給某人或某事物很大的支持，而且是願意冒著如果不成功就會損失錢財或其他事物的風險。

• International investors are **betting big** on a strong U.S. dollar. 國際投資人在強勢的美元下了很大的賭注。

sit up and take notice 刮目相看

sit up 是指「挺起腰桿，打起精神」，sit up and take notice 表現出觀眾等忽然坐直注意看的樣子，也就是「刮目相看」。

• The young actor's performance in the film made critics **sit up and take notice**.
這位年輕演員在電影裡的表現讓影評人刮目相看。

ahead of one's/its time 思想超前

某人所生活或工作的年代、或某事物被發明的年代，過於前衛或現代化，而不被理解或欣賞。

• That director was really ahead of his time. 那位導演真的思想超前。

後面可接名詞或動名詞的動詞

本文的一開頭就是動詞後接動名詞的例子，Imagine putting on a virtual reality (VR) headset and going to a meeting...，imagine 後面不能接不定詞，英文中還有類似這樣的動詞後面只能接名詞或動名詞，以下是例舉的列表，看到時須格外留意：

avoid	celebrate	consider	delay	dread
enjoy	escape	excuse	finish	forgive
keep	involve	mind	miss	pardon
postpone	prevent	resist	save	stop

EZpedia

virtual reality (VR) 虛擬實境

是利用電腦類比產生一個三維空間的虛擬世界，提供使用者視覺等感官的類比，讓使用者彷彿身歷其境，可以即時、沒有限制地觀察三維空間內的事物。使用者移動時，電腦可以立即進行複雜的運算，將精確的三維世界影像傳回以產生臨場感。該技術整合了電腦圖形、電腦仿真、人工智慧、感應、顯示及網路並列處理（parallel processing）等技術的最新發展成果，是一種由電腦技術輔助生成的高技術類比系統。

Big Tech 科技巨擘

或譯作科技巨頭，也被稱作 Tech Giants、Big Four、Four Horsemen、Big Five 和 S&P 5，是對資訊科技（IT）行業最大、最具主導地位的公司合稱，尤其指美國的 Amazon、Apple、Google（Alphabet）、Facebook（Meta）及 Microsoft。這些公司不只在美國，在世界的資訊科技產業也佔有龍頭地位。

AR (augmented reality) 擴增實境

指透過攝影機影像的位置及角度精算加上圖像分析，讓螢幕上的虛擬世界能夠與現實世界場景進行結合與互動的技術，始於 1990 年。隨著隨身電子產品運算能力的提升，用途也越廣。

first-person shooter 第一人稱射擊遊戲

是射擊遊戲的一個類型，以第一人稱視角的槍支和其他武器的戰鬥為主，玩家通過主角的眼睛體驗做動作並控制玩家角色。

NFTs Made Simple
非同質化代幣 NFT 懶人包

▲ 比特幣為近年來許多人的熱門投資選項。

全文朗讀 ∩ 049　單字 ∩ 050

Over the past year, NFTs, or non-***fungible** 1)**tokens**, have taken the world by storm. These digital 2)**assets** have been 3)**embraced** by artists, celebrities and 4)**investors**, with some selling for millions of dollars. In 2021 alone, the market for NFTs was worth $41 billion! Although they may seem like a 5)**fad**, NFTs have been around much longer than most people realize.

過去一年來，所謂的非同質化代幣 NFT，如旋風般席捲全世界。有許多藝術家、名人和投資人均欣然接受此類數位資產，有些 NFT 還出售上百萬元。光是 2021 年，NFT 市場價值就高達 410 億美元！雖然看起來像是曇花一現的潮流，但是 NFT 問世的時間，其實比多數人以為的還要久。

But first, what exactly is an NFT? Simply put, NFTs are bits of data that represent digital objects like art, music, videos or even tweets. NFTs are bought and sold 6)**online**, often with **cryptocurrency**, and are created with the same type of 7)**software** used to create cryptocurrencies. How are the two different? Cryptocurrencies, like other forms of money, are fungible, which means they can be freely exchanged or replaced. One **Bitcoin** always has the exact same value as any other Bitcoin. NFTs, on the other hand, aren't fungible. Each NFT has a 8)**unique** digital 9)**signature**, and exists on a blockchain, which is a record of 10)**transactions** stored on a computer network.

但首先，NFT 到底是什麼？簡單來講，NFT 是代表藝術品、音樂、影片、甚至是推文等數位物品的資料位元。NFT 通常藉由加密貨幣而在網路進行買賣，並且是使用與創建加密貨幣一樣的軟體來建立。那麼兩者有何不同？加密貨幣就像其他形式的貨幣，具有同質化特性，也就是可自由交換或替換。一塊比特幣的價值永遠會跟其他任何比特幣完全相同。NFT 則具有非同質化的特性。每個 NFT 都有獨特的數位簽章，並且存在於區塊鍊，而區塊鍊就是在電腦網絡上儲存交易的一種記錄機制。

As you may know, most of the objects 11)**associated** with NFTs can be viewed online—even ***downloaded** or copied—for free. So why would people be willing to spend millions on something they could enjoy without paying a cent? Because buying the NFT allows them to own the original item, giving them "digital <u>bragging rights</u>." Anyone can view the NFT, but only the buyer has the 12)**status** that comes with being the official owner.

大家也許知道，和 NFT 有關的多數物件均可免費上網觀看，甚至還能免費下載或複製。那麼為什麼有人願意花上百萬元來購買可以不花一毛錢就能享有的東西呢？因為購買 NFT 能讓他們擁有原作，給了他們「在數位世界炫耀自己的本錢」。任何人都能觀看 NFT，但是只有買家擁有官方所有人的地位。

The idea of linking digital assets to blockchains was first proposed in 2012, and in 2014 artist Kevin McCoy created the first NFT—a short animation called Quantum that sold for the 13)**bargain** price of $4. But it wasn't until March, 2021 that NFTs <u>became a household name</u>. That's when Everydays: The First 5000 Days—a ***collage** of 5,000 digital images created by digital artist Mike Winkelmann, better known as Beeple—sold for a record $69.3 million in an online 14)**auction**. Later that same month, Twitter 15)**founder** Jack Dorsey's first tweet, "just setting up my twttr," sold for $2.9 million.

將數位資產連結至區塊鍊的構想，首次出現於 2012 年。而藝術家凱文麥考伊於 2014 年首創 NFT——是一部名為《量子》的動畫短片，以 4 美元的低價出售。不過直到 2021 年 3 月，NFT 才成為家喻戶曉的名詞。當時由數位藝術家邁克溫克曼（筆名 Beeple 更為人知），以 5000 張數位影像所拼貼而成的「每一天：前

---

11. associate (with)
[əˋsoʃɪˌet] (v.)
與……有關

12. status [ˋstætəs] (n.)
地位，身分

13. bargain [ˋbɑrgɪn] (n.)
划算的價格、商品

14. auction [ˋɔkʃən] (n.)
拍賣會

15. founder [ˋfaundə] (n.)
創立者，創辦人

16. immense [ɪˋmɛns] (a.)
極大的，巨大的

17. risky [ˋrɪskɪ] (a.)
高風險的

Advanced Words
fungible [ˋfʌndʒəbəl] (a.)
同質化的，可取代的

download [ˋdaunˌlod]
(v.) 下載

collage [kəˋlɑʒ] (n.)
拼貼畫

「5000 天」作品，於線上拍賣會創紀錄售出 6 億 9300 萬美元。同一個月份不久後，推特創辦人傑克多西的第一則推文「我剛設定好我的推特」則以 290 萬美元售出。

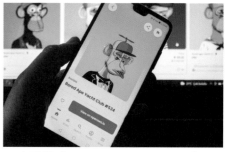

Since then, the market for NFTs has continued to grow. Celebrities like Justin Bieber and Paris Hilton have turned NFTs from the Bored Ape collection into expensive status symbols, and sports fans are buying and trading NFTs related to their favorite teams and players in ever greater numbers. While not everyone is a fan—some have complained about the [16]**immense** amounts of electricity required for blockchain transactions, and others view NFTs as [17]**risky** investments—it looks like non-fungible tokens are here to stay.

▲ 無聊猿（Bored Ape Yacht Club）可說是當今世界上價格最高的 NFT 收藏品，該系列的地板價高達 28 萬美元（約 800 萬台幣）。

從那時起，NFT 市場就持續成長。小賈斯汀和派瑞絲希爾頓等名人，讓「無聊猿」系列的 NFT 變成昂貴的地位象徵，而運動賽事的粉絲則以不斷增加的數量，買賣交易與自己最愛球隊與球員有關的 NFT。但也不是人人都愛 NFT，有些人抱怨區塊鍊交易需要耗用龐大的電量，有些人則視 NFT 為高風險的投資——不過看來非同質化代幣已經被廣為接受了。

Phrase

take (the world, etc.) by storm 旋風般席捲 (全世界等等)

在特定地方或在特定團體裡非常成功。這將原本軍事用法 "assault in a violent attack" 的原始含義轉為更和平的用法。

• The author **has taken the literary world by storm**. 這名作者如旋風般席捲了文學界。

simply put 簡單來講

以更清楚、直接或易於了解的名詞來說明（可於討論複雜主題或情境時運用）。

• **Simply put**, a root canal is the removal of infected tissue inside the tooth.
簡單來講，根管治療就是去除牙齒裡受感染的組織。

bragging rights 自吹自擂、炫耀的本錢

有機會驕傲的張揚自己做了某件了不起的事；享有吹噓某事物（通常是某技能或成就）的權利

• Robert earned **bragging rights** by completing his project ahead of schedule.
羅伯特因為超前進度完成專案，而有辦法炫耀。

become/be a household name 成為家喻戶曉的名詞

意指某人、產品、公司、品牌等非常熱門與知名，而變得家喻戶曉。

• Coca-Cola **is a household name** all over the world. 可口可樂是全世界家喻戶曉的名詞。

How/What 用法

英文中的 How/What 有時用法容易搞混，例如我們可以說：

• What do you think of the restaurant? 你對這個餐廳的看法是？

但是不能說：

• How do you think of the restaurant? 因為思考當然是用頭腦。

本文中所出現的例句： How are the two different?

是問兩者如何 / 有何不同？

如果要改成 What 開頭，句子需要變動為：

What is different about the two?

EZpedia

cryptocurrency 加密貨幣

是一種使用密碼學原理來確保交易安全及控制交易單位創造的交易媒介。

跟平常使用的紙幣需要防偽設計一樣，加密貨幣的防偽是利用數位貨幣和虛擬貨幣使用密碼學及數字雜湊而成並與智慧型合約的綁定之下的新型通證。比特幣在 2009 年成為全世界第一個去中心化的加密貨幣，這之後加密貨幣一詞多指此類設計。自此之後數種類似的加密貨幣被創造，它們通常被稱作 altcoin。加密貨幣基於去中心化的共識機制，與依賴中心化監管體系的銀行金融系統相對。

去中心化的性質源自於使用分散式賬本的區塊鏈（blockchain）技術。

bitcoin 比特幣

是一種基於去中心化，採用點對點網路與共識主動性，開放原始碼，以區塊鏈作為底層技術的加密貨幣，比特幣由中本聰（Satoshi Nakamoto）於 2008 年 10 月 31 日發表論文，2009 年 1 月 3 日，創世區塊誕生。在某些國家、央行、政府機關、學術界則將比特幣視為虛擬商品，而不認為是貨幣。貨幣金融學認為貨幣具有交易媒介、記賬單位、價值儲藏三種基本職能，但由於其高度波動性因此不具有後兩種基本職能從而不是貨幣。

Bored Ape 無聊猿

是建立在以太坊區塊鏈上的不可替代代幣 (NFT) 集合。該系列包含由算法 程序生成的卡通猿個人資料圖片。Bored Ape Yacht Club 的母公司是 Yuga Labs。該項目在 2021 年 4 月 20 日首次鑄造後，於 2021 年 4 月 23 日進行現場預售 Bored Ape NFT 的所有者可以訪問私人在線俱樂部、獨家現場活動、和圖像的知識產權。截至 2022 年，Bored Ape NFT 的銷售額已超過 10 億美元。許多名人都購買了這些不可替代的代幣，包括小賈斯汀、吉米法倫、史努比狗狗、阿姆、格溫妮絲帕特洛、麥當娜、內馬爾、帕麗斯希爾頓、提姆巴蘭、和 DJ 史蒂夫青木。

The Promise and Danger of Deepfakes
Deepfake 技術的前景和危險

Tiktok / deeptomcruise

全文朗讀 | 🎧 051   單字 | 🎧 052

Deepfake technology has been around for several decades, but it didn't enter the ¹⁾**mainstream** until a series of Tom Cruise deepfake videos <u>caused a stir</u> on TikTok last year. In the videos, Cruise can be seen laughing ***manically** while doing things like playing golf, performing a magic trick and biting into a lollipop. "Mmm, that is ²⁾**incredible**," says Cruise. "How come nobody ever told me there's bubblegum?" Millions of views later, 61 percent of users couldn't ³⁾**distinguish** the fake Tom Cruise from <u>the real McCoy</u>.

雖然 deepfake 技術已存在數十年，但是直到一系列的湯姆克魯斯 deepfake 影片去年在 TikTok 造成轟動後，此技術才開始進入主流。在這些影片中，阿湯哥一邊瘋狂大笑，一邊打高爾夫球、表演魔術和咬碎棒棒糖等等。阿湯哥說：「嗯，這真太不可思議了。怎麼都沒人跟我說過裡面有泡泡糖？」觀看人次達幾百萬後，有 61% 的用戶竟然無法分辨山寨阿湯哥和阿湯哥本尊。

The TikTok videos were so realistic that they prompted wild ⁴⁾**speculation**—until Belgian ⁵⁾**visual** effects artist Chris Umé revealed they were deepfakes created by him with **AI** software and the assistance of Miles Fisher, an American actor who'd already <u>made a name for himself</u> by *impersonating Tom Cruise. First, Fisher made videos of himself [6]imitating Tom Cruise, and then Umé used a deepfake model to replace Fisher's face with Cruise's.

這些 TikTok 影片實在太真實,而讓大眾議論紛紛──直到比利時視覺特效師克里斯烏米,揭露這些 deepfake 影片是由他運用人工智慧軟體,並於邁爾斯費雪的協助下所製作。而費雪已經是靠模仿阿湯哥走紅的美國演員。首先,費雪先錄製自己模仿阿湯哥的影片,烏米再用 deepfake 模型來將費雪的臉替換為阿湯哥的臉。

How are deepfake models created? AI software is provided with images of the subject, and then two *algorithms compete to build an ever more realistic model, with one algorithm producing new images and the other trying to determine whether they are real or fake. To create deepfake Tom Cruise, Umé collected over 6,000 images of the actor, including all possible angles and [7]facial expressions, and let his algorithms run for over two months until the model was perfect.

那麼要如何創造 deepfake 模型?首先,必須向人工智慧軟體提供被仿者的影像,然後由兩個演算法去較勁建立一個更真實的模型,也就是一個演算法負責產生新影像,另一個演算法則試著判斷影像的真假。為了創造阿湯哥的 deepfake,烏米收集超過六千張的阿湯哥影像,包括所有可能的角度和臉部表情,然後讓演算法運行超過兩個月的時間,直到模型無懈可擊。

Sensing the commercial potential of deepfake technology, Umé recently founded his own company to create deepfakes for use in advertising, television and film. So far, he's worked on a Super Bowl ad featuring [8]retired football player Deion Sanders shaving with Gillette's latest razor—on NFL Draft Night in 1989, as well as an ad campaign for the Belgian Football Association that brings two *deceased team managers back to life.

烏米嗅到 deepfake 技術的潛在商機後,即於最近成立自己的公司,而將 deepfake 運用在廣告、電視和電影。目前為止,他的作品包括超級盃的電視廣告,廣告中出現已退休的美式足球員迪恩桑德斯,在參加 1989 年美式足球聯盟選秀夜前,使用吉列最新的刮鬍刀剃鬍。還有一部比利時足球協會的宣傳廣告,讓兩位已故球隊經理起死回生。

[9]Intelligence and security [10]agencies, on the other hand, are much more concerned about the potential of deepfakes being used for *disinformation or fraud. While deepfakes of politicians have been around for a few years—examples include a deepfake of Barack Obama

10. **agency** (n.) [ˋedʒənsi]
（政府機構的）局、署、處等

11. **fragile** (a.) [ˋfrædʒəl]
脆弱的,虛弱的

12. **viewer** (n.) [ˋvjuɚ]
電視觀眾,觀看者

Advanced Words

manically (adv.)
[ˋmænɪkli] 瘋狂地

impersonate (v.)
[ɪmˋpɝsə͵net] 模仿,冒充

algorithm (n.)
[ˋælgə͵rɪðəm] 演算法

deceased (a.) [dɪˋsist]
已故的

disinformation (n.)
[dɪs͵ɪnfɚˋmeʃən]
不實資訊

slur (v.) [slɝ]
含糊地發音

calling Donald Trump names in 2018, and another of Nancy Pelosi **slurring** her speech as if drunk in 2019—they were mostly easy to detect <u>with the naked eye</u>.

情報及國安機關則很擔憂 deepfake 可能被用來散播不實資訊或詐騙。雖然政治人物的 deepfake 影片已行之多年——例如 2018 年有歐巴馬辱罵川普的 deepfake 影片，還有裴洛西於 2019 年的 deepfake 影片中，看似喝醉而說話含糊不清——但還是能以肉眼輕易發現破綻。

▲ 假阿湯哥使用黑科技 Deepfake 在 Tiktok 上變魔術給網友們看。

But the technology is improving so rapidly that when deepfakes of Kim Jong-un and Vladimir Putin warning about how [11)]**fragile** American democracy is were created for the 2020 presidential election, television stations refused to air them because they feared [12)]**viewers** would believe they were real. And earlier this year, the FBI made an announcement that criminals are using deepfakes to apply for work-from-home IT jobs so they can gain access to sensitive customer and financial data.

不過，deepfake 技術日新月異的速度之快，因應 2020 年的總統大選，而推出金正恩和普丁警告大家美國的民主制度有多麼脆弱的 deepfake 影片時，電視台均以深怕觀眾信以為真為由而拒播。今年初，美國聯邦調查局則宣布許多罪犯運用 deepfake 來申請在家工作的資訊科技職務，以便取得敏感的顧客與財務資料。

(Phrase)

cause a stir 引起軒然大波，引起騷動

stir 是指「攪拌」的動作，這句話是指某事件因爭議性高，而在人群中引起騷動，就像在靜止的湖面忽然投入一顆大石頭而引起水波，使湖面不平靜一樣。

• The protesters **caused** quite **a stir**.　示威者引起了不小的騷動。

the real McCoy 本尊

本人或真實的人事物、非複製版、同類裡最棒的。其來源是 "The real MacKay"，MacKay 是一種蘇格蘭威士忌。

• I've never seen **the real McCoy** of the Mona Lisa. 我從來沒看過「蒙娜麗莎」的真品。

make a name for oneself 出名，走紅

在特定領域變得有名或廣為人知。

• I hope to **make a name for myself** as a sports photographer. 我希望能以運動攝影師的身分出名。

with/to the naked eye 肉眼

只用眼睛觀察，不需要借助望遠鏡或顯微鏡等器具的幫助。

• Some cells are large enough to be seen **with the naked eye**. 有些細胞大到可以用肉眼看見。

so + a./adv. + that... 的用法

so...that... 有「強調」的用法，強調是「如此這般…以至於…」，所以中間的詞是用來加強強度，例如：（"that" 可以省略）

• I'm so tired (that) I might sleep till noon. 我是如此的累以至於可能睡到中午。

• She is so hungry (that) she could eat a horse. 她是如此的餓以至於可以吃下一頭馬。

deepfake 深偽技術

專指基於人工智慧的人體圖像合成技術的應用。此技術可將已有的圖像或影片疊加至目標圖像或影片上。偽造面部表情並將其彩現至目標影片的技術。2016 年出現，此技術逼真地偽造現有 2D 影片中的面部表情。

AI 人工智慧

可模擬人工智慧執行任務的系統或機器，並且可以根據收集的資訊來反覆改善自身。相較於特定格式或功能，AI 的重點在於超級思維與數據分析的過程和能力。雖然人工智慧會讓人聯想到高功能機器人佔領全世界的畫面，但人工智慧的出現並非為了取代人類。因為人類進一步解讀、分析資料的能力，已無法負荷現在的龐大資訊量——這個時候，就能請人工智慧代勞。像是在醫療產業，就已開始協助臨床決策或疾病判斷，交通方面，已有自駕車、路況安全預警等，生活中，也有 AI 客服辨識客戶想法，提供個人化回覆。AI 應用早已無所不在，持續改善你我生活品質。

Brazil Sets New Deforestation Record
巴西創下毀林新紀錄

全文朗讀 | ∩ 053　單字 | ∩ 054

Vocabulary

1. **denounce** [dɪˋnaʊns]
   (v.) 譴責，指責

2. **exploit** [ɪkˋsplɔɪt] (v.)
   剝削，利用

3. **research**
   [ˋrisɜtʃ / rɪˋsɜtʃ] (n./v.)
   研究，調查

4. **destruction**
   [dɪˋstrʌkʃən] (n.)
   毀滅，破壞

5. **reservation**
   [ˏrɛzɚˋveʃən] (n.)
   保留地，保護區

6. **congress** [ˋkɑŋgrəs]
   (n.) 議會，國會

7. **presidential**
   [ˏprɛzɪˋdɛnʃəl] (a.)
   總統的，總裁的

8. **mining** [ˋmaɪnɪŋ] (n.)
   採礦，礦業

9. **exporter** [ˋɛksportɚ]
   (n.) 出口國，出口商

10. **generate** [ˋdʒɛnəˏret]
    (v.) 產生，發生

Thousands of people from over 100 ***indigenous** tribes gathered in Brazil's capital city of Brasilia this month to demand greater protection for their lands and [1)]**denounce** proposed laws that would allow the government to further [2)]**exploit** the Amazon rainforest, where most make their home. The protest came as Brazil set a new record for ***deforestation** during the first quarter of 2022 compared to a year earlier, according to government data.

數千名屬於 100 多個原住民部落的人，本月聚集在巴西首都巴西利亞，要求政府加強保護他們的土地，並譴責將可能讓政府進一步剝削亞馬遜雨林的法律草案，亞馬遜雨林也就是多數原民的家園。之所以會有此抗議行動，是因為根據政府資料顯示，與 2021 年同期相比，巴西在 2022 年第一季的毀林率創下新紀錄。

From January to March, deforestation of the Brazilian Amazon rose 64% from last year to 363 square miles, data from the country's national space [3)]**research** agency, INPE, showed. That area, larger in size than New York City, is the most rainforest lost in the first three months of the year since data collection began in 2015.

根據巴西國家太空研究院的資料顯示，單以今年一月至三月來看，巴西亞馬遜的毀林率就比去年多了 64%，達到 363 平方英里。今年頭三個月所流失的雨林面積比紐約市還大，可說是 2015 年開始收集資料以來，流失最多雨林的一次。

⁴⁾**Destruction** of the world's largest rainforest, 60% of which lies within Brazil, has <u>picked up pace</u> since President Jair Bolsonaro took office in 2019. Elected on a promise not to create any more indigenous ⁵⁾**reservations**, Bolsonaro has also weakened existing environmental protections in the Amazon, arguing that they *****hamper** economic development that could reduce poverty in the region. The current bills, which Bolsonaro hopes to push through ⁶⁾**congress** before the next ⁷⁾**presidential** election in October, would open up indigenous lands to agriculture and ⁸⁾**mining**.

全球最大的亞馬遜雨林有 60% 位於巴西境內，而總統波索納洛於 2019 年當選後，其毀林率不斷上升。因為不再設立原住民保留地的承諾而當選的波索納洛，亦削弱了亞馬遜現有的環境保護措施。波索納洛認為這種措施會妨礙可降低該區貧窮率的經濟發展。而波索納洛目前希望在十月的總統大選前，促使國會通過的法案，將開放原住民土地進行農業耕種與採礦。

In Brazil, the world's leading ⁹⁾**exporter** of beef and soy, most deforestation is driven by agriculture. The concern among scientists is that if the deforestation continues, the forest will <u>reach a tipping point</u> after which it would no longer ¹⁰⁾**generate** enough rain to ¹¹⁾**sustain** itself. Reduction in the number of trees would lower moisture levels in the rainforest, resulting in the further loss of trees because of the lack of rain. In this <u>vicious cycle</u>, the rainforest would gradually ¹²⁾**transform** into dry grassland, a process that would release huge amounts of ¹³⁾**carbon** and ¹⁴⁾**accelerate** global warming.

巴西是全球最大的牛肉和大豆出口國，而多數的毀林作業都是為了農業發展。科學家擔心如果繼續砍伐森林，就會到達無法產生足夠雨量來維持森林生態的臨界點。林木數量減少，會降低雨林的水分，而在缺乏雨量的情況下，就會流失更多林木。如此惡性循環，雨林就會逐漸轉變為乾草地，此過程會造成龐大的碳排放並加快全球暖化的速度。

A UN climate ¹⁵⁾**panel** report released on April 6 warned that governments around the world are not doing enough to reduce greenhouse gas

11. **sustain** [sə`sten] (v.)
維繫，維持

12. **transform**
[træns`fɔrm] (v.)
轉變，改變

13. **carbon** [`kɑrbən] (n.)
碳

14. **accelerate**
[ək`sɛlə‚ret] (v.)
（使）加快

15. **panel** [`pænəl] (n.)
專家小組，委員會

16. **enforcement**
[ɪn`fɔrsmənt] (n.)
執行，實施

Advanced Words

indigenous [ɪn`dɪdʒənəs]
(a.) 本地的，原住民的

deforestation
[di‚fɔrəs`teʃən] (n.)
毀林，森林砍伐

hamper [`hæmpɚ] (v.)
妨礙，阻礙

emission [ɪ`mɪʃən] (n.)
（光、熱、氣等）排放

*emissions in order to avoid the most harmful effects of global warming. Although most of the blame goes to the burning of fossil fuels, deforestation accounts for about 10% of global emissions, according to the report.

4 月 6 日發佈的聯合國氣候委員會報告，警示全世界的政府，沒有為了避免全球暖化最有害的效應，而盡力降低溫室氣體排放量。根據該報告，雖然多數究責落在燃燒石化燃料，但毀林作業對全球碳排放量的影響仍佔 10% 左右。

Some scientists believe deforestation will continue to rise ahead of Brazil's October election, as it has ahead of the last three elections. Environmental [16)]**enforcement** usually weakens during election years, and criminals may rush to cut down trees before a new government takes office.

有些科學家認為，在巴西十月大選之前，毀林問題仍會持續攀升，因為前三次的選舉均如此。環境方面的執法效力，通常會在選舉期間削弱，而罪犯可能會在新政府當選前，急著砍伐林木。

Phrase

pick up (the) pace 急起直追

亦可寫作「pick up speed」；pace 等於 speed，「pick up the pace」意指加快速度。

- Car sales are expected to **pick up pace** in the third quarter. 汽車銷售量可望於第三季加速成長。
- If we want to finish on time, you're going to have to **pick up the pace**.
  如果我們想準時完工，你就要加快速度。

reach/approach/near a tipping point 達到、靠近臨界點

tipping point（臨界點）意指某情況、程序或體制的關鍵點，如果超越這個點，就會發生無法阻擋的重大影響或改變。

- Some experts believe we will soon **reach a tipping point** in the transition to electric vehicles.
  某些專家認為，我們即將到達要改用電動車的臨界點。

vicious cycle 惡性循環

亦可寫作「vicious circle」；意指兩種以上的因素所產生一系列的因果關係，更放大彼此的影響力，導致整個情況惡化。

- We need to create jobs to help pull people out of the **vicious cycle** of poverty.
  我們必須創造就業機會，來讓大家擺脫貧窮的惡性循環。

英文中的 **of which** [介詞加關係代名詞]，有「其中部分」、「而其中的」的意思：

"of which" 可以接在量詞後面，例如：all, both, each, many, most, neither, none, part, some...

• There are thousands of books in the school library, many **of which** I'm interested in reading.
  學校圖書館裡有上千本書籍，其中有很多本我都有興趣閱讀。

或是數字、序數後面，例如：one, two...; the first, the second...; half, a third....

• Dan watched four movies over the weekend, two **of which** he really enjoyed.
  丹在週末看了四部電影，其中兩部他非常喜歡。

以及接在最高級後面，例如： the best, the biggest....

• I caught a lot of fish, the biggest **of which** was over 20 pounds. 我釣到過很多魚，最大的一隻超過 20 磅。

EZpedia

greenhouse gas 溫室氣體

指大氣中促成溫室效應的氣體成份。自然溫室氣體包含水蒸氣（H_2O）、二氧化碳（CO_2）約佔所有溫室氣體的 26%。溫室氣體的共同點，在於它們都能夠吸收紅外線（infrared）。太陽輻射穿透大氣以可見光居多，可直接穿透大氣層，到達地面。而地面有溫度就會發射紅外線釋放熱量，但紅外線不能穿透大氣層，因此熱量就保留在地面的大氣中，造成溫室效應（greenhouse effect）。

fossil fuel 化石燃料

一種碳氫化合物（hydrocarbon）或其衍生物，包括煤炭、石油和天然氣（natural gas）等。化石燃料之間的差異很大，可以從低碳氫比的揮發性物質如甲烷（methane）、到液態的石油到無揮發性的煤油（kerosene）。目前仍是主要能源來源之一，但是屬於耗竭性能源，需要數百萬年才能生成，而消耗速度又遠遠超過生成速度。因此供應量不足會造成能源危機。特別是從石油提煉出來的汽油（gasoline）影響最大。現時全球正趨向發展可再生能源（renewable energy），這可以有所幫助。每年燃燒化石燃料產生的二氧化碳約有 213 億噸，但自然界只能吸收其中的一半，因此每年在大氣中約增加 107 億噸的二氧化碳。二氧化碳是溫室氣體的主來源之一，因此也是加快全球暖化的因素之一。

Heat Wave Brings Wildfires to Europe
熱浪席捲歐洲帶來野火肆虐

全文朗讀 | 🎧 055 　單字 | 🎧 056

Vocabulary

1. **worsen** [`wɜsən] (v.)
   惡化，變得更糟

2. **drought** [draʊt] (n.)
   乾旱

3. **rage** [redʒ] (v.)
   肆虐，猖獗

4. **firefighter** [`faɪr,faɪtə]
   (n.) 消防隊員

5. **blaze** [blez] (n.)
   火焰，火災

6. **intense** [ɪn`tɛns] (a.)
   激烈的，強烈的

7. **induce** [ɪn`dus] (v.)
   引起，導致

8. **suppress** [sə`prɛs] (v.)
   壓制，抑制

9. **scramble** [`skræmbəl]
   (n.) 急忙、賣力地做某事

10. **evacuate** [ɪ`vækju,et]
    (v.) 撤離，疏散

As a record heat wave has ¹⁾**worsened** ²⁾**drought** conditions in Europe, wildfires are ³⁾**raging** across the continent. Although temperatures have begun to cool in France and England, ⁴⁾**firefighters** are still fighting ⁵⁾**blazes** in Greece, Spain and Italy.

由於破紀錄的熱浪使歐洲的乾旱情況更為惡化，野火在整片大地上肆虐。儘管法國和英國的溫度已開始降低，消防人員仍在與希臘、西班牙和義大利的火勢搏鬥。

According to climate scientists, heat waves have become more frequent, more ⁶⁾**intense**, and longer lasting because of human-⁷⁾**induced** climate change. The world has already warmed by more than 1 degree Celsius (1.8 degrees Fahrenheit) since the beginning of the Industrial Revolution, and temperatures will continue to rise unless governments around the world make steep cuts to emissions.

根據氣候科學家的說法，由於人類引起的氣候變化，熱浪變得更頻繁、更強烈、持續時間也更長。自工業革命開始以來，世界已經升溫超過攝氏1度（華氏1.8度），除非世界各國政府大幅削減碳排放，否則氣溫將繼續上升。

In Greece, firefighters are working to [8)]**suppress** a wildfire on Mount Penteli, which lies northeast of the capital Athens. In the nearby town of Pallini, electricity workers are [9)]**scrambling** to remove damaged *pylons. Winds <u>in excess of</u> 80 kph have made it harder to contain the fire.

在希臘，消防員正在努力撲滅位於首都雅典東北部彭特利山上的野火。在附近的帕里尼鎮，電力工人趕著拆除損壞的高壓電塔。超過每小時 80 公里的風速使火勢更難控制。

With almost all the fire engines in the area already *deployed, fire authorities have asked for additional support from other regions. Hundreds have been [10)]**evacuated** from surrounding communities, including the Athens suburb of Gerakas, which <u>is home to</u> nearly 30,000 people. A children's hospital and an *observatory have also been evacuated.

由於該地區幾乎所有的消防車都已被調動，消防當局已要求其他地區提供額外支援。數百人已從周邊社區撤離，包括雅典郊區人口約 30,000 的葛拉卡斯。一家兒童醫院和天文台也被疏散。

In Spain, firefighters are battling multiple wildfires. While one blaze in the central province of Zamora has been <u>brought under control</u>—after burning at least 24,000 *hectares—two large wildfires are still <u>out of control</u> in the northwestern region of Galicia. Another fire in the Sierra de Gredos mountain range is advancing east towards the Madrid region. Over 5,000 hectares of land have also been burned in the northeastern region of Aragon.

在西班牙，消防員與多場野火纏鬥。雖然中部薩莫拉省的一場大火在燃燒了至少 24,000 公頃土地之後已經得到控制，但西北部加利西亞地區的兩場野火仍然持續蔓延。格雷多斯山脈的另一場火勢正在向東往馬德里地區推進。東北部阿拉貢地區也有超過 5,000 公頃的土地被燒毀。

In Portugal, some 900 firefighters were fighting two active fires in the country's far north. An elderly couple was found dead inside a burned car in the town of Murça. More than 1,000 deaths have been linked to the extremely high temperatures in Portugal, and at least 500 in Spain.

在葡萄牙，大約 900 名消防員正在對抗該國最北部的兩場大火。在穆爾薩鎮，一對老夫婦被發現死在一輛被燒毀的汽車內。葡萄牙有超過 1,000 人死於極端高溫，西班牙則至少有 500 人死亡。

11. **alert** [əˋlɝt] (n.)
    警戒，警報

12. **impact** [ˋɪmpækt]
    (v./n.) 影響，衝擊

13. **closure** [ˋkloʒɚ] (n.)
    關閉，結束

14. **route** [rut / raʊt] (n.)
    路線，路徑

15. **despite** [dɪˋspaɪt]
    (prep.) 雖然，儘管

16. **forecast** [ˋforˏkæst]
    (v./n.) 預報，預測

Advanced Words

pylon [ˋpaɪlɑn] (n.)
鐵塔，電塔

deploy [dɪˋplɔɪ] (v.)
部署，配置

observatory
[əbˋzɝvəˏtori] (n.)
天文台，觀測所

hectare [ˋhɛktɛr] (n.)
公頃

Major fires have also affected Italy over the past few days, causing the country to be put on its highest heat wave [11]**alert**. Italian infrastructure has also been heavily [12]**impacted**, with temporary [13]**closure** of a key train [14]**route** between Rome and Florence.

過去幾天，義大利也飽受大火之苦，導致該國進入最高熱浪警報。義大利的基礎建設也受到嚴重影響，臨時關閉羅馬和佛羅倫斯之間的主要火車路線。

As the heat wave moves to the northeastward, parts of Germany have recorded temperatures as high as 38 C, according to the German Weather Service. [15]**Despite** the hot temperatures, heavy rain and winds of up to 100 kmh are [16]**forecast**.

根據德國氣象局的數據，隨著熱浪向東北移動，德國部分地區的氣溫高達攝氏 38 度。儘管氣溫攀高，但預報將會有大雨和時速高達 100 公里的強風。

Phrase

in excess of 大於（特定數字），多於（特定數量）

excess 有過量的、多餘的意思，此片語指大於特定數字，多於特定數量。

• The novel sold **in excess** of a million copies. 那本小說的銷售量超過 100 萬本。
• There's a higher tax rate for those earning **in excess of** $40,000. 那些收入超過 4 萬美金的人有較高的稅率。

(be) home to ……的所在／發源地

表示事物的起源，或是其家園、所在之處。

• San Francisco **is home to** the Giants and the 49ers. 巨人隊和四九人隊都是舊金山的球隊。
• The island **is home to** many different species of birds. 這個島是很多不同種類鳥類的家園。

bring (sth.) under control 控制住

主張對某事或某人的控制，特別是限制其或他們的行為或潛在的負面影響。

• The new government has promised to **bring inflation under control** 新政府承諾控制通貨膨脹
• The substitute teacher wasn't able to **bring the screaming kids under control**.
  代課老師無法控制尖叫的孩子

out of control 失控

不再可能管理，不受控制，（人）狂野或不守規矩。

• Housing costs in the city are **out of control**. 市內的住房成本已經失控。
• The children have been **out of control** since their father left. 自從父親離開後，孩子們一直失控。

With/Without + N (+ Ving or Ved)..., S + V 或是 S + V with/without + N (+ Ving or Ved) 的用法

以 with 或 without 開頭或結尾的句法，用來引導一個情境或是解釋一種原因，例如文中例句：

• **With** almost all the fire engines in the area already deployed, fire authorities have asked for additional support from other regions.
  由於該地區幾乎所有的消防車都已被調動，消防當局已要求其他地區提供額外支援。

with 帶入的子句解釋了消防當局需請求額外支援的原因，本句也可改寫為：

Fire authorities have asked for additional support from other regions **with** almost all the fire engines in the area already deployed.

Industrial Revolution 工業革命

約於 1760 年代興起，一直持續到 1830 至 1840 年代。而後所謂的第二次工業革命（1870 年至 1914 年）和 20 世紀以來的第三次工業革命。這段時間裡，人類生產與製造的方式逐漸以機械化取代，是以機器取代人力、畜力為趨勢，大規模的工廠生產取代手工生產的一場革命，也引發現代的科學革命。

工業革命在 1759 年左右開始，但直到 1830 年前仍尚未真正蓬勃發展。大多數觀點認為，工業革命發源於英國中部地區，當地富藏的煤礦成為工業化的土壤，以及大規模生產羊毛，農民湧向城市等因素結合起來，紡織（textile）產業轉向工業化。1769 年，蘇格蘭人瓦特（James Watt）改良蒸汽機（steam engine）之後，一系列技術革命引起了從手工勞動向動力機器生產轉變的重大飛躍。隨後自英國擴散到整個歐洲大陸，19 世紀傳播到北美地區。此前哥倫布大交換（Columbian exchange）導致歐洲人口爆炸，社會生產需求大增，蒸汽機、煤、鋼和金融是促成工業革命技術加速發展的四項主要因素。英國為最早開始工業革命也是最早結束工業革命的國家。

在瓦特改良蒸汽機之前，生產所需動力為人力、畜力、水力和風力。伴隨蒸汽機的發明和改進，很多以前依賴人力與手工完成的工作，被機械化生產取代。工業革命是一般政治革命不可比擬的巨大變革，與 1 萬年前農業革命（agricultural revolution）一樣，革命其影響涉及各個方面，使社會發生了巨大的變革，對人類的現代化進程推動起到不可替代的作用，把人們推向了一個嶄新的「蒸汽時代」。

kph 公里 / 小時

是速率（標量）和速度（矢量）的單位，國際單位制符號為 km/h，譯為公里 / 小時。

Senate Moves to Make Daylight Saving Time Permanent
美國參議院決議使日光節約時間永久化

全文朗讀 🎧 057　單字 🎧 058

The U.S. **Senate** has passed a [1)]**measure** that would make daylight saving time [2)]**permanent** across the entire country. The ***bipartisan** Sunshine Protection Act passed the [3)]**chamber** Tuesday, but still needs to be approved by the **House of Representatives** and signed by President Joe Biden to become law. If the bill is signed into law, it would mean an end to the "spring forward, fall back" routine of [4)]**adjusting** clocks twice a year. "Hopefully, this is the year that this gets done," said Senator Marco Rubio of Florida, one of the bill's [5)]**sponsors**, on the Senate floor. "And pardon the ***pun**, but this is an idea whose time has come."

美國參議院通過了一項使日光節約時間在全國永久生效的法案。兩黨陽光保護法週二在議院通過，但仍需得到眾議院批准並由拜登總統簽署才能正式生效。如果該法案通過，這將表示不用再進行每年兩次「春天往前，秋天往後」調整時鐘的例行公事。「希望今年能完成這項工作」該法案的提案人之一，佛羅里達州參議員盧比歐在參議院表示。「請原諒我的雙關語，但這是一個時機成熟的想法。」

Daylight saving time was first 6)**implemented** in the U.S. during WWI and WWII to 7)**conserve** energy for the war effort. By setting clocks forward an hour during the spring and summer months, the goal was to move extra sunlight from the morning to the evening when the days are longer, thus reducing the need for 8)**artificial** lighting. After 1945, some states and cities continued the practice, while others didn't, but the Uniform Time Act of 1966 9)**imposed** a national standard for DST—an hour forward in April and an hour back in October. Since passage of the Energy Policy Act of 2005, DST lasts from the second Sunday in March until the first Sunday in November.

美國歷史上，日光節約時間最早實行於第一次和第二次世界大戰期間，為戰爭而節約能源。藉由在春季和夏季將時鐘撥快一小時，白天較長時將額外的陽光從早晨轉移到晚上，減少人工照明的需求。1945 年以後，一些州和城市延續這種做法，其他則沒有，但 1966 年的統一時間法案規定了 DST 的國家標準，即 4 月提前一個小時，10 月往後一個小時。自 2005 年能源政策法案通過以來，日光節約時間從 3 月的第二個星期日持續到 11 月的第一個星期日。

So why extend DST to the entire year? In addition to the potential to save even more energy, the Sunshine Protection Act also holds the promise of making people's lives more convenient. According to a 2019 poll, 71% of Americans would prefer to avoid the *hassle of switching their clocks twice a year. The bill has also received strong support from business leaders, who believe more light in the evenings will encourage 10)**consumers** to spend more on 11)**retail** and leisure activities. Other *proponents of the legislation argue that Americans exercise more frequently during DST, reducing the risk of 12)**stroke** and heart attack.

那麼為什麼要將日光節約時間延長至全年呢？除了有機會節省更多能源之外，《陽光保護法》也可能讓人們的生活更方便。根據 2019 年的一項民意調查，71% 的美國人希望避免每年調整兩次時鐘的麻煩。該法案還得到了商界領袖的大力支持，他們認為晚間有更多陽光會鼓勵消費者在零售和休閒活動上花更多錢。其他該法案的支持者認為，美國人在 DST 期間運動得更頻繁，從而降低了中風和心臟病發作的風險。

But not everybody is on board with the health benefits of permanent DST. While sleep scientists support the 13)**elimination** of clock changes in March and November, they believe that permanent standard time— the "fall back" part of "spring forward, fall back"—is a better choice.

11. retail [`ritel] (a./n.)
零售的；零售（業）

12. stroke [strok] (n.) 中風

13. elimination
[ɪ.lɪmə`neʃən] (n.)
消除，排除，淘汰

14. facilitate [fə`sɪlə.tet]
(v.) 促進，使便利

15. outcome [`aut.kʌm]
(n.) 結果，後果

Advanced Words

bipartisan [baɪ`pɑtəzən]
(a.) 兩黨的

pun [pʌn] (n.)
雙關語，俏皮話

hassle [`hæsəl] (n.)
麻煩，困難

proponent [prə`ponənt]
(n.) 支持者，擁護者

align [ə`laɪn] (v.)
相符，一致

According to the American Academy of Sleep Medicine, standard time ***aligns** with the body's circadian rhythm, which [14)]**facilitates** better sleep quality and leads to positive health and safety [15)]**outcomes**. The DST debate, it seems, is far from over. Will the Sunshine Protection Act end up on the books? Only <u>time will tell</u>.

▲ 溫和派的馬克宏和極右派的勒龐在第二輪投票中競爭

但並不是每個人都同意永久 DST 對健康的益處。雖然睡眠科學家支持取消 3 月和 11 月的時鐘調整，但他們認為永久標準時間「春天往前，秋天往後」的「秋天往後」部分是更好的選擇。根據美國睡眠醫學學會的說法，標準時間符合體內的生理時鐘，有助於提升睡眠品質並帶來正面的健康和安全結果。DST 的相關辯論似乎離結束還很遙遠。《陽光保護法》最終會正式生效嗎？只有時間會給出答案。

Phrase

spring forward, fall back 春天往前，秋天往後

春天時把時鐘往前移一個小時，秋天時把時鐘往後移一個小時，從 3 月的第二個星期日持續到 11 月的第一個星期日，這個片語幫助人們記得如何為了日光節約時間調整時鐘。

• A: We're supposed to adjust the clocks tomorrow, but is it forward or back?
　明天我們應該調整時鐘，但到底是向前還是向後？
• B: Remember, **spring forward, fall back**. It's March, so they go an hour forward.
　記住，春天往前，秋天往後。現在是三月，所以時鐘要往前一個小時。

sth./sb. whose time has come 某事 / 某人時機成熟了

表達現在正是做某事或是某人最好的時機。

• There is nothing more powerful than an idea **whose time has come**.
　沒有什麼比一個時機成熟的想法更強大的了。
• Our party's candidate is a man **whose time has come**. 我們黨的候選人是一個時機成熟的人。

be on board (with) 同意，贊成

很多人知道 on board 可指「搭乘（車、船、飛機等）」或「到職」，但很少人知道老外還會以 be on board with sth. 來表示「同意、贊成某事」，最常聽到的就是 I'm on board with it.「我同意」。

• A: How about grabbing a burger after the movie? 我們看完電影去吃個漢堡怎麼樣？
• B: **I'm on board with** that. 我同意。

(only) time will tell 時間會證明一切

用來表示一件事情的真相或是結果只有在未來當事情發生後才會知道。

• A: Do you think we made the right decision? 你認為我們做出了正確的決定嗎？
• B: I don't know. **Time will tell**. 我不知道。時間會證明一切。

pardon the pun 的用法

一般常見的 pardon 用法為 I beg your pardon? 或是 Pardon me? 其實都是有請對方再說一次的意義，或若是說話時言語中有出現不雅字眼，我們可以用 Pardon my French. 此用法始於 1880 年代的美國，人們為了展示自己的階級向可能聽不懂法文的人說聲抱歉，略帶高傲意味。而文中的 pardon the pun，代表接下來要說的話，可能有雙關的意味，例如：

• **Pardon the pun**, but when I asked my French friend if she likes video games, she said, "Wii."
  原諒我的雙關語，但當我問我的法國朋友是否喜歡電動遊戲時，她說是。

因為法文的「是」= "Oui" 跟 "Wii" 的讀音一樣。

EZpedia

Senate 參議院

美國的參議院也稱「上院」（Upper Chamber），被視為具有比眾議院更大的審議權。由 100 名議員（senator）組成（每州兩名），參議員每一任期為 6 年，可連任。基於選舉需要，參議院中一向有在任年度不等的三組議員，從而每兩年就有三分之一的議員任期屆滿，需卸任或經選舉連任。這可以確保參議院中始終有一定比例的資深議員。

參議院與眾議院有著很多相同的立法權力，但它同時具有一些特殊權力：

1. 參議院負責批准總統提名的最高法院大法官、下級聯邦法院法官以及行政機構重要職位的人選。總統提名人必須通過參議院批准才能就任。
2. 參議院負責批准或否決總統簽署的國際條約。
3. 在發生彈劾總統或最高法院大法官的情況時，由參議院主持審判，全體參議員擔任陪審員。

House of Representatives 眾議院

眾議院被視為「民眾之議院」（House of the People），有 435 名議員，各州議員人數按人口比例決定。美國的五個特區或屬地——哥倫比亞特區（District of Columbia）、美屬薩摩亞（American Samoa）、關島（Guam）、波多黎各（Puerto Rico）、美屬維爾京群島（U.S. Virgin Islands）——在眾議院也有代表，但這些代表沒有投票權。

所有眾議員的任期均為兩年，可連任。眾議員是從各個州內按地理區域劃分的所謂國會選區（Congressional District）中選出，補缺要通過專門選舉或隨大選進行。眾議院議長由眾議院議員選舉而產生，故來自多數黨。眾議院具有的與參議院不同的職權包括：

1. 有權對總統和最高法院大法官提出彈劾案。
2. 所有涉及增加稅收的提案必須從眾議院產生。
3. 如果在總統大選中沒有任何一位候選人贏得選舉人多數票，眾議院負責決定總統當選人，一州一票。

Sri Lankan President Flees [1)]Amid Economic Crisis
斯里蘭卡總統於經濟危機期間出逃

全文朗讀 | 🎧 059   單字 | 🎧 060

Over the past week, scenes of Sri Lankan protesters taking over the president's house and climbing the walls of the prime minister's office have captured global attention. Sri Lanka, [2)]**gripped** by economic crisis and political ***unrest**, has [3)]**descended** into chaos.

過去一週，斯里蘭卡抗議民眾攻佔總統府、攀爬總理官邸圍牆的種種景象，吸引了全球的目光。被經濟危機和政治動盪不安處境所困的斯里蘭卡，已陷入混亂狀態。

Since March, the South Asian nation's 23 million people have faced an economic crisis that has caused daily power cuts and [4)]**severe** shortages in medicine, food and fuel. As conditions grew more [5)]**desperate**, so did anger at the decades of political corruption. The country has been run by one family, **the Rajapaksas**, for most of the past 20 years.

自三月起，此南亞國家的 2300 萬人民，面臨了造成每天斷電與醫藥、糧食和燃油嚴重短缺的經濟危機。隨著情況越發危急，人民對於數十載的政治貪腐也越發憤怒。該國一直是由同一個拉賈帕克薩家族治理將近 20 年。

In one year, Sri Lanka's inflation rate grew by more than 50%. Protests in late March against President Gotabaya Rajapaksa's government pushed him to declare a state of emergency, giving police more power to crack down on dissent. In Mid-April, security forces [6]**clashed** with [7]**demonstrators**, injuring 12 and killing one in Rambukkana, a town near the capital of Colombo.

斯里蘭卡一年內的通膨率漲到超過 50%。三月下旬，民眾反對拉賈帕克薩總統的政府所進行的抗議，迫使他宣布進入緊急狀態，讓警方擁有更多鎮壓反對聲浪的權力。四月中旬，保安人員和示威民眾發生衝突，在首都可倫坡附近的倫布卡納小鎮，造成 12 人受傷、1 人死亡的憾事。

Five days later, students in Colombo gathered to demand the president and prime minister resign in the face of soaring inflation. In May, Prime Minister Mahinda Rajapaksa, Gotabaya's brother, announced his resignation. The [8]**hardships** faced by Sri Lankans have worsened since then. Last week the World Food Programme said over six million residents don't have enough to eat.

五天後，可倫坡的學生聚集要求總統和總理為高漲的通膨率負責而下台。五月，身為總統戈塔巴亞的弟弟——總理馬辛達拉賈帕克薩，宣布辭職。斯里蘭卡人所面臨的困境從那時起更是每況愈下。世界糧食計畫署上週表示，有超過六百萬的居民沒有足夠的糧食。

Months of struggle came to a head as Sri Lankans [9]**stormed** the president's house on July 9. They took a dip in his pool, cooked in his kitchen, and lifted weights in his gym. Less than a week later, Rajapaksa fled to Singapore and resigned his office. For a brief moment, protesters appeared [10]**victorious**. But the country remains in a deep crisis, and it's not clear who will fill the power [11]**vacuum**.

數月的掙扎來到了高峰，斯里蘭卡人於 7 月 9 日攻佔總統府。他們在泳池游泳、用他的廚房煮飯，在他的健身房練舉重。不到一週之後，拉賈帕克薩就逃到新加坡並辭職。有那麼一瞬間，抗議民眾看似勝利了。但是該國家仍深陷危機，該由誰來填補這個權力空窗期仍不明朗。

What led to the economic crisis? The government blames the Covid pandemic, which [12]**crippled** Sri Lanka's tourist trade—one of its main sources of foreign [13]**currency**. It also says tourism numbers were affected by the Easter bombings in 2019. Many experts, however, blame

11. **vacuum** [ˋvækjum] (n.)
真空，空窗期

12. **cripple** [ˋkrɪpəl] (v.)
重創，使癱瘓

13. **currency** [ˋkɝənsi] (n.)
貨幣，錢

14. **reserve** [rɪˋzɝv] (n.)
存底，儲備

15. **fertilizer** [ˋfɝtə͵laɪzə] (n.) 肥料

16. **organic** [ɔrˋgænɪk] (a.)
有機的

17. **widespread** [ˋwaɪd͵sprɛd] (a.)
大規模的，廣泛的

Advanced Words

unrest [ʌnˋrɛst] (n.)
不安，動盪

mismanagement [͵mɪsˋmænɪdʒmənt] (n.)
管理不當

deficit [ˋdɛfəsɪt] (n.)
逆差，赤字

Rajapaksa's economic *mismanagement.

是什麼原因導致此經濟危機？政府怪罪新冠肺炎疫情，重創了斯里蘭卡的旅遊業，而這是此國的主要外幣來源之一。政府亦表示，觀光人次受到 2019 年復活節連環爆炸案的影響。然而，許多專家將事件歸咎於拉賈帕克薩經濟管理不當。

As its civil war ended in 2009, Sri Lanka began to focus on its domestic market instead of promoting foreign trade. This meant falling income from exports and a growing bill for imports. The resulting annual trade *deficit caused the country's foreign currency [14)]reserves to drop from $7.6 billion in 2019 to around $250 million today. Rajapaksa was also criticized for large tax cuts in 2019, which cost the government more than $1.4 billion a year.

斯里蘭卡內戰於 2009 年結束時，就開始著重國內市場，而非推廣國外貿易。這表示出口收入下滑，進口開銷增加，進而造成每年貿易逆差的問題，使得該國的外匯存底從 2019 年的 76 億美元，掉到現在約 2.5 億美元。拉賈帕克薩亦因 2019 年大幅減稅而受到批評，此舉讓政府每年少了 14 億美元的稅收。

To make matters worse, when Sri Lanka's foreign currency shortage became serious in early 2021, the government responded by banning imports of chemical [15)]fertilizer. Farmers were told to use local [16)]organic fertilizers instead, which led to [17)]widespread crop failure. The country had to import more food from abroad, making its foreign currency shortage even worse.

更糟的是，當斯里蘭卡外幣短缺問題在 2021 年變得嚴重時，政府卻以禁止進口化學肥料的方式來應對。政府告知農人應改用當地的有機肥料，結果導致大規模的作物歉收問題。該國不得不從國外進口更多糧食，讓外幣短缺問題雪上加霜。

Phrase

crack down (on) 鎮壓，制裁

以更嚴厲的方式應對不良或非法行為；以更具武力的方式去管制、壓制或限制；採取紀律方面的措施。

• The new mayor has promised to **crack down** on drug dealing. 新任市長承諾要打擊毒品交易。
• The police launched a campaign to **crack down** on drunk driving. 警方發動了取締酒駕的行動。

come to a head 達到緊要關頭

到達危機狀態；某情況已經到了必須有所行動的地步。

• Tensions between Russia and Ukraine **came to a head** when Russian troops crossed the border on February 24. 俄羅斯和烏克蘭之間的緊張情勢，在俄羅斯步兵於 2 月 25 日跨越國界時到達高峰。

however 的插入句用法

however 通常用來表達轉折的語氣，但前後的標點符號用法就會有所差異，例如：

- I would love to go to lunch with you. **However,** I need to make a phone call.
  我很想跟你去吃午餐。但是，我需要打通電話。

- I would love to go to lunch with you; **however,** I need to make a phone call.
  我很想跟你去吃午餐，但是我需要打通電話。

- You can go out to lunch if you like. I, **however,** need to make a phone call.
  你想的話可以去吃午餐。但是，我需要打通電話。

前兩句是一樣的意思，只是標點符號的位置不同。第三種則是本文中的用法，however 前面是主詞，是強調第一、二句主詞的對比。

EZpedia

the Rajapaksas 拉賈帕克薩家族

是斯里蘭卡政壇的顯赫家族。它是馬欣達拉賈帕克薩（Mahinda Rajapaksa）擔任總統期間斯里蘭卡最有權勢的家族之一，當時該家族的許多成員都在斯里蘭卡國家擔任要職。隨著他們政治權力的增長，有報導稱國家在他們的統治下正走向專制。繼馬欣達拉賈帕克薩 (Mahinda Rajapaksa) 在 2015 年總統大選中意外落敗後，他們被指控專制、腐敗、任人唯親和治理不善。在 2019 年的總統選舉中，馬欣達拉賈帕克薩的弟弟戈塔巴亞拉賈帕克薩參選並獲勝。拉賈帕克薩家族的行為引發了始於 2019 年的經濟危機，導致斯里蘭卡在上台後短短 30 個月內首次出現獨立後歷史上的債務違約，導致拉賈帕克薩家族的聲望一落千丈。據信，拉賈帕克薩大家族積累了大量財富，雖然財富的數量和規模不詳，但該家族的幾名成員已在國際調查中被揭露，例如潘多拉文件將利用空殼公司和信託網絡將其財富隱藏在離岸避稅天堂，這導致人們指責拉賈帕克薩斯將斯里蘭卡變成盜賊統治。

World Food Programme 世界糧食計畫署

原名糧食援助政策與計劃委員會，是屬於聯合國的食品援助組織，成立於 1961 年，總部設於義大利羅馬，為全世界最大的人道救援組織，為世界上 9 千萬有需要人士提供糧食，其中包括了大約 5800 萬名的孩童。世界糧食計劃署在全球擁有超過 80 個國家辦公處，他們成立的目標是幫助無法生產與獲得糧食的人和家庭。2020 年因對抗飢餓問題及避免其演變成戰爭和衝突而獲頒諾貝爾和平獎。

Easter Bombings

2019 年 4 月 21 日復活節星期日，斯里蘭卡的三座教堂和商業首都科倫坡的三座豪華酒店成為一系列斯里蘭卡籍伊斯蘭教恐怖分子自殺式爆炸的目標。當天稍晚，科倫坡郊區的一個住宅區和一個賓館發生了規模較小的爆炸。共 269 人遇難，至少 500 人受傷。被炸的酒店有香格里拉、肉桂大酒店、金斯伯里酒店和熱帶酒店。據國家情報局稱，本有第二波攻擊，但因政府突襲而停止。

U.S. Stocks Enter Bear Market
美股進入熊市

全文朗讀 🎧 061　單字 🎧 062

U.S. [1]**stocks** took a dive on Monday, with the **S&P 500** entering **bear market** territory, defined as a fall of 20% or more from a recent record high. This marks the first time the S&P 500 has confirmed a bear market since the 2020 **Wall Street** [2]**slump** resulting from the Covid-19 pandemic. The [3]**plunge** adds to fears that expected [4]**aggressive** interest rate hikes by the **Federal Reserve** could tip the [5]**economy** into a [6]**recession**.

美國股市週一暴跌，標準普爾 500 指數進入熊市，即從近期新高下跌 20% 以上。這表示自 2020 年華爾街新冠疫情導致的暴跌以來，標準普爾 500 指數首次確認為熊市。股市暴跌加劇了人們對聯準會預期激進升息將可能導致經濟陷入衰退的擔憂。

The S&P 500 closed Monday at 3,749.63, down 3.9% for the day and 21.8% below its Jan 3 record closing high of 4,796.56. The Dow Jones Industrial Average dropped 2.79% to close at 30,516.74, while the Nasdaq Composite fell 4.68% to end the day at 10,809.23. Last

Friday, the [7]**indexes** posted their biggest weekly [8]**percentage** drops since January and ended sharply lower after an inflation report showed consumer prices rising 8.6% in May, the fastest since 1981.

標準普爾 500 指數週一收於 3,749.63，當日下跌 3.9%，比 1 月 3 日創下的收盤新高 4,796.56 低 21.8%。道瓊工業平均指數下跌 2.79%，以 30,516.74 作收，而納斯達克綜合指數下跌 4.68%，以 10,809.23 作收。上週五，在通膨報告顯示 5 月消費者物價上漲 8.6% 為 1981 年以來最快後，三大指數寫下自 1 月以來的最大週線跌幅，並大幅收低。

Stocks have been *volatile since the start of the year, with Russia's invasion of Ukraine in late February <u>taking a heavy toll on</u> markets. But much of the recent *sell-off has been [9]**fuelled** by increasing worries about inflation and the tightening of *monetary policy as the Fed attempts to <u>rein it in</u>.

自今年年初以來，股市持續波動，2 月下旬俄羅斯入侵烏克蘭對市場也造成了沉重打擊。但最近大部分的拋售是因為對通膨的擔憂加劇以及聯準會為了抑制通膨收緊貨幣政策而造成的。

When it concludes its two-day meeting on Wednesday, the Fed is expected to hike interest rates by 50 basis points to [10]**curb** inflation, and some economists [11]**speculate** that the Fed could even raise rates by 75 basis points. Many worry that a more aggressive rate hike could send the economy into recession.

當聯準會週三結束為期兩天的會議時，預計將升息 2 碼以抑制通膨，有的經濟學家推測聯準會甚至可能升息 3 碼。許多人擔心，更激進的升息可能會使經濟陷入衰退。

The [12]**yield** on the two-year U.S. Treasury note, a *benchmark for borrowing costs, rose briefly above the 10-year yield on Monday. Many market [13]**analysts** see this as a reliable signal that a recession could come in the next year.

2 年期美國國債殖利率，也就是藉貸成本的基準，週一短暫升至 10 年期國債收益率之上。許多市場分析師將此視為明年可能出現衰退的可靠徵兆。

This year's *downturn is a major shift for the market after its strong post-pandemic [14]**rally**. The S&P 500 rose 114.38% from its closing low on March 23, 2020 to its record closing high on January 3 this year. The

11. **speculate** [ˈspɛkjəˌlet]
(v.) 推測，揣測

12. **yield** [jild] (n.)
殖利率，收益（率）

13. **analyst** [ˈænəlɪst] (n.)
分析師

14. **rally** [ˈræli] (n./v.)
（股市）反彈

15. **prior** [ˈpraɪə] (a.)
在先的，在前的

Advanced Words

volatile [ˈvɑlətəl] (a.)
不穩定的，異變的

sell-off [ˈsɛlˌɑf] (n.)
（股市）拋售

monetary [ˈmʌnəˌtɛri]
(a.) 貨幣的，幣制的

benchmark
[ˈbɛntʃˌmɑrk] (n.) 基準

downturn [ˈdaʊnˌtɜn]
(n.)（經濟）衰退

Nasdaq fell into bear market territory earlier this year, the first of the three major U.S. indexes to do so.

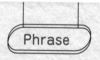

DOW JONES	16,314.67
S&P 500	1,931.34
NASDAQ	4,686.50
NYSE COMPOSITE	9,857.25
DOW COMPOSITE	5,825.39

今年的低迷是市場在疫情後強勁反彈之後的重大轉變。標準普爾 500 指數從 2020 年 3 月 23 日的收盤低點上漲 114.38%，至今年 1 月 3 日的收盤新高。納斯達克指數今年稍早跌入熊市，是美國三大指數中的第一個。

The longest S&P 500 bear market lasted just over five years, starting in March 1937 ending in April 1942, while the shortest lasted just over a month, beginning on Feb 19, 2 and ending on March 23. It's taken a little over a year on average for the index to <u>hit r</u> <u>bottom</u> during bear markets, and then about another two years to return to its [15)]**prior** hi

最長的標準普爾 500 熊市持續了五年多，從 1937 年 3 月開始，到 1942 年 4 月結束，而最短的持 一個多月，從 2020 年 2 月 19 日開始，到 3 月 23 日結束。熊市期間，該指數平均花了一年多一點 間跌至谷底，然後大約再過兩年回到其之前的高點。

Phrase

take a dive 大跌，放水

在股票市場中，「跳水」以突然變得更低，就像公司或整個市場的股票一樣;拳擊是假裝被對方擊倒來操縱比賽結 足球是假裝被對方擊倒來罰點球。

• The stocks I bought all **took a dive** this week. 我這週買的股票都大跌了。

take a toll (on) 對⋯⋯造成負面影響

toll 是「損害」的意思。take a toll 或 take its/their toll 是「造成負面影響」，後面介系詞常用 on。

• All those years of sunbathing have really **taken a toll** on her skin. 多年來狂做日光浴真的很傷她的皮膚。

rein in 控制，勒住

"rein" 是駕馭、韁繩的意思，此片語指控制情緒，活動或情況以防止它變得過於強大。

• That candidate promised to **rein in** government spending. 那個候選人承諾控制政府開支。

hit rock bottom 觸底

"rock bottom" 是最低點的意思，此片語指處於極低的水平，不能再低了。

• People's confidence in the government's ability to manage the economy has **hit rock bottom**. 人民對政府管理經濟能力的信心已跌至谷底。

do so / do it / do that 的用法

這三種說法都屬於動詞性替代詞的用法,用來代替實際的動詞和它的受詞或補語,以避免跟前方重複。例如:

• I promised to send a Christmas card and I **did so**. 我答應要寄出一張聖誕卡片而我也這麼做了。

• I'd like to go snorkeling. I've never **done that** before. 我想要去浮潛,我從沒那麼做過。

• She asked her kids to do their homework and they **did it**. 她要求她的孩子們做作業而他們也做了。

要注意的地方是,助動詞中只有 do 可以如此使用,我們不能說 I can so,或是 She must that,而必須要說 I can do so 或是 She must do that。

S&P 500 標準普爾 500

簡稱 S&P 500 、標普 500 或史坦普 500,是由 1957 年起記錄美國股市的平均記錄,觀察範圍達 500 支的一個普通股,佔總市值約 80%。標準普爾 500 指數由標普道瓊指數公司(S&P Dow Jones Indices LLC,標準普爾全球控股公司控制的合資公司)開發並維持。指數內的 500 支普通股(包括不動產投資信託)都是在美國股市的兩大股票交易市場,紐約證券交易所和納斯達克 (Nasdaq) 中有多個交易的公司。幾乎所有標準普爾中的公司都是全美最高金額買賣的 50 支股票。這個股票指數由標準普爾公司創建並維護。

bear market 熊市

又稱為空頭市場,指證券市場上,價格走低的市場。其相反為牛市(多頭市場 bull market)。此處的證券市場,泛指常見的股票、債券、期貨、選擇權、外匯、可轉讓定存單、衍生性金融商品及其它各種證券。史上最有名的熊市是 1930 年代的美國經濟大蕭條(Great Depression)。

Wall Street 華爾街

是一條位於美國紐約市下曼哈頓的狹窄街道。今日,「華爾街」一詞已超越這條街道本身,成為對整個美國經濟具有影響力的金融市場和金融機構的代稱。

華爾街是紐約證券交易所與納斯達克的總部所在,美國證券交易所、紐約商品期貨交易所和紐約貿易局也曾將總部設在這裡。紐約市依靠華爾街成為了世界最具經濟活力的城市和首屈一指的金融中心。不過,現時許多金融公司已經把總部遷離華爾街,取而代之的是曼哈頓的中城,以及紐約市其他外圍地帶。

Federal Reserve 聯邦儲備系統

美國的中央銀行系統。創建於 1913 年 12 月 23 日,隨著一系列金融恐慌(特別是 1907 年的恐慌)導致人們希望中央控制貨幣體系以緩解金融危機促成美聯儲法案的頒布。 諸如 1930 年代的大蕭條和 2000 年代的大衰退等事件導緻美聯儲系統的作用和責任這些年來逐漸擴大。

Shoppers Struggle with Soaring Food Prices
食品物價高漲令消費者吃不消

全文朗讀 | 🎧 063   單字 | 🎧 064

Vocabulary

1. **browse** [braʊz] (v.)
   逛逛，流覽

2. **aisle** (n.) [aɪl]
   通道，走道

3. **staple** [`stepəl] (n.)
   主食，主要產品

4. **spike** [spaɪk] (n./v.)
   （價格等）飆漲、劇增

5. **add up** (phr.)
   加起來（很多）

6. **analyze** [`ænə,laɪz] (v.)
   分析

7. **detergent** [dɪ`tɜdʒənt]
   (n.) 洗潔劑，洗衣粉

8. **ground** [graʊnd] (a.)
   磨碎的，絞（肉）

9. **category** [`kætɪ,gɔri]
   (n.) 種類，範疇

10. **ounce** [aʊns] (n.) 盎司

As shoppers [1)]**browse** the [2)]**aisles** of their local supermarket these days, they're finding that the prices of items they used to toss into their carts <u>without a second thought</u> have soared. Just how expensive have [3)]**staples** like peanut butter and potato chips become? The annual inflation rate hit 9.1% last month. But that doesn't mean Americans are seeing their grocery store bills increase by 9% across the board. In fact, the rise in prices has been far greater for most food items.

現在當消費者逛當地超市時，他們發現過去毫不猶豫地扔進購物車的商品價格飆升了。花生醬和洋芋片等主食到底變得多貴？上個月的年通膨率達到了 9.1%。但這並不意味著美國人看到他們超市賬單全面增加了 9%。事實上，大多數食品的價格上漲幅度要大得多。

On average, food prices have been ***outpacing** the Consumer Price Index, with grocery prices showing a 12.2% [4)]**spike** over the last year— the largest 12-month increase since 1979. This may not seem like a huge jump, but it can really [5)]**add up** when every item on your shopping list is more expensive.

平均而言，食品價格超過了消費者價格指數，超市商品價格過去一年上漲了12.2%，這是自1979年以來12個月內的最大漲幅。雖可能看起來不是巨大的躍升，但當你的購物清單上每件商品都更貴的時候，加起來可不便宜。

To better understand what American shoppers are experiencing, a Washington D.C. market research firm [6]**analyzed** the average price of eight *****everyday** grocery products, including Kraft cheese slices, Birds Eye frozen corn, Jif peanut butter, Cheerios cereal, Coca-Cola, Lay's potato chips, Wonder sandwich bread, and Tide laundry [7]**detergent**. Products like eggs, milk and [8]**ground** beef weren't included, as items in these [9]**categories** are mostly sold under local brands.

為了更加了解美國消費者的購物體驗，華盛頓特區的一家市場研究公司分析了八種日常超市商品的平均價格，包括卡夫奶酪片、雀目牌冷凍玉米、JIF 花生醬、Cheerios 穀片、可口可樂、樂事洋芋片、Wonder 吐司麵包和汰漬洗衣精。雞蛋、牛奶和牛絞肉等產品不包括在內，因為這類別中的商品大多以本地品牌銷售。

As it turns out, price increases for grocery products are <u>all over the place</u>. Some items are seeing annual jumps of more than twice the CPI rate. For example, the cost of a 13-[10]**ounce** bag of Lay's potato chips shot up 38% over the past 12 months, and the price of a package of Kraft cheese slices rose almost 15%. But other items saw much lower price [11]**surges**, like an 18-ounce box of Cheerios cereal, which increased by only 2.6%.

結果發現，超市商品的價格漲幅參差不齊。有些項目的年度漲幅是 CPI 的兩倍以上。例如，一袋 13 盎司的樂事洋芋片價格在過去 12 個月中飆升了 38%，一包卡夫奶酪片的價格上漲了近 15%。但其他商品的價格上升卻少得多，例如一盒 18 盎司的 Cheerios 穀片，僅上漲 2.6%。

Food prices are rising at such different rates because the CPI is a cost [12]**calculation** based on average prices for Americans in major [13]**metropolitan** areas, while shoppers in [14]**rural** areas are seeing much bigger increases. Inflation <u>kicked into high gear</u> after the start of the COVID-19 pandemic, with the prices of the eight everyday grocery products analyzed *****skyrocketing** nearly 24% since January 2020.

食品價格以如此不同的速率上漲，因為 CPI 是一項基於美國人在主要都市地區平均價格的成本計算，而鄉村地區的消費者則看到更大的漲幅。通膨率在新冠疫情爆發後迅速上升，八種日常超市商品的價格自 2020 年 1 月以來飆升了近 24%。

---

11. **surge** [sɝdʒ] (v./n.)
激增，暴漲

12. **calculation**
[ˌkælkjəˈleʃən] (n.)
計算，計算結果

13. **metropolitan**
[ˌmɛtrəˈpɑlɪtən] (a.)
大都市的

14. **rural** [ˈrʊrəl] (a.)
鄉間的，農村的

15. **counterpart**
[ˈkaʊntɚˌpɑrt] (n.)
相對應者，相配對者

16. **insight** [ˈɪnˌsaɪt] (n.)
洞察，見解

17. **charity** [ˈtʃærəti] (n.)
慈善，慈善事業

Advanced Words

outpace [ˌaʊtˈpes] (v.)
超過，勝過

everyday [ˈɛvriˌde] (a.)
日常的，每天的

skyrocket [ˈskaɪˌrɑkɪt]
(v.) 飛漲，猛漲

And Americans aren't experiencing the burden of inflation equally. Not only are rural residents seeing bigger surges, but younger households are also feeling more economic pressure. **Gen Z** Americans are struggling more to <u>put food on the table</u> than their older [15)]**counterparts**, according to the Consumer Food [16)]**Insights** Report. One third of

Gen Z households report seeking groceries from a church or [17)]**charity** in the last month, compared to just 8% of **Baby boomer** households, the report said.

美國人也沒有平等地承受通膨的壓力。不僅鄉村居民看到通膨激增，年輕家庭也感受到了更大的經濟壓力。根據《消費者食品洞察報告》，Z 世代美國人比他們上一代的人更難維持家計。報告指稱，上個月有三分之一的 Z 世代家庭從教堂或慈善機構尋求食品雜貨，而嬰兒潮一代家庭的這一比例僅為 8%。

Phrase

without a second thought 不假思索

"second thought" 是重新考慮的意思，此片語指（做某事）不停止思考，不猶豫，不考慮後果

- Michelle spends hundreds of dollars on makeup **without a second thought**.
  蜜雪兒不假思索地在化妝品上花費了數百美元。
- **Without a second thought**, Daniel chased after the pickpocket.
  丹尼爾沒有多想，就追捕扒手。

(be) all over the place 七零八落，亂無章法

all over the place 字面上是説東西散亂得「到處都是、亂七八糟」，也可以用來形容事物「參差不齊、荒腔走板」。

- A: How did your students do on the quiz? 你的學生小考考得怎樣？
- B: Their answers **were all over the place**. 他們答得亂七八糟的。

kick into high gear 進入全盛狀態

字面上 high gear 是指車子的最高檔速，此用語引申為將事情和某種狀態帶入或推向如日中天的最佳境界。

- A: How's your election campaign coming along? 你的競選活動進行得如何？
- B: It's **kicking into high gear**. 正要邁進最好的狀態。

put food on the table 維持家計，賺錢養家

賺取足夠的錢來為自己和（通常）家人提供基本必需品。

- A: Do you want to pursue a high-paying career? 你想追求高薪的職業嗎？
- B: No. I just want to do something I enjoy and be able to **put food on the table**.
  不，我只是想做我喜歡的事情，並且能夠自給自足。

分數的讀法

中文的分數可能讀作幾分之幾，英文中的分數讀法則不盡相同，例如文中出現的 one third 就是 **1/3**（三分之一）的意思，分母用序數，其他讀法包括：

1/2 : a/one half

2/3 : two thirds

40% : forty percent

13.01% : thirteen point zero one percent

3/4 : three quarters

17/824 : seventeen over eight hundred and twenty four

0.3% : (zero) point three percent

EZpedia

Consumer Price Index (CPI) 消費者物價指數

在經濟學上，是反映居民生活產品及勞務價格統計出來的物價變動指標，以百分比變化來表示。它是衡量通貨膨脹的主要指標之一。一般定義超過 3% 為通膨，超過 5% 就是嚴重的通貨膨脹。CPI 往往是市場經濟活動與政府貨幣政策的重要參考指標。CPI 穩定、就業充分及 GDP 成長往往是最重要的社會經濟目標。指數過高的升幅往往不被市場歡迎，解決的手段有升息、財政緊縮、採取穩健的財政政策、增加生產、平抑物價等。

Gen Z Z 世代

口語稱作 zoomers。特指在 1990 年代末葉至 2010 年代前期出生的人。約是 1994 年－ 2014 年之間出生。Z 世代受到網際網路、即時通訊、智慧手機、平板電腦等科技產物影響很大。Z 世代是自小生活在電子虛擬、現實世界的原生世代，由科技發展形塑的社群關係與價值觀深深影響了此世代的自我認同。近年，關於此世代在職場上與其他世代人們的互動關係受到關注，其中 Z 世代以獨特的文化與能力，為組織注入活水，但亦有許多的矛盾浮現，例如比起前世代（千禧一代 Millennials）傾向求教權威，Z 世代更依賴網路搜尋而來的資訊。

Baby boomers 嬰兒潮

「嬰兒潮一代」是用來描述西方國家 1946 年至 1964 年間出生之人的術語。嬰兒潮一代佔世界人口的很大一部分。根據最新的人口普查報告，至 2019 年 7 月，它代表了美國 7300 萬人口。作為美國歷史上最大的一代群體，嬰兒潮一代已經並將繼續對經濟產生重大影響。因此，它們通常是行銷活動和商業計劃的重點。

PART 3

Life News

Simone Leigh 2019 年
的作品 Brick House

Black Women Make History at the 2022 Venice Biennale
非裔女性藝術家留名威尼斯雙年展

Two black woman, one British, one American, have made history by winning top honors at the 59th Venice Art Biennale, which was delayed by a year due to the pandemic. British artist Sonia Boyce and American [1]sculptor Simone Leigh were not only the first black women in the Biennale's 127-year history to take home Golden Lion, but also the first to represent their countries at the [2]prestigious art event.

兩名非裔女性，一位為英國人，另一位為美國人，在因疫情而延後一年舉辦的第 59 屆威尼斯美術雙年展中贏得最高榮譽，締造歷史佳績。來自英國的藝術家索尼婭博伊斯與美國雕塑家西蒙雷伊是在雙年展長達 127 年的歷史中，首兩位贏得金獅獎的非裔女性，她們也是首兩位代表自己國家參與這場藝術盛會的非裔女性。

Boyce, who is [3]Professor at University of the Arts London, won the Golden Lion for her Feeling Her Way [4]exhibition at the Biennale's British Pavilion. In her exhibition, the artist uses videos, [1]sculptures and *memorabilia to celebrate five black British female singers representing different generations and musical styles, from jazz to the blues.

博伊斯是倫敦藝術大學的教授，因為《她摸索前進》展覽，她代表英國館贏得威尼斯雙年展金獅獎肯定。在該展中，這位藝術家使用影像、雕塑與紀念物來歌頌五名非裔英國女歌手，呈現出不同世代及音樂風格，從爵士到藍調音樂。

Chicago-born Leigh won the Golden Lion for her giant [5]bronze statue, Brick House, which greets visitors in the opening [6]gallery of the Biennale's central exhibition at Venice's famous Arsenale. The 16-foot-tall figure, which combines the head of a black woman with a *torso in the form of an African clay hut, was originally exhibited in New York's High Line park.

出生於芝加哥的雷伊以巨型銅雕《紅磚屋》獲得金獅獎殊榮，這件作品展示在雙年展中央主題館展區，也就是威尼斯著名的軍械庫展區中，在開幕展廳迎接到訪的觀眾。這件高達 16 英尺的人像上半部為非裔女性的頭部，軀幹則是非洲陶土屋的造型，該作品最初在紐約的高架公園中展示。

1. sculptor [ˋskʌlptɚ] (n.) 雕塑家，雕刻家
   sculpture [ˋskʌlptʃɚ] (n.) 雕塑品，雕像
2. prestigious [prɛsˋtɪdʒəs] (n.)
   著名的，有名望的
3. professor [prəˋfɛsɚ] (n.) 教授
4. exhibition [ˌɛksəˋbɪʃən] (n.) 展覽，展示館
5. bronze [brɑnz] (a./n.) 青銅製的，青銅色
   的；青銅
6. gallery [ˋgælərɪ] (n.) 美術館，畫廊

Advanced Words

memorabilia [ˌmɛmərəˋbɪlɪə] (n.)
紀念品，收藏品

torso [ˋtɔrso] (n.) 人體軀幹，軀幹雕像

EZpedia

make history 締造歷史

完成某件之前沒有人做過，但非常重要或有名的事情，因此在歷史上留下紀錄，為後人所知。

- The two scientists **made history** by discovering the structure of DNA. 這兩名科學家因為發現了 DNA 結構而名留青史。
- Margaret Thatcher **made history** when she became Britain's first female prime minister.
  柴契爾夫人因成為英國首位女性首相後而名留青史。

feel one's way 摸索前進，小心翼翼

藉由觸覺而非視覺來摸索找到行進方向；小心翼翼地進展，特指在不熟悉的環境中。

- Richard **felt his way** through the dark living room.
  理查在黑漆漆的客廳中摸索著前進。
- Kim is new at the company, so she's still **feeling her way**.
  金是公司的新人，因此她仍然在謹慎地適應當中。

Venice Art Biennale 威尼斯美術雙年展

威尼斯雙年展（意大利語：La Biennale di Venezia）是一個擁有上百年歷史的藝術節，奇數年為藝術雙年展，在偶數年為建築雙年展。它與德國卡塞爾文獻展（Kassel documenta）、巴西聖保羅雙年展（São Paulo Art Biennial）並稱為世界三大藝術展。展覽一般分為國家館與主題館兩部分，主要展覽當代藝術和建築藝術。第 59 屆威尼斯雙年展 2022 年 4 月至 11 月開展，本屆主題展為「夢之乳」（The Milk of Dreams）；臺北市立美術館策劃的台灣館，則以「不可能的夢」為題參展。

Golden Lion 金獅獎

是威尼斯雙年展的最高榮譽獎項，分為個人獎與主題展獎等。另外，威尼斯影展（Venice Film Festival）中的金獅獎（義大利語：Leone d'oro）則是該影展的最高榮譽，從 1949 年開始頒發，由該屆評審團自正式競賽單元中選出得獎作品。1970 年開始另外頒發榮譽金獅獎，表揚對於電影有重要貢獻的工作者。

British Pavilion 英國館

本屆雙年展英國館策展主題為《The Garden of Privatised Delights》，聚焦在英國社會中「私有化的公共空間」，展覽由跨領域策展團隊 Unscene Architecture 策劃。

Arsenale 威尼斯軍械庫

是一個歷史悠久的建築群，前身是造船廠和軍械庫，聚集在威尼斯。軍火庫歸國家所有，負責威尼斯共和國從中世紀晚期到近代早期的大部分海軍力量來源。

High Line 紐約高架公園

紐約空中鐵道公園（High Line Park/High Line）是位於美國紐約市曼哈頓廢棄的中央鐵路西區線，一高架橋上的綠道和帶狀公園，設計理念來自法國巴黎的綠蔭步道。它一度面臨被拆除的命運，但在當地居民的努力經營與活化之下，它與一旁的雀兒喜市場（Chelsea Market）成為紐約著名觀光景點之一。

▶ 風靡全球的超級英雄漫畫

全文朗讀 🎧 067　單字 🎧 068

Comic Book Artist Neal Adams Dies at 80
漫畫家尼爾亞當斯逝世，享壽 80 歲

[1]**Legendary** comic book artist Neal Adams, famous for bringing a new realistic look to Batman and other superheroes, has died at the age of 80. According to his wife, Marilyn Adams, he [2]**passed away** in New York from [3]**complications** due to *sepsis. In a statement, DC Comics called Adams "one of the most *acclaimed artists to have [4]**contributed** to the comic book industry."

著名漫畫家尼爾亞當斯逝世，享壽 80 歲。他以為蝙蝠俠及其餘超級英雄們帶來更真實的新樣貌而聞名。據遺孀瑪麗蓮亞當斯表示，亞當斯在紐約因敗血症所引發的併發症而過世。在一份聲明中，DC 漫畫稱亞當斯為「對漫畫界貢獻最傑出的藝術家之一」。

Born in New York City on June 15, 1941, Adams graduated from Manhattan's School of Industrial Art in 1959. After cutting his teeth in advertising, he joined DC Comics in the late 1960s, where he started out drawing war comics. He later graduated to illustrating superheros like Deadman and Superman, and *freelanced for Marvel Comics, where he worked on The Avengers and X-Men stories.

亞當斯 1941 年 7 月 15 出生於紐約市，並在 1959 年畢業於曼哈頓的工藝學校。在廣告業初試啼聲磨練後，他在 1960 年代末加入 DC 漫畫，並在那裡開始繪製戰爭類漫畫。之後，他更進一步繪製像是死俠及超人等超級英雄，並擔任漫威漫畫的自由繪師，負責畫復仇者聯盟及 X 戰警系列。

But it was at DC that Adams really made his mark. Working together with writer Dennis O'Neil, he brought new life to the Batman character, giving him a darker image and *gritty, realistic look. The duo also created new [5]**villains** like Ra's al Ghul and his daughter Talia, who became Batman's lover.

但在 DC 漫畫公司，亞當斯才真正聲名大噪。他和作家丹尼斯歐尼爾一起工作，為蝙蝠俠角色注入新生命，給予他更黑暗、寫實逼真的形象。他們倆同時也創造了新的反派，例如拉斯奧古與其女塔莉亞，後者成為蝙蝠俠的戀人。

Adams is also remembered as a strong [6]**advocate** for the rights of comic book creators. He helped make it standard practice for [7]**publishers** to return original art to the artists, and led the fight for fair pay in the industry.

亞當斯同時也因強力提倡漫畫家權益而為人所知。他協助設立業界標準，也就是出版社該將原始作品歸還藝術家，且帶頭爭取漫畫業界的合理薪資。

1. legendary [`lɛdʒən‚dɛri] (a.) 著名的，傳奇的
2. pass away (phr.) 過世
3. complication [‚kɑmplɪ`keʃən] (n.) 併發症
4. contribute [kən`trɪbjut] (v.) 做出貢獻，出力
5. villain [`vɪlən] (n.) 反派，壞蛋
6. advocate [`ædvəkɪt/`ædvə‚ket] (n./v.) 提倡者，擁護者；提倡，擁護
7. publisher [`pʌblɪʃə] (n.) 出版社，發行人

Advanced Words

sepsis [`sɛpsɪs] (n.) 敗血症

acclaimed [ə`klemd] (a.) 受到讚賞的

freelance [`fri‚læns] (v./a.) 當自由業者；自由業的

gritty [`grɪti] (a.) 寫實的，呈現人生現實、黑暗面的

EZpedia

Batman 蝙蝠俠

是一名出現於 DC 漫畫中的虛構超級英雄角色，最初被稱為「蝙蝠人」（Bat-Man），後被稱為「黑暗騎士」等。蝙蝠俠的真實身份為布魯斯韋恩（Bruce Wayne），是一位美國的億萬富翁。蝙蝠俠主要在高譚市（Gotham）行動，並和其他配角一起對付各種職業罪犯，如小丑、企鵝人等。他和其他超級英雄不同，並沒有任何超能力。

Deadman 死俠

是美國 DC 漫畫旗下一超級英雄，首次登場於《奇異冒險》（Strange Adventures）第 1 卷 205 期（1967 年 10 月）。死人本名波士頓布蘭德（Boston Brand），原是一名馬戲團雜技演員。被謀殺後，他與死亡女神交易，成為一名行俠仗義的超級英雄，並參與創立了黑暗正義聯盟（Justice League Dark）。

---

cut one's teeth 開始學習

要表示某人在特定工作領域的初體驗，只要在 cut one's teeth 後面加上「in + 特定領域」，如：cut one's teeth in business「開始學習從商」、cut one's teeth in politics「開始學習從政」等。

- A: How did you manage to get a position working at a major paper? 你為什麼有辦法在大型報社找到工作？
- B: Well, first I **cut my teeth** working at a small local paper. 這個嘛，我是從一間地方小報社開始學起。

---

make one's mark 成名，成功

mark 在這裡指「印記」。在某處留下記號，是不是會很引人注目，讓大家都知道你呢？

- Sean Connery **made his mark** playing James Bond. 史恩康納萊以飾演詹姆士龐德而成名。

The Avengers 復仇者聯盟

是一個超級英雄團體，由漫威漫畫公司創造，首次出現於《復仇者》第一期（1963 年）。最初成員為蟻人、黃蜂女、雷神索爾、鋼鐵人以及浩克。然而《復仇者》第二期中浩克就離隊改由美國隊長加入。目前復仇者聯盟電影系列共有四集。

X-Men X 戰警

是漫威漫畫的超級英雄團體，由史丹李和傑克科比創作，初次登場於 1963 年 9 月漫畫 X-Men #1 中。2000 年推出同名電影，主要角色包括 X 教授、金鋼狼、萬磁王等，迄今已拍攝多部系列電影。

Texas School District Removes Over 40 Books from Shelve.
德州校區將 40 餘本讀物列為禁書

A school [1]**district** in Texas is removing all books from libraries and classrooms that were challenged by parents, community members and [2]**legislators** over the past year, including the Bible.

德州的一個學區正在將圖書館和教室中過去一年受到家長、社區成員和立法者質疑的書籍列為禁書,包括《聖經》。

The day before students returned to class in Keller Independent School District, which serves students in the suburbs of Fort Worth, Jennifer Price, [3]**executive** director of [4]**curriculum** and instruction, told school [5]**administrators** and librarians to remove 41 books while they undergo review.

凱勒獨立學區位於沃思堡郊區,當地學生開學前一天,課程與教學執行主任珍妮弗普萊斯交代校務人員和圖書館員將 41 本正接受審查的書暫列禁書。

Some of the books under review are the Bible, a [6]**graphic** novel [7]**version** of The Diary of Anne Frank, The Bluest Eye by Nobel Prize winner Toni Morrison, and [8]**Gende**r Queer: A *Memoir, by Maia Kobabe. Kobabe's book is No. 1 on the American Library Association's list of most banned books in 2021.

受審查的書籍包括聖經、《安妮日記》的漫畫版、諾貝爾獎得主童妮摩里森的《最藍的眼睛》,和瑪雅科巴貝的《性別酷兒:一本回憶錄》。科巴貝的書在美國圖書館協會 2021 年禁書排行榜上排名第一。

The decision comes at a time when book bans are <u>on the rise</u> in schools and libraries across the United States. The American Library Association, which <u>keeps track of</u> book challenges and bans, reported more than twice as many challenges in 2021 than 2020, with actual numbers likely being much higher.

此決定宣佈之際,美國各地學校和圖書館的禁書數量也持續上升。紀錄著書籍相關質疑和禁令的美國圖書館協會指稱,2021 年提出的質疑是 2020 年的兩倍多,而實際數字可能還要高得多。

Parents, politicians, and members of the public have been challenging books at increasing rates as mostly conservative legislators raise concerns about what students are being taught in schools about topics like race, *sexuality, and gender identity.

家長、政治人物和社會大眾一直在以越來越高的頻率質疑書籍,因為多為保守派立法者開始擔憂學校對於種族、性和性別認同等主題教給了學生什麼。

1. district [`dɪstrɪkt] (n.) 區，行政區

2. legislator [`lɛdʒɪsˌletə] (n.) 立法者，國會議員

3. executive [ɪg`zɛkjətɪv] (a.) 執行的，常務的

4. curriculum [kə`rɪkjələm] (n.)（學校全部的）課程

5. administrator [əd`mɪnəˌstretə] (n.) 管理人，行政官員

6. graphic [`græfɪk] (a.) 圖解的，圖畫的

7. version [`vɜʒən] (n.) 版本

8. gender [`dʒɛndə] (n.) 性別

Advanced Words

memoir [`mɛmwɑr] (n.) 回憶錄，傳記

sexuality [ˌsɛkʃuˈælətɪ] (n.) 性，性行為

on the rise 在上升

rise 是上升的意思，此片語指數量、數字、頻率水平增加；變得更有名或成功。

• Violent crime is **on the rise** in Chicago.
芝加哥暴力犯罪率呈上升趨勢。

• The young actor's career is **on the rise**.
這位年輕演員的演藝事業越走越順。

keep track (of) 紀錄，掌握訊息

track 有軌跡、歷程的意思。此片語指保持對某事或某人的充分了解或知情，擁有你需要的關於某事或某人的所有訊息。

• We use this software to **keep track of** our expenses.
我們使用這個軟體來記帳。

• It's hard to **keep track of** all the characters in War and Peace.
很難記住戰爭與和平中的所有角色。

EZpedia

The Diary of Anne Frank 安妮的日記

由猶太少女安妮法蘭克所寫，此書發行版的內容摘錄自安妮在納粹佔領荷蘭的時期所寫的日記，並於戰後由她倖存的父親加以整理出版。

內容是寫成給幾個想像中朋友的信件，她也幫同樣在避難的親友和協助隱匿的友人取了假名，避免暴露他們的真實身分。安妮和許多青少年一樣，和家人相處上會有些矛盾情緒和衝突，也會因為愛上別人而煩惱，對於人生的想法也不斷變化。但日記中展現了難得的深度和文學才華，結合安妮面對逆境的樂觀開朗，讓她的記述成為文學和歷史上的瑰寶。

「我到現在還未放棄所有理想，也算奇蹟了，」她在被納粹逮捕之前不久寫道，「它們看起來如此荒謬而且不切實際。但我緊緊攀住它們，因為我仍相信，無論如何，人們的內心是善良的……我看見世界慢慢變成一片荒野，我聽見總有一天也會將我們毀滅的雷聲逐漸逼近，我感受到幾百萬人在受苦。然而，當我望向天空，不知怎麼的，我覺得一切都將好轉，而殘酷終將結束，和平和寧靜將會再臨。」

Nobel Prize 諾貝爾獎

是根據因發明炸藥而聞名的瑞典化學家阿佛烈諾貝爾（Alfred Nobel）遺囑於 1901 年開始每年頒發的 5 個獎項，包括：物理、化學、生理學 / 醫學、文學、和平。1968 年，瑞典中央銀行設立了瑞典銀行來紀念諾貝爾經濟科學獎，通稱「諾貝爾經濟學獎」。諾貝爾獎普遍被認為是其頒獎領域內最有聲望的獎項

Toni Morrison 童妮摩里森

美國非洲裔女性作家，是世界文學最重要的作家之一，其選集於 1993 年獲得諾貝爾文學獎。另外有著名的著作 Song of Solomon (1977) 和 Beloved (1987)。摩里森獲得過許多文學獎項，其中包括國家圖書評論獎（National Book Critics Circle Award）、普立茲獎（Pulitzer Prize），以及 1993 年諾貝爾文學獎。

美國教育測驗結果顯示，
疫情影響了孩童的學習成效

全文朗讀 🎧 071　　單字 🎧 072

Pandemic Erases Decades of Academic Progress
疫情使孩童學業成績退步數十年

National test results released on Thursday showed how ***devastating** the pandemic has been for American children, with the math and reading performance of 9-year-olds falling to levels not seen in decades. The exams were **1)administered** in early 2020 before the pandemic and then again in early 2022.

週四公佈的全國測驗結果顯示這次疫情對美國兒童造成了多麼嚴重的負面影響，9 歲兒童的數學和閱讀能力下降到幾十年來未見的水準。測驗是在疫情之前的 2020 年初舉行，然後在 2022 年初再次舉行。

This year, for the first time since the National **2)Assessment of Educational Progress** exams began measuring **3)academic** performance in the 1970s, 9-year-old students <u>lost ground</u> in both math and reading. Exam scores fell <u>across the board</u>, but were much worse for the lowest-performing students, with their math scores falling by up to 12 points and reading scores by up to 10 points.

今年，自 1970 年代全國教育進步測驗開始衡量學業成就以來，9 歲的學生首次在數學和閱讀方面都失利。測驗成績全面下降，但學習成就低落的學生退步最嚴重，他們的數學成績最多下降 12 分，閱讀成績最多下降 10 分。

Black students lost 13 points in math, while white students lost five points, increasing the gap between the two groups. Research has revealed the **4)profound** impact school **5)closures** had on poor and minority students, who were more likely to continue remote learning for longer periods.

非裔學生在數學科丟了 13 分，而白人學生丟了 5 分，拉大了兩族群之間的差距。研究顯示學校停課對貧困和少數族群學生產生了深遠的影響，他們較可能繼續更長時間的遠距學習。

The declines in exam scores show that although many 9-year-olds have a basic understanding of what they're reading, fewer can **6)infer** a character's feelings. In math, students can perform simple arithmetic, but fewer are able to add **7)fractions**.

測驗成績的下降顯示，儘管許多 9 歲的孩子對他們閱讀的內容有基本的了解，但能夠推斷人物角色的感受卻佔少數。至於數學科，學生可以進行簡單的算術，但能夠做分數加法的則較少。

These academic **8)setbacks** could have serious **9)consequences** for a generation of children as they continue their education and prepare for their future careers.

這些學業上的退步可能會在這一代孩子繼續接受教育並為未來的職涯做準備時產生嚴重的後果。

1. **administer** [ədˋmɪnɪstə] (v.)
   舉行，執行，實施

2. **assessment** [əˋsɛsmənt] (n.) 評價，估計
   assess [əˋsɛs] (v.) 評估

3. **academic** [ˌækəˋdɛmɪk] (a.)
   學術的，學業的

4. **profound** [prəˋfaʊnd] (a.)
   深遠的，深刻的

5. **closure** [ˋkloʒə] (n.) 停業，關閉

6. **infer** [ɪnˋfɜ] (v.) 推斷，推論

7. **fraction** [ˋfrækʃən] (n.) 分數

8. **setback** [ˋsɛtˏbæk] (n.) 挫折，退步，失敗

9. **consequence** [ˋkɑnsəˏkwɛns] (n.)
   後果，結果

Advanced Words

devastating [ˋdɛvəˏstetɪŋ] (a.) 極具破壞性
的，毀滅性的

lose ground 失利，退步

變得不那麼成功、先進或強大；變得不那麼受歡迎或得到更少的支
持這原本是一個軍事術語，相反詞是 gain ground。

- The scientist claims we are **losing ground** in the fight against climate change.
  這位科學家聲稱，我們在應對氣候變化方面正在失利。
- The Democratic Party is **losing ground** among working class voters.
  民主黨在工人階級選民中的地位正在下降。

across the board 全面

包含或影響所有級別或類別，涉及一個地方或情況中的每個人或所
有事物；用作形容詞時寫成 across-the-board，此用法原先來自於
賽馬。

- Prices for goods and services are increasing **across the board**.
  商品和服務的價格全面上漲。
- The school district is facing **across-the-board** budget cuts.
  學區正面臨全面的預算削減。

EZpedia

National Assessment of Educational Progress
美國國家教育進展評測

是對美國學生在各個學科中的知識和能力進行的最
大具有全國代表性的評估。NAEP 是美國國會授權
的評測，由美國教育部教育科學研究所內的國家教
育統計中心管理。國家評估管理委員會（National
Assessment Governance Board）是一個獨立的兩黨
委員會，負責為 NAEP 制定政策、框架和測試規範。
其成員由美國教育部長任命，包括州長、州立法者、
地方和州學校官員、教育工作者、企業代表和公眾成
員。國會於 1988 年設立了由 26 名成員組成的管理
委員會。

疫情下，學生多半透過網路視訊上課

全文朗讀 ○ 073　單字 ○ 074

Rafael Nadal Wins 14th French Open Title
納達爾贏得第 14 屆法網冠軍

Rafael Nadal defeated Norwegian Casper Ruud 6-3 6-3 6-0 on Sunday, [1]**extending** his record with yet another French Open title, his 14th.

拉斐爾納達爾在周日以 6-3 6-3 6-0 擊敗挪威好手卡斯珀魯德，以第 14 次法網冠軍頭銜延續他的輝煌紀錄。

Although Nadal was beaten by Novak Djokovic in the semifinals of last year's French Open, he defeated his rival in the quarterfinals this year before an easy win against Alexander Zverev in the semifinals.

儘管納達爾在去年的法網半決賽中敗給了諾瓦克喬科維奇，但他在今年的四分之一決賽中擊敗了對手，然後在半決賽中輕鬆戰勝了亞歷山大茲維列夫。

The King of Clay [2]**dominated** the men's singles final, winning 11 *consecutive games in the second and third sets to *clinch his 22nd Grand Slam title, one more than Djokovic and two more than Roger Federer. The victory also makes the 36-year-old Nadal the oldest men's singles champion at Roland Garros.

紅土之王主導了男單決賽，在第二盤和第三盤連續贏下 11 局，奪得個人的第 22 座大滿貫冠軍，比喬科維奇多 1 場，比羅傑費德勒多 2 場。這場勝利也讓 36 歲的納達爾成為法國網球公開賽最年長的男單冠軍。

In the *showdown between Nadal and Ruud on Sunday, it was master against *apprentice. Ruud greatly admired the Spanish superstar while growing up, and has risen through the tennis ranks since he began training at the Rafael Nadal [3]**Academy** in Mallorca in 2018.

週日納達爾與魯德的對決，是師傅與徒弟的對決。魯德在成長過程中非常欽佩這位西班牙超級巨星，並且自 2018 年開始在馬略卡島的拉斐爾納達爾學院接受訓練以來，他的網壇排名不斷上升。

This was the first time the two players faced off against each other in [4]**competition**, and despite a [5]**chronic** foot injury and a recent rib [6]**fracture**, Nadal ended the 23-year-old Norwegian's French Open dream in just three sets. Having led 3-1 at the start of the second set, Ruud quickly fell behind and failed to win a single game in the final set.

這是兩位球員第一次在比賽中交鋒，儘管受長期的腳傷和近期肋骨骨折所擾，納達爾還是僅用三盤就結束了這位 23 歲挪威好手的法網美夢。第二盤開局以 3-1 領先的魯德卻隨即落後，而決勝盤則一局未得。

1. extend [ɪk`stɛnd] (v.) 延伸，延續
2. dominate [`dɑmə.net] (v.) 主導，佔優勢
3. academy [ə`kædəmɪ] (n.) 學院，學會
4. competition [.kɑmpə`tɪʃən] (n.) 競賽，競爭
5. chronic [`krɑnɪk] (a.) 慢性的，久病的
6. fracture [`fræktʃə] (n./v.) 骨折；斷裂

Advanced Words

consecutive [kən`sɛkjətɪv] (a.)
連續的，連貫的

clinch [klɪntʃ] (v.) 贏得，得勝

showdown [`ʃo.daʊn] (n.) 對決，決賽

apprentice [ə`prɛntɪs] (n.) 徒弟，學徒

rise through the ranks 一步一步往上爬

rank 是指「等級，地位」，相同的說法還有 rise from the ranks、come up through the ranks、rise in the ranks，都用來表示「在企業、社會階級的提升」。

- A: How did Bradley get to be CEO?
  布萊德里是怎麼當上執行長的？
- B: He did it the old-fashioned way—he started at the bottom and **rose through the ranks**. 他靠著老方法 —— 從基層做起，一步一步往上爬。

face off (against) 面對，對峙

"face" 當動詞時有面對的意思，此片語指與某人競爭、爭鬥或爭論，開始競爭或對抗。

- If you make it to the final, you'll have to **face off** against the no. 1 player.
  如果你進入決賽，你將不得不面對排名第一的球員。
- The two presidential candidates **faced off** on the debate stage.
  兩位總統候選人在辯論台上對峙。

EZpedia

French Open 法國網球公開賽

是一項為期兩週的大型網球賽事，因於法國巴黎的羅蘭加洛斯球場 (Roland Garros Stadium) 舉行也被稱為羅蘭加洛斯（Roland Garros），於每年五月下旬開始。法網是世界上首屈一指的紅土錦標賽，也是目前唯一在這個場地舉行的大滿貫賽事。按時間順序，它是四項年度大滿貫賽事中的第二項，舉辦在澳大利亞公開賽之後、溫布頓網球公開賽和美國公開賽之前。至 1975 年以前，法網是唯一沒有在草地上進行的大型賽事。法網被廣泛認為是世界上對體力要求最高的網球賽事。

King Of Clay 紅土之王

納達爾的法網紀錄至今無人能敵。連續出場 18 次，14 場決賽中有 14 場勝利。有一年納達爾在錦標賽期間退出法網，另外三年他被擊敗。115 場比賽，納達爾贏了 112 場，這是另一個記錄。納達爾是法網年齡最大的男單冠軍，他於 2005 年 6 月 5 日贏得了他的第一個法網冠軍，並於 2022 年 6 月 5 日贏得了他的第 14 個法網冠軍。這就是為什麼納達爾被稱為紅土之王的原因。

Grand Slam 大滿貫賽事

網球四大賽事：

澳洲網球公開賽（Australian Open）

硬地（hard court）賽事，是網球硬地賽事中聲望最高的 2 大賽事之一。

法國網球公開賽（French Open）

紅土（clay court）賽事，是網球紅土賽事裡的最高榮譽。

溫布頓網球錦標賽（Wimbledon Championship）

草地（grass court）賽事，是網球草地賽事裡的最高榮譽；也是全世界聲望最高、歷史最久的網球賽事。

美國網球公開賽（U.S. Open）

硬地賽事，是硬地賽事中聲望最高的 2 大賽事之一。

金洲勇士隊的柯瑞拿下人生首座
總冠軍戰最有價值球員

全文朗讀 ∩ 075　單字 ∩ 076

Stephen Curry Wins 1st NBA Finals MVP
柯瑞榮獲生涯首座 FMVP

In the third quarter of Game 6 of the **NBA Finals** on Thursday, Stephen Curry sank a three-pointer from 29 feet out before pointing at his right ring finger. But the star point guard didn't just <u>put another ring on it</u> that night at TD Garden [1])**arena**, he [2])**cemented** his future Hall of Fame [3])**legacy** with his first NBA Finals **MVP** [4])**trophy**.

週四 NBA 總冠軍賽第 6 戰的第 3 節，史蒂芬柯瑞投中了一記 29 英尺外的三分球，然後指了指他的右手無名指。但那天晚上在 TD 花園球場這位明星控衛並不只有再戴上一枚戒指，他用首座 NBA 總冠軍賽 MVP 獎盃為他的未來名人堂事蹟錦上添花。

After leading the Golden State Warriors to a 103-90 victory to eliminate the Boston Celtics on Thursday night, Curry won his fourth [5])**championship** ring and the one honor that had ***eluded** him when he was [6])**unanimously** named the NBA Finals Most Valuable Player. As the game ended, an emotional Curry was seen embracing his father in tears.

週四晚上在率領金州勇士以 103-90 淘汰波士頓賽爾提克之後，柯瑞贏得了他的第四枚總冠軍戒指，並當被一致評為 NBA 總冠軍賽最有價值球員時達成了一項之前沒有的榮譽。隨著比賽結束，有人看到情緒激動的柯瑞哭著擁抱他的父親。

"It's good to get another championship and <u>top it off</u> with a Finals MVP," said Curry's brother, Seth Curry, who plays for the Nets. "That's one of the few things he didn't have."

「再次贏得總冠軍加上總冠軍賽 MVP 是很好的，」柯瑞為籃網隊效力的弟弟賽斯說。「這是他原本沒有的少數東西之一。」

The NBA's most ***prolific** 3-point shooter now has four rings, two [7])**league** MVPs, two scoring titles, one **All-Star Game** MVP, and a Finals MVP. With four championship wins and [8])**multiple** MVP awards, Curry joins an elite group that includes LeBron James, Michael Jordan, Magic Johnson and Kareem Abdul-Jabbar.

NBA 最多產的三分射手現在擁有四枚戒指、兩個聯盟 MVP、兩個得分王、一個全明星賽 MVP 和一個總冠軍賽 MVP。憑藉四次總冠軍和多個 MVP 獎項，柯瑞加入了包括勒布朗詹姆士、麥可喬丹、魔術強森和天鉤賈霸在內的精英陣容。

1. **arena** [ə`rinə] (n.) 體育場，球場

2. **cement** [sə`mɛnt] (v.)
   加強、鞏固（地位、關係等）

3. **legacy** [`lɛgəsi] (n.) 歷史遺，事跡

4. **trophy** [`trofi] (n.) 獎盃，獎品

5. **championship** [`tʃæmpiən,ʃip] (n.)
   錦標賽，冠軍頭銜

6. **unanimously** [ju`nænəməsli] (adv.)
   全體一致地，無異議地
   unanimous [ju`nænəməs] (a.)
   一致同意的

7. **league** [lig] (n.) 聯盟，聯合會

8. **multiple** [`mʌltəpəl] (a.)
   多重的，不只一個的

Advanced Words

elude [ɪ`lud] (v.) 使達不到
prolific [prə`lɪfɪk] (a.) 多產的，得分多的

put a ring on it 求婚，贏得冠軍戒指

在一般口語中，put a ring on it 的意思是給某人訂婚戒指並承諾與他們結婚，此表達方式來自 Beyoncé 的歌曲 Single Ladies；在體育運動中，這個片語指的是贏得一枚總冠軍戒指。

- A: Hey, what do you say we move in together?
  嘿，妳說我們同居怎麼樣？
- B: Sure, but you're gonna have to put a ring on it first.
  可以啊，但你得先向我求婚。

- A: Do you think the Rams are gonna put a ring on it this year?
  你認為公羊隊今年會得到總冠軍戒指嗎？
- B: I hope so. They haven't won a Super Bowl since moving back to L.A.
  但願如此。自從搬回洛杉磯後，他們還沒有贏得過超級盃。

top it off (with) 更 ... 的是

以令人難忘或引人注目的方式完成某事；以特別積極或消極的方式結束經歷或情況。

- A: How was your date with Elizabeth last night?
  昨晚你和伊麗莎白的約會怎麼樣？
- B: Great. We went for dinner and a movie, and then topped it off with drinks at my favorite bar. 很棒。我們去吃晚飯和看電影，然後在我最喜歡的酒吧喝了一杯。

- A: Did you have fun on your camping trip?
  你的露營之旅玩得開心嗎？
- B: No. It rained the whole time, and to top it off, my car broke down on the way home.
  沒有。一直在下雨，最糟糕的是，我的車在回家的路上拋錨了。

EZpedia

NBA Finals NBA 總冠軍賽
是美國國家籃球協會（National Basketball Association）總冠軍系列賽，由東、西區（Eastern/Western Conference）的冠軍球隊角逐 NBA 總冠軍，系列賽贏家可榮獲賴瑞奧布萊恩冠軍獎盃（Larry O'Brien Championship Trophy）。此系列賽最初為 2-2-1-1-1 的形式，1985 年起為了減少跨國移動次數而改成 2-3-2 的形式，2014 年起改回 2-2-1-1-1 的形式。

MVP 最有價值球員
Most Valuable Player 的縮寫，是給予體育運動表現最佳運動員的榮譽。早期主要在職業運動賽事中使用，但後來亦廣泛運用於業餘體育活動中，甚至如媒體、商業及音樂獎項等非體育活動。

類似的獎項包括足球先生及賽事最佳球員。最有價值球員一般較常用於美國體育運動。

All-Star Game 全明星賽
全明星賽是 NBA 每年 2 月舉辦的一場籃球表演賽，由聯盟的 24 名明星球員參加。這是 NBA 全明星週末的特色賽事，為期三天，從周五到週日。全明星賽於 1951 年 3 月 2 日在波士頓花園首次舉行。每支球隊的首發陣容由球迷、球員和媒體投票共同選出，而主教練則選擇預備隊，七名球員來自各自的球隊，所以每一方都有一個 12 人的名單。教練不得為自己的球員投票。如果被選中的球員因傷不能參加，NBA 總裁將選擇一名替補球員。

◀ 「費爸」費德勒宣布退休，
令球迷十分不捨

全文朗讀 ∩ 077　單字 ∩ 078

Roger Federer Announces Retirement
網球天王費德勒宣布退休

Swiss great Roger Federer has [1)]**affirmed** that he will retire from [2)]**professional** tennis, with next week's **Laver Cup** in London set to be his final appearance. The first male player to win 20 Grand Slam titles, Federer dominated men's tennis for nearly two decades, sharing the glory with his two greatest rivals, Rafael Nadal and Novak Djokovic. The *****trio** share an [3)]**astonishing** 63 Grand Slam titles among them.

瑞士巨星羅傑費德勒宣佈將從職業網球生涯退役，下週在倫敦舉行的拉沃盃將是他的最後一次亮相。作為第一位獲得 20 次大滿貫冠軍的男性球員，費德勒稱霸男子網壇近二十年，與他的兩個最大對手拉斐爾納達爾和諾瓦克喬科維奇分享了榮耀。這三人共有驚人的 63 個大滿貫冠軍頭銜。

"Every time people <u>write me off</u>, or try to write me off, I'm able to <u>bounce back</u>," Federer once said in an interview. But when it comes to [4)]**athletic** careers, retirement is [5)]**inevitable**.

「每次有人否定我，或者試圖否定我，我都能重振旗鼓，」費德勒曾在一次採訪中說。但是當談到運動生涯時，退休是不可避免的。

"As many of you know, the past three years have presented me with challenges in the form of injuries and [6)]**surgeries**," said Federer in a social media statement on Thursday. "I've worked hard to return to full [7)]**competitive** form. But I also know my body's capacities and limits, and its message to me lately has been clear."

「你們很多人都知道，過去三年我面臨了傷病和手術的困擾，」費德勒在週四的社交媒體聲明中說。「我嘗試努力恢復到最佳的競技狀態，但我也了解自己身體的能力和極限，它最近給我的訊息很清楚。」

"I am 41 years old," the Swiss [8)]**ace** continued. "I have played more than 1,500 matches over 24 years. Tennis has treated me more generously than I ever would have dreamt, and now I must recognize when it is time to end my competitive career."

「我今年 41 歲，」這位瑞士球王繼續說道。「24 年來，我參加了超過 1,500 場比賽。網球運動賦予我的比我想像中要更富足，而現在是必須認知到是時候該結束我的職業生涯。」

Federer leaves with 103 **ATP** singles titles on his *****résumé** and 1,251 wins in singles matches, both second only to **Jimmy Connors** in the Open Era, which began in 1968.

費德勒在他的職業生涯獲得了 103 個 ATP 單打冠軍和 1,251 場單打比賽的勝利，自從 1968 年的公開賽時代以來，這兩項都僅次於吉米康納斯。

Vocabulary

1. **affirm** [əˋfɝm] (v.) 聲明，斷言
2. **professional** [prəˋfɛʃənəl] (a.) 職業的，專業的
3. **astonishing** [əˋstɑnɪʃɪŋ] (a.) 令人驚嘆的
4. **athletic** [æθˋlɛtɪk] (a.) 體育的，運動的
5. **inevitable** [ɪnˋɛvɪtəbəl] (a.) 不可避免的，必然（發生）的
6. **surgery** [ˋsɝdʒəri] (n.)（外科）手術
7. **competitive** [kəmˋpɛtətɪv] (a.) 參加比賽的，有競爭力的
8. **ace** [es] (n.) 高手，名手

Advanced Words

trio [ˋtrio] (n.) 三人組

résumé [ˋrɛzə͵me] (n.) 履歷

---

write sb./th. off 否定某人 / 某事價值

將某人或某事視為微不足道而不理會；決定某人或某事不再有用、重要或成功。write off 原先是會計用語，意為勾銷。

- Many companies seem to **write off** workers when they're over fifty.
  許多公司似乎在員工超過 50 歲時就否定其價值。
- After months of work, we **wrote the project off** and decided to try something new.
  經過幾個月的努力，我們捨棄了這項專案並決定尋找新的方向。

---

bounce back 重振旗鼓，反敗為勝

在困難的情況或事件後迅速恢復正常狀態；在一段例如經歷失敗、失去信心、疾病或不快樂的困難時期之後重新開始成功。

- After several early losses, the team **bounced back** to win the series.
  經過幾次早期的失利，球隊重振旗鼓並贏得了系列賽。
- I was glad to see Marilyn **bounce back** quickly after her surgery.
  我很高興看到瑪麗蓮在手術後迅速恢復。

EZpedia

Laver Cup 拉沃盃
是一個國際室內硬地球場的男子網球比賽。比賽由兩個小組對決：歐洲隊和世界隊，後者的球員來自非歐洲國家，每年舉辦一次。該比賽在美國網球公開賽的兩周後舉行，歐洲城市和世界其他地區城市每年輪流舉辦。獲勝隊伍的每個成員可以獲得 250,000 美元的獎金，但比賽本身並不計算在球員當年 ATP 世界巡迴賽的積分。2019 年 5 月，拉沃盃成為一個正式批准的 ATP 世界巡迴賽項目。

ATP ATP 世界巡迴賽總決賽
職業網球協會 (ATP) 是男子職業網球巡迴賽——ATP 巡迴賽、ATP 挑戰賽和 ATP 冠軍巡迴賽的管理機構。自 1990 年以來，該協會組織了 ATP 巡迴賽，是僅次於網球四大滿貫的錦標賽，在每年的年底舉行，參賽者是當年男子網球 ATP 冠軍賽（ATP Champion Race）排名前八的選手。但根據規則，如果一名選手是當年四大滿貫賽事冠軍之一且排名在前 20 名以內（但排名在第八名以外），那他就可取代排名第八的選手進入比賽，如果超過一名球員符合上述條件，則以冠軍排名較高者為優先。因為獲得參賽資格的難度和贏得比賽帶來的聲望，這項賽事有時被稱為「第五個大滿貫」。

Jimmy Connors 吉米康諾斯
前美國職業網球運動員，首位連續五年（1974-78 年）成為 ATP 年終單打世界排名第一，並曾佔據世界第一寶座達 268 週之久的球員。 他亦是網壇歷史上職業生涯最長的球員之一，從上個世紀 70 年代初到 90 年代中，見證了網壇由木球拍年代到碳鋼球拍年代。他也是公開賽年代中較早採用碳鋼球拍的球員。 他是 70 年代中至 80 年代初男子網壇最有競爭力球員之一，其職業生涯共奪 109 個 ATP 巡迴賽單打冠軍，是公開賽年代以來最多，當中包括八項大滿貫錦標。

Must-see Movies and TV Series of 2022
2022 年必看電影與電視影集

The Batman 《蝙蝠俠》

The Batman 《蝙蝠俠》

If you're a Batman fan, you'll be sure to love The Batman, which many [1)]**critics** are calling the best film in the ***franchise** since 2008's *The Dark Knight*. In addition to Robert Pattinson in the starring role, the cast includes other big names like Paul Dano, John Turturro and Colin Farrell. Directed by Matt Reeves, who gave us the hit monster movie *Cloverfield*, the film follows Batman on his hunt for the Riddler (Dano), a [2)]**brutal** criminal who is killing Gotham City politicians one by one, starting with the mayor. But as he gets closer to the Riddler, Batman is forced to investigate the [3)]**corruption** that touches every level of society, and possibly even his own family. Since its release in March, The Batman has become the highest-earning film of 2022.

如果你是蝙蝠俠粉絲，一定會愛上這部《蝙蝠俠》電影。許多影評將這部電影譽為 2008 年《黑暗騎士》以來，蝙蝠俠系列最棒的續作。除了主演的羅伯派汀森之外，卡司陣容還包括保羅迪諾、約翰特托羅與柯林法洛等大明星。由賣座怪物電影《科洛弗檔案》的導演麥特李維斯執導，帶領大家跟著蝙蝠俠追查「謎語人」（由迪諾飾演）。謎語人是殘忍的罪犯，他先從市長下手，一一殺害高譚市的政客。但是隨著蝙蝠俠越接近謎語人的真相，就等於被迫調查觸及社會各階層的腐敗問題，甚至可能與他自己的家族有關。而《蝙蝠俠》自三月上映以來，至今已成為 2022 年票房最高的電影。

The Tinder Swindler 《Tinder 大騙徒》

The Tinder Swindler
《Tinder 大騙徒》

The Netflix true crime [4)]**documentary** *The Tinder Swindler* tells the story of Israeli ***con man** Simon Leviev, who used the dating [5)]**app** Tinder to trick women into giving him money to support his expensive lifestyle. Born Shimon Hayut, he later changed his name to Simon Leviev so people would think he was related to Lev Leviev, an Israeli billionaire known as the King of Diamonds. After wining and dining the women he met, he would pretend he'd been attacked by his "enemies," and ask them to lend him money to get out of trouble. By the time he was jailed for ⁶⁾**fraud** in 2019, he'd stolen millions from his victims. True crime is always popular, but The Tinder Swindler hit the top 10 on Netflix in 92 countries.

Netflix 所推出的真實犯罪紀錄片《Tinder 大騙徒》，講述以色列騙子賽門列維夫，以交友軟體 Tinder 來用計誘導女性金援他的豪奢生活。本名為西蒙海約特的這名騙子，爾後改名為賽門列維夫，來讓大家以為他與以色列億萬富翁、人稱「鑽石國王」的里維列維夫有親戚關係。他請許多女性大啖美酒佳餚後，就會假裝自己被「敵人」攻擊，並要求女性借錢給他以便脫離險境。他在 2019 年因詐騙罪名而入獄時，早已從受害者身上竊走上百萬美元。真實犯罪類一直都很受歡迎，不過《Tinder 大騙徒》竟然名列 92 個國家 Netflix 平台的前 10 名影片。

Everything Everywhere All at Once《媽的多重宇宙》

As *Everything Everywhere All at Once* begins, we meet Evelyn Wang (played by Michelle Yeoh), a Chinese-American woman who runs a struggling *laundromat with her husband Waymond. Things aren't going well, <u>to say the least</u>. Waymond wants a ⁷⁾**divorce**, her daughter Joy hates her, and their laundromat is being investigated by the IRS. But just as you think you're watching a typical family drama, Evelyn meets another ⁸⁾**version** of Waymond from a ⁹⁾**parallel** universe and learns that she is the only one who can keep a powerful being from causing the destruction of the multiverse. Is this science fiction? Fantasy? Black comedy? In any case, it's fun to watch!

Everything Everywhere All at Once
《媽的多重宇宙》

電影《媽的多重宇宙》一開頭，帶著我們認識美國華裔移民王秀蓮（由楊紫瓊飾演）和先生威門，經營著岌岌可危的洗衣店。一切都不順利，這樣說還客氣了，因為威門想離婚，女兒喬伊恨她，洗衣店還被國稅局稽查。當你以為只是在看一部典型的家庭劇情片，秀蓮就遇見了來自平行宇宙的另一個威門，還發現自己是能夠阻擋某強大人物造成多重宇宙毀滅的唯一人選。這是科幻片、奇幻片抑或黑色喜劇片呢？無論是哪一種類型，都能讓人看得樂在其中！

1. **critic** [ˋkrɪtɪk] (n.) 評論家，影評

2. **brutal** [ˋbrutəl] (a.) 殘忍的，粗暴的

3. **corruption** [kəˋrʌpʃən] (n.) 腐敗，貪污

4. **documentary** [ˌdɑkjəˋmɛntəri] (n.) 紀錄片

5. **app** [æp] (n.) 手機軟體（原為「application 應用程式」的簡寫）

6. **fraud** [frɔd] (n.) 詐騙，詐欺，騙局

7. **divorce** [dɪˋvors] (n./v.) 離婚

8. **version** [ˋvɝʒən] (n.) 版本

9. **parallel** [ˋpærəˌlɛl] (a.) 平行的，並行的

Advanced Words

franchise [ˋfræntʃaɪz] (n.)
系列作品，授權商品

con man (phr.)（以贏得信任而騙取錢財的）騙子

laundromat [ˋlɔndrəˌmæt] (n.) 自動洗衣店

Phrase

wine and dine 以飲宴款待

以昂貴的美酒佳餚來娛樂某人，一般是以此做法來請對方於私或於公來幫忙自己。

- A: Did you end up signing a deal with that client?
  你跟客戶的交易合約最後有簽成功嗎？
- B: Yes, but it took days of **wining and dining**.
  有，但是是在招待好幾天的美酒佳餚後成功的。

to say the least 這樣說已經很客氣了

the least 是「最少」的意思。這句話表示完全同意對方的説法，也可以接在一句話後面，用來強調「這樣説已經很客氣了」。例如：The movie was boring, to say the least.

- A: A ten-hour flight in economy class? What was that like?
  你在經濟艙度過十小時的飛行時間？感覺怎麼樣？
- B: It was uncomfortable, **to say the least**.
  不舒服，但這樣説已經很客氣了。

EZpedia

The Dark Knight 黑暗騎士
一部於 2008 年上映的超級英雄電影，由克里斯多福諾蘭編劇、監製及執導。本片是諾蘭所執導的黑暗騎士三部曲中的第二部，以 DC 漫畫旗下角色蝙蝠俠為主角，是 2005 年電影《蝙蝠俠：開戰時刻》的續集。電影中，布魯斯韋恩／蝙蝠俠（貝爾飾演）、詹姆斯高登（歐德曼飾演）與哈維丹特（艾克哈特飾演）聯手打擊高譚市的黑幫，但其行動被高智商罪犯小丑（萊傑飾演）所破壞，後者企圖削弱蝙蝠俠的影響力，並讓高譚市陷入混亂。導演對本片的基本概念，分別來自小丑在 1940 年首次登場的漫畫章節，另外包含著名漫畫《蝙蝠俠：致命玩笑》及《蝙蝠俠：漫長的萬聖節》中的故事。

Cloverfield 科洛弗檔案
一部 2008 年的美國偽紀錄片怪物恐怖電影。本片由麥特李維斯執導，並由影集《LOST 檔案》製作人傑弗瑞亞柏拉罕擔任製片。電影首次在《變形金剛》前的預告中向大眾公開，並宣布 2008 年 1 月 18 日在美國本土上映。針對本片，發行公司派拉蒙影業推出了一系列病毒式行銷的宣傳活動。

Tinder
是一款手機交友 app，常用於約會與一夜情。根據使用者的 Facebook 和 Spotify 資料，雙方只有互相表示感興趣才能開始聊天。

IRS 國稅局
是美國聯邦政府的稅務機構，隸屬於美國財政部，受國稅局局長的直接領導。國稅局局長由美國總統任命，一屆任期為五年。負責徵收稅款以及執行美國國內稅收法，該法構成了美國聯邦成文稅收法律的主體。其職責包括向納稅人提供稅務相關幫助，以及調查並解決偷稅漏稅問題；同時，它還監管過許多補助計劃，並負責患者保護與平價醫療法案部分內容的執行。

Must-see Movies and TV Series of 2022
2022 年必看電影和電視影集

Doctor Strange in the Multiverse of Madness
《奇異博士 2：失控多重宇宙》

©Wikipedia

Doctor Strange in the Multiverse of Madness
《奇異博士 2: 失控多重宇宙》

Doctor Strange in the Multiverse of Madness is a ***sequel** not only to 2016's Doctor Strange, but also to *Avengers: Endgame* and the hit TV series *WandaVision*. This time around, Doctor Strange (Benedict Cumberbatch) <u>joins forces with</u> America Chavez, a teenager with the ability to travel the multiverse, on a [1]**quest** for the Book of Vishanti, which contains spells that can help him defeat the monster that's chasing her. But the monster kills Strange first, and Chavez opens a doorway that transports her to Earth-616, a world where another version of Strange [2]**rescues** her from another monster with the help of Wong, the ***Sorcerer** [3]**Supreme**. Together, the three must now face an even greater enemy—Wanda Maximoff, the Avenger who became the Scarlet [4]**Witch** in WandaVision.

《奇異博士 2：失控多重宇宙》不僅是 2016 年《奇異博士》的續集，亦為《復仇者聯盟：終局之戰》與熱門電視影集《汪達幻視》的續集。這一次，奇異博士（班奈迪克康柏拜區飾演）和能夠穿梭多重宇宙的青少女「美國小姐」艾美莉卡查韋斯聯手，踏上探尋「維山帝之書」的旅程。此書含有的咒語，能協助他擊敗追捕查韋斯的怪物。但是該怪物先殺了奇異博士，查韋斯則開啟了傳送自己到 616 號地球的通道，而這個世界另一版本的奇異博士，則在至尊法師「王」的協助下，在另一隻怪物的襲擊下救了查韋斯。他們三人則必須面對更強大的敵人──汪達，也就是在《汪達幻視》裡成為緋紅女巫的復仇者。

Death on the Nile 《尼羅河謀殺案》

Based on the 1937 Agatha Christie mystery novel of the same name, *Death on the Nile* is the sequel to 2017's *Murder on the Orient Express*. Both films were directed by Oscar winner Kenneth Branagh, who also ***reprises** his role as the Belgian [5]**detective** Hercule

Poirot—Christie's most famous character. While on vacation in Egypt, Poirot and his friend Bouc are invited on a cruise down the Nile. Their hosts are 6)**newlyweds** Linnet Ridgeway, a wealthy 7)**heiress**, and her husband Simon. Their 8)**honeymoon** is cut short, however, when Linnet is found dead in a pool of blood. Suspicion naturally falls on Jackie de Bellefort, who planned on marrying Simon before Linnet stole him away—but she has an *alibi. Will Poirot be able to follow the clues and solve the murder? You'll have to see the movie to find out!

Death on the Nile
《尼羅河謀殺案》

以 1937 年阿嘉莎克莉絲蒂所著同名小說而改編的《尼羅河謀殺案》，是 2017 年《東方快車謀殺案》的續集。兩部電影均由奧斯卡得主肯尼斯布萊納所執導，他亦再次演出自己於該片的角色：比利時偵探赫丘勒白羅，也就是克莉絲蒂筆下最著名的人物。白羅與朋友布克在埃及度假時，受邀搭乘航行尼羅河的遊輪。招待他們的人是新婚夫妻，富二代琳妮瑞奇威和先生賽門。然而，他們的蜜月卻好景不常，因為琳妮被發現死在血泊中。嫌疑目光自然落到賈姬貝弗身上，因為她原本打算要嫁給賽門，琳妮卻捷足先登，但是她又有不在場證明。白羅有辦法循線來破解此謀殺案嗎？一定要看完電影才會知道！

Turning Red 《青春養成記》

Directed by Domee Shi, who won an Oscar for her short film *Bao*, Turning Red is a Pixar 9)**animated** comedy about a 13-year-old Chinese-Canadian girl named Mei who is torn between being an 10)**obedient** daughter and the joys of 11)**adolescence**. Mei makes her strict mother Ming proud by taking care of the family's temple to their 12)**ancestor**, Sun Yee, but at the same time struggles to hide her new interest in boy bands—and boys in general—knowing she wouldn't approve. And then one morning Mei wakes up from a 13)**nightmare** to find that she's turned into a giant red panda—

Turning Red
《青春養成記》

something that starts happening whenever she experiences strong emotions. Mei learns from her father that the red panda spirit—which comes from Sun Yee—can be trapped inside a *talisman, but then she starts to enjoy her new ability. Now she has decisions to make....

由《包・子》贏得奧斯卡短片獎的石之予導演，所執導的《青春養成記》是皮克斯公司出品的喜劇動畫電影，講述一名住在加拿大的 13 歲華裔女孩美美，在當個順從的乖女兒與享受青春期之間左右為難的故事。美美以妥善打理家族供奉祖先新怡的寺廟，而讓虎媽李明引以為傲。但她同時也掙扎於隱藏自己喜愛男孩團體的新嗜好——還有對一般男孩有興趣的事——因為她知道媽媽不會認同。某天早上，美美從惡夢中醒來，發現自己變成巨大的小熊貓，而且只要她開始出現激動情緒，就會變這樣。美美的爸爸告訴她，傳承自新怡的小熊貓靈，可以封印在護身符，但是她開始享受她的新能力，於是面臨了抉擇……

1. **quest** [kwɛst] (n.) 尋找，探索
2. **rescue** [`rɛskju] (v./n.) 拯救，解圍
3. **supreme** [sə`prim] (a.) 至尊的，至上的
4. **witch** [wɪtʃ] (n.) 女巫，巫婆
5. **detective** [dɪ`tɛktɪv] (n.)
   （私人）偵探，警探
6. **newlywed** [`nuli,wɛd] (n.) 新婚丈夫、妻子
7. **heiress/heir** [`ɛrɪsəɛr] (n.)
   女繼承人 / 男繼承人
8. **honeymoon** [`hʌni,mun] (n.)
   蜜月，蜜月旅行
9. **animated/animation**
   [`ænə,metɪdə, ænə`meʃən] (a./n.)
   動畫的；動畫
10. **obedient** [ə`bidiənt] (a.) 順從的，聽話的
11. **adolescence** [,ædə`lɛsəns] (n.)
    青春期，青少年時期
12. **ancestor** [`ænsɛstə] (n.) 祖先，祖宗
13. **nightmare** [`naɪt,mɛr] (n.) 惡夢，夢魘

join forces (with) （和……）合作

這個說法原來是指「聯合、會師軍隊」的意思，在這裡引申為「和他人合作」，以達成共同的目的。

- City and county police officers are **joining forces** to fight crime. 縣市警力一起合作，打擊犯罪。

---

be torn (between) 左右為難，難以取捨

torn 原意為「痛苦得難以下決定」，torn between 即表示難以在兩者中做出抉擇。

- A: What color did you choose for your new car?
  你的新車選了什麼顏色？
- B: I haven't decided yet. I'm **torn between** silver and white.
  我還沒決定。我難以取捨要銀色還是白色。

sequel [`sikwəl] (n.) 續集

sorcerer [`sɔrcərə] (n.) 巫師，魔術師

reprise [rɪ`priz] (v.) 重複（表演），再次演出

alibi [`ælə,baɪ] (n.) 不在場證明

talisman [`tælɪsmən] (n.) 護身符，法寶

Bao 《包·子》

一部 2018 年美國動畫短片，由石之予（Domee Shi）編劇和導演，皮克斯動畫工作室製作。這是第一部由女性導演執導的皮克斯短片。它在翠貝卡電影節（Tribeca Film Festival）上映，然後於 2018 年 6 月 15 日與超人總動員 2 一起正式上映。這部電影講述了一位患有空巢綜合症的年邁而孤獨的加拿大華裔母親，她意外地獲得了第二次做母親的機會，因為她做了一個有生命的包子。該片在第 91 屆奧斯卡頒獎典禮上獲得最佳動畫短片獎。

red panda 喜馬拉雅小熊貓

小熊貓（Ailurus fulgens）是一種小型哺乳動物，原產於喜馬拉雅山脈東部和中國西南部。它有濃密的紅棕色皮毛，黑色的腹部和腿部，白色的耳朵、嘴巴和環狀的尾巴。其靈活的關節和彎曲的半伸縮爪，非常適合攀爬。

EZ TALK

2022年度新聞英文：疫情下的台灣
EZ TALK 總編嚴選特刊

總　編　審：Judd Piggott
作　　　者：Judd Piggott、EZ TALK編輯部
譯　　　者：劉嘉珮、EZ TALK編輯部
責　任　編　輯：賴祖兒、簡巧茹、劉怡欣
繪　　　者：嘰哩呱啦真
封　面　設　計：林書玉
內　頁　設　計：林書玉
內　頁　排　版：簡單瑛設
錄　音　後　製：純粹錄音後製有限公司
錄　音　員：Jacob Roth、Leah Zimmermann
照　片　出　處：shutterstock.com

副　總　經　理：洪偉傑
副　總　編　輯：曹仲堯
法　律　顧　問：建大法律事務所
財　務　顧　問：高威會計師事務所
出　　　版：日月文化出版股份有限公司
製　　　作：EZ 叢書館
地　　　址：臺北市信義路三段151號8樓
電　　　話：(02)2708-5509
傳　　　真：(02)2708-6157
客　服　信　箱：service@heliopolis.com.tw
網　　　址：www.heliopolis.com.tw
郵　撥　帳　號：19716071日月文化出版股份有限公司

總　經　銷：聯合發行股份有限公司
電　　　話：(02)2917-8022
傳　　　真：(02)2915-7212
印　　　刷：中原造像股份有限公司
初　版　一　刷：2023年1月
定　　　價：420 元
I　S　B　N：978-626-7164-88-4